M.C. Ray

The Unveiled

by M.C. Ray

The Unveiled

M.C. Ray aka McSellin Ray II
www.mcsellin.com
Cover Art by JD&J Book Cover Design

The Unveiled / M.C. Ray aka McSellin Ray II – 1st ed
ISBN – 978-0-692-17897-3

Thank you to Brianna, Ashley, Aubrey, Tiffany, and Myla.

Dedicated to my sister, Alexis, for just like Alya, I hope that you find your light. Remember – "You have to keep your mind open to the possibilities."

M.C. Ray

Book One

Chapter One

It was dark. The moon and stars glistened through the treetops. I darted through the foliage trying to outrun my pursuers. My leg got caught on a vine that snaked around my ankle from the ground, sending me trapped to the ground, but I fought myself free. The trees whispered and writhed as I ran along the soft moss that layered the forest floor. I stopped and listened. Footsteps were approaching from a couple of meters away. There was only one option: I had to climb.

I picked a honey locust, a tree as dark as night and bearing sharp thorns that were unavoidable to anyone over the size of a small ape—perfect for a young sprite with my talent. I closed my eyes, and after a few moments, began my ascent. Branches began to sprout and the thorns retreated as I made my way up. I reached the middle of the tree before refusing to go any farther. I felt nauseous. Before I could attempt to resume my climb, a spark lit beneath me. My breath became slow and steady, almost nonexistent.

"I don't see her!" he shouted.

I was just out of view. The flame was small, a bright red, but not bright enough to reveal my position. I began to relax until I saw the tree's shadow from the flame. The silhouette of my long hair and petite frame could be easily seen along the slender trunk of the honey locust tree. All it would take was for my pursuer to evaluate his surroundings for me to be discovered. The only things protecting me were the thorns that resurfaced after I had passed. All I could do was wait. I looked down nervously. The ground spun beneath me as I waited for the flame to either go out or move on into the distance.

What seemed like a lifetime went by before the flame moved off into the brush. A few moments later, I heard a rustle in some bushes a little ways off from the tree I clung to. I sighed in relief and began making my way down past the poison-tripped thorns. The same thing happened. The thorns retracted and branches aligned to the placement of my hands and feet. My chest was burning as I neared the ground. My body jerked. Corn beans and yam yokes spewed from my mouth onto the forest floor. As I touched solid earth, a skinny sprite with dark skin and hair like sheep's wool bolted toward me.

"We found you!" he yelled.

The flame began to approach again. I spat up the remainder of my meal. My vision blurred and my throat was scorching dry. I needed something to drink.

"Segun! I need water." He paused and pondered the request before removing something from his side, hoping it wasn't a trick.

"Here." He held out a cloth sleeve and gave it to me to drink.

The flame came between the two of us. Maintaining its life was a fiery-haired lad with tanned brown skin and eyes the color of unripe pecans. He swirled his hands to keep the flame going. For his age, he was strong in stature and his eyes showed that he feared nothing.

"We said no talents, Alya. You're a cheat. Now you have to be the shadow man," said the sprite with the flame.

I wiped my lips, stood up, and smiled.

"I will be the shadow *woman*," I said. Segun and I laughed.

"Besides, Rayloh, you used yours," I said, nodding at the lad's hands, which whirled with fire. He glared.

"How did you know I was in the tree?" I asked.

"Segun saw your shadow. I told him to stay put and I'd walk off into the brush. I knew you'd eventually come down."

"It's only been nine months since the start of the rotation. We haven't even learned whatever . . . specialization that is," Segun said as he imitated Rayloh's hands encompassing the calm heat.

"I guess I'm more clever than you think," Rayloh said. He chuckled and turned to lead us back though the forest when he tripped on a vine, just as I had before. He fell to the ground, extinguishing the flame and leaving us in darkness. Segun and I laughed again.

3

"Not so clever now, are you?" I said.

The sprite got up and twisted his hands, trying to bring back the flame.

"Look at what you did, Alya! You put my flame out. How will we get home?" He knew the vine being raised was my doing. I didn't want to admit it, but like most sprites my age, my talent wasn't altogether controlled either. I couldn't tell them that I had nearly tripped earlier in the night.

"He hasn't mastered a specialization, Segun. Just off to a blessed start." I turned back to the sprite who once held the flame. "Calm your mind, Rayloh. We'll follow the stars, as we normally do."

The three of us laughed and joked as we made our way home. We came out of the edgewoods and began crossing the great stone bridge. Below us was a large gorge. At the base of the gorge lay sharp rocks and geodes the size of pumpkins that protruded out of a thick mist produced from the river that flowed through our city, into the rocky stomach below.

In the distance, the light of the moon revealed a spectacle of gold at the zenith of the city, that showed both beautifully and frightening in the night. Trailing from the tallest tower was a thin line of fuchsia light that subtly tinted the night sky a dark purple hue. There were gates of oakwood, with iron strapping and tips of silver that stood at the opening of the city, locked. My comrades and I slipped in through a hole dug under the wall, a little ways down from the gate, which we referred to as *the tunnel*. The

4

Guards of Candor were patrolling as usual, and if any one of them was to spot us outside of the city limits, there would be *consequences*. I wasn't sure what would actually happen, just that there would be punishment. We didn't worry so much about that. The guards near the gate were few, and lazy at that.

The tops of high towers glimmered in the starlight, sending shots of gold and white into the sky. This city belonged to the great nation of Keldrock, a community of elves and humans, which had come to call home the face of a small but mighty mountain. We crept through the streets, trying our best to go unnoticed. Before I could spot it, a displaced brick reprimanded my large toe for helping me to creep out of my home at this hour of the night. I couldn't tell which toe was hurt or if all of them took the blow because my entire foot was throbbing from the collision. I saw blood and reached to feel for a gash or an uprooted nail, but found nothing. I moved into the light of the moon, trying to make sense of the situation. I didn't think I hit the brick that hard.

Once I got into a good position, where the moonlight showed bright on my skin, I realized that the blood was not from my toe, but was trickling down my leg from my right knee. I recalled that when I was running during our game of "shadow man," I had tripped and fallen. That must have been when it happened. Then a thought came to me. I stood up and turned excitedly to Segun.

5

"You should try," I urged him. "Rayloh and I used our talents tonight. Let's see if you've gotten any better. I'm sure you have."

Segun looked uncertain but eventually walked over to me, and with some reassurance from Rayloh, knelt and closed his eyes to focus. His talent hadn't come as naturally as Rayloh's or mine but was a great gift nonetheless. Segun's hand began to glow blue. Even through the bright glow, his teeth shone full in the darkness from his overly anxious grit. He ran his hands over the gash, and the blood rescinded up my leg and back into the scrape. I began to cry, quietly. The pain was increasing—not unbearable, but indeed there. As the pain increased, so did my tears, unintentional as they were.

Segun looked up at my face, and as he did, his hands ceased their glowing. "My apologies, Alya."

I bent over to look at my leg. No more blood flowed from the wound, and I felt no more pain, but left behind was a small, thin scar in the shape of a cross.

"With all good things come a price, I suppose," I muttered as I ran my hand over the small ridges that formed the scar.

"Please pardon me, Alya! I didn't mean to cause you harm. I told you I wasn't ready. This happens every time. I'm afraid I'm a—"

"It's all right, Segun. I actually fancy it." I stared at it, smiling, feeling the scarred skin with my fingertips. It felt smooth and coarse all at once. "When I become a warrior, I'm going to

6

have many more scars from battles won and lands conquered that will be much bigger than this," I said, joking, knowing it would never happen, since we were confined to the city.

I patted Segun on the shoulder to reassure him that I had no anger toward him. The truth is that the scar was actually interesting to me. Its two lines were perfect in every way, like the two straights that formed the shape of a cross. The longer, pointing north to south, and the shorter, east to west, seemed to give direction to the blood that flowed through my body. With the scar on my knee I thought I looked combative and well experienced in the trials and tribulations that the mighty suffer in battle— although that was more likely a stretch. Yet it made me feel more intimidating. Most likely it would go unnoticed, but it comforted me to rely heavily on these hopes.

"Misses can't be warriors."

I turned around and met the eyes of children. Human children. They appeared slightly older than my thirteen years. They were the children of the Dwala clan, born with no talents, and were the sons and daughters of men and women. Their parents worked as servants throughout the city. This was the fate of their race. I looked in disgust at the children. Their legs were scraped and bumpy from insect bites and street wanderings. Their hair was coarse and their skin mottled with welts and bruises from sleeping on hard pallets atop rocky or worn wood floors. Their clothes were nothing more than strung- together rags and scraps. Some of their makeshift garments were either too tight or too large, undoubtedly passed down from an older relative or outgrown and should be passed down to a younger one.

My father warned me of the Dwala. Street urchins. Our history with the Dwala had unforgivable roots. For it was they who betrayed the elves of Keldrock, and so began the days of refuge among my people. They were lucky their remaining number were allowed to continue living among us after such treachery. These children were trouble, and some, I had heard, made special efforts to show it.

"A she-elf can't be a warrior," one of them said. A boy stepped forward into the moonlight. His head was shaved and although his body was full and strong, his chest proud, his face was gentle, almost like that of a young woman.

"You have no business in the streets after dark," Rayloh said sternly.

"The streets are my business." The Dwala boy began to move toward Rayloh. "The streets are like us, rugged and worn, but still strong enough to support an entire civilization. Even the melon that rolls atop your shoulders." The boy and his comrades laughed obnoxiously.

Rayloh's eyes widened and his nostrils flared. "You have a wide mouth to be so wretched. If your kind could possess a talent, yours would be producing nonsense from that large gourd of yours." He pointed at the boy's mouth. I laughed convincingly enough to make the boy's comrades express obvious annoyance. Although Rayloh's banter was long strung and the boy's was much more humorous, I couldn't let them address my dearest of friends in such a manner.

Rayloh lunged at the boy, and I prepared myself for a fight. Rayloh's hot temper had gotten us into worse situations, but his brute strength and leadership had gotten us out of those situations and some of Segun's and my own matters as well. Rayloh grabbed the Dwala boy and lifted him into the air and just held him. I got ready. Any second now, he would send the boy down to the ground, unleashing the forces of savagery that stood behind the young leader of the band of misfits.

But instead, after holding him for a moment, Rayloh put him down gently and they locked wrists, a custom of welcome in our culture.

"It's good to see you, my friend. Even after all this time, you still grasp like a girl," the boy said.

"It's good to see you too, Nazda."

The sky was beginning to lighten. The sun hadn't begun to kiss the hills yet, but I could tell morning was near as the moon was losing its luster and the shadows were no longer dark as coal. I stood there staring as the other children gathered to greet Rayloh. I didn't understand it. *How could Rayloh know these infidels?* I thought.

In our city, there were rings. Four rings, to be exact, which worked their way up to the zenith of our great nation, where the gold-crested towers stand and the spouts of fuchsia bring beauty to the sky. At the topmost and most inner ring was the home of the royal family, who had no distinct duties other than addressing the public through formal appearances. Our advisory body, called the Courts, also worked here. This was called the purple ring. I had never seen or met the members of the Courts, and from the stories my father told, I don't think I'd want to. My father always seemed stressed from his work and I made a point to not bog him with questions or make his load any heavier than it was.

The second ring, the yellow ring, is where my friends and I belonged. The section of the city consisted of minor government officials, like my father, medics, and the few high-ranking honored officers who had served their nation in battles past, if they so chose to live there, although most chose to remain in the barracks within the blue ring. Below us was the blue ring, which was divided into halves. To one side was Shiloh's school of talents, where my friends and I attended, the markets along with little cottages, and the fort belonging to the Guards of Candor, the law enforcers of our city. Other elves lived there as well. To the other side was the militia division, where those chosen to serve in the Guerr, the warriors of Keldrock, resided. The members of the Guerr weren't vast in number, like the Guards of Candor, but because of their training, elite skills, and great sacrifice, they were catered to. Last was the black ring, the biggest and outermost of the rings in Keldrock. This is where the Dwala lived. This is where we were currently standing.

In all my years of knowing Rayloh, I never knew him to be humble enough to associate with the Dwala. I never had seen him address any of the ones that worked in our estate in such a friendly manner as this, but then Rayloh didn't speak much to anyone other than those he called friend or kin. Segun and I stood confused. The other children were embracing Rayloh, some introducing themselves. I scowled in disgust at the very thought of such association. Rayloh turned toward us grinning and waved his hand to beckon us over.

"Segun. Alya. This is Nazda."

Segun smiled and walked over. I tried to glare and catch his attention before he left my side but it was too late. He had already wrapped his hand around the boy's wrist. I couldn't believe it. The boy turned to me and began walking my way. He held out his hand.

"Nazda," he said with a smile. "It means 'pretty soul,' in case you were wondering," he added, as if this would make me all the more interested to speak to him.

I scoffed. Nazda meant "pretty soul," and for a boy that was strange. I would never make a point of it to spare the feelings of another, but in this case, I made an exception. His appearance as well as his comments only made me all the nastier in my reaction. As he held out his hand, I slapped his wrist away.

"No thank you. I like to shake the hands of formidable men. Not ones with soft faces and pretty names." I laughed, raking my hair over my shoulder.

Rayloh's eyes widened. Some of the boys stared in awe. It's almost as if I had cursed the boy. I had challenged his

11

manhood, so my goal was accomplished. I, a miss, had cut down their brave leader, stating what half of them were too scared to even think. I turned for reassurance to Segun, who was smiling at me, assuming it was all mindless banter. His smile turned to concern and before he could shout any words of warning, I turned around to find the boy's fist meeting my left cheek.

I spun around, my hair flying into the air. I pitifully tumbled to the ground. My face was throbbing, and I couldn't believe the boy had hit me so hard. For a human to hit an elf was reprehensible beyond reason. I could have his life for such an assault. In a daze, I sat up. I didn't want to stand, for fear I'd fall from a fit of dizziness.

"You dare to strike me, you Dwala scum? I was right about you . . . you, like your name, are weak. You'll regret this day."

The boy stepped to me and I shivered, sinking my tongue back behind my teeth. He crossed his arms and began pulling up his shirt. This was it. This was when I expected Rayloh to rescue me. This was when his brute strength should emerge tenfold and save the day, but he stayed put. I looked at him, pleading, but he seemed to be holding himself back, as if he were unsure who to side with. His allegiance couldn't be in limbo between this street vermin and myself. It couldn't be.

The boy was wearing layers. It was chilly out, but there was no reason for him to have all of these clothes on his person. He was now on his second garment. He aggressively pulled away at his clothes as I sat waiting, shivering from the cool air as well as my vibrating fear. My face, however, held, as did his. His eyes never left mine but for the quarter blink it took for him to pull a garment over his head. If I were to lose this meaningless street brawl today, I was going to lose with dignity, looking my oppressor in the eyes, blow after blow. He finally reached his final garment. As the shirt came over his head, I saw what I was intended to see. It all made sense, his naming and his face. Hot tears began to run down my face. I didn't want to cry, or perhaps I did. I couldn't be feeling sorry for my words.

I hung my head in not only shame but also disbelief at the thought of someone doing this. Under Nazda's shirt were two indentions. One was over his heart; the other was over his lung. The tears started coming faster as I felt him staring at me. He had the last garment in his hand. He threw it to his feet.

"Look at me."

I took in a deep breath. To see such pain and mutilation was unbearable. Nazda was not a boy with a girl's name, but a girl made to look like a boy. Nazda had been punished. Her breasts were missing from her body. I could tell by the scars and the craters of her absent parts that this was not self-inflicted but done by someone else. As tears rushed down my face, I could barely make out the words.

"I am . . . sorry." Oddly enough I meant it, the conflicting forces of my feelings about the Dwala and this altercation having resolved. Even though I could still feel hate beating within me, I was remorseful to this Dwala.

I felt her footsteps walking toward me. She reached down, her hand hovered in the air in front of me. She wasn't smiling or anxious, just following through on her initial intent. I reached up and took her hand and wrist, gripping it kindly.

"Nice to meet you, Alya."

Emotions of hate left me and for a moment I thought of her as something more than what I had been told. No, she was not a friend, but in that moment, I sympathized with her. So many thoughts circled in my head. Feeling her pain. Her sorrow, now mine.

"A pleasure to meet you as well, Nazda."

Chapter Two

Rayloh, Segun, and I crept through the streets, trying to make it home before the chime of the mornowl. Every morning, the sacred bird awakened the people of our city with a powerful hoot. Its call marked the beginning of a new day, and it is said that without the call of the mornowl, our sun wouldn't rise. People held that bothersome fowl in such high regard, although to me, it was no more than an annoyance.

The three of us lived in a large, beautiful estate called the Remni. We slipped in through the door of Coor, the entrance closest to Segun's family quarters. We would sneak out through this door, leaving it unhitched, because we often would spend nights in our estate's study, playing and eating corn leaves until we fell asleep atop the wool pillows, or, if chance be had, slipped out into the night.

The Remni employed a few Dwala to assist its many residents. Our estate was grand. The he-elves and the she-elves had separate, luxurious quarters for grooming. The dining area contained some of the finest cutlery in the city, and every morning, if we were not already awakened by the mornowl, we'd be brought back to life by the smells of a bountiful breakfast. Every night, personal attendants came to the ladies of each family, and ask what meals they wanted to be served the next day before leaving for their homes in the black ring.

15

Although Madja was not a servant, she-elves were still expected to serve the lords and the household. Soon I would be forced to embark toward this tradition my society had set for me, departing from Segun and Rayloh, with a coming-of-age ceremony called a Kei. This ceremony celebrated more than the beginnings of elfhood and my day of birth, but also my readiness for marriage. Lord Calo, a council official, like my father, and who lived with his sister in the Remni, said that age fourteen was when a lady was fully ripe and ready for the picking. When he said this, the biggest grin stretched across his face and his eyes would grow exceedingly warm. I always got an odd feeling when we had these conversations, but I appreciated his old humor along with the fact that he was one of the more relaxed tenants of the Remni. His sister, however, was awkward or snooty, I hadn't decided, refusing to speak to anyone. She spent her days in her quarters in solitude, and whenever I saw her, she was either alone playing with her collection of random trinkets or with her brother. My friends and I jested that some young spirit had been trapped in her body on its way out of this world, and her mind was so dull that the spirit was constantly being tortured and the only thing that brought it comfort was when she played with small trinkets she carried, like a little sprite with her toys. I kept my distance from her.

My own sister was all too anxious to make the rite of passage into the tiring rituals of adult she-elves. Mira, at nine years, already shared Madja's idle interests in keeping a home along with the other ladies of the Remni. I found it more enjoyable to go out on scavenging adventures and play shadow man in the edgewoods with my friends than participating in such tasks.

Madja burst into the study to find me and my comrades battling between looking like we were asleep and being refreshed from a good night's rest. I was exhausted but I had gone more than a day without sleeping before, so I was sure that I could handle a couple more hours. I sat up before she could awaken me.

"Good morning, Madja!" I shouted. Madja was an endearing term for mother in our tongue and one I called her often.

She put her hands on her hips. "You would know it is a good morning, wouldn't you. Since you almost came in with the sun." I was in trouble now. This was the second time this month I had been caught leaving the Remni at night.

"Madja . . . I only went to—"

"Save your lies, Alya. I saw you come in after the chime of the mornowl. I warned you. I'm going to discuss this with your father and see what punishment he feels is most befitting for a sprite that won't follow her mother's orders."

She set down the basin of water she had been carrying along with the towels she had draped over her shoulder for the lads and me to wash our faces. Before storming out, she snatched the pillow I was leaning on, pounded out the indentations, and returned it to its place on the lounge chair.

I turned to see Rayloh and Segun still lying on the floor atop their pillows, sleeping. They both could drift off in mere blinks, but the reprimand Madja just gave would bring the

17

deceased back to life. Rayloh rolled over with a smile on his face.
He'd heard the whole conversation. Segun was asleep for sure—
his right foot was thumping as it did when he slept. I got up,
grabbed a red rag off the top of the towel stack, and dipped it into
the steaming hot water. I wiped my face, rubbing over my sore left
cheek with care as to not cause any further pain. Nazda had hit me
hard. Despite what I'd heard about the Dwala, I was intrigued,
especially if Rayloh, our unspoken leader, found her interesting
enough to form a friendship.

I headed to the grooming quarters, where a bath was
prepared as usual. I put warm maple flower petals and cinnapine
stem sap in the water. Even though there were many petal
fragrances and sweet saps to choose from, I always picked the
maple flower and cinnapine sap scents. I sprinkled the autumn red
leaves though my hot bath and got in. I had to be at lessons, soon
so I washed in haste.

After my bath, I had one of the Dwala braid my hair. She
took my locks of hair and weaved them into two braids that ran
from the two sides of my head down to my lower back. I beamed
at myself in the mirror. My hair was long and I was proud of it.

I put on my swelk, the uniform for school, a dark brown
clothing set pinned with gold and iron fasteners, and went down to
the main hall for breakfast. When I arrived, I saw that Rayloh and
Segun were already there. I hated that I had to do so much to
prepare myself for the day and the lads had to do so little. I always
thought, since it took she-elves longer to bathe and manage

themselves, that the he-elves should have the duty of preparing the children and completing other household duties before attacking their personal work. Still, I was just a sprite, and after my Kei, I would become just an elf. Madja made sure that I kept my ideas to myself.

I sat next to Segun. His family had melon and wolf nuts for breakfast. Segun's father worked as a medic in the purple ring. They moved to the Remni when I was but a little sprite. He was a brilliant physician and was chosen by the Courts based off his reputation, to aid the purple ring's residents in daily treatments ranging from vitamins and herbal teas to body ailments and broken bones. Madja and Segun's mother were close friends.

Rayloh's family had snake fruit and honeysuckle tarts. Rayloh loved snake fruit because of its protein potency and its charming flavor, as reflected in its naming. His family consisted of himself and his father. His mother died after giving birth to him. His father, Lord Fueto, told him his strength was so great and his life was so highly favored that she was able to pass into the afterlife with her mission complete, knowing her son would go on to do great things. I believed his father told this story not solely to quell Rayloh's questioning but also to convince him that it was the will of something greater for his wife to pass. Rayloh's father worked as the chief architect in our city. His beautiful work graced all throughout the city. He was strong in stature and had the ruggedness that most mistresses would find attractive in a sir. He was another one of the entertaining, kind adults in the Remni.

Rayloh's father, unlike my own, was open about life, and at times
when he wasn't busy would sit down with us sprites and impart
wisdom or a comical story from Rayloh's younger years. Rayloh
hated these conversations, but having him as a father was different
than having him as a benevolent neighbor. I hoped Rayloh would
grow up to have the same charisma and looks as his father. The
charisma I found so inviting.

In my place at the table sat colored river greens and
foxtrits, a popular biscuit consisting of cheese and sweet herbs.
We sprites usually sat separate from our parents and the other
elves of the Remni. My sister, carrying fresh flowers from the
garden, came in with Madja. I sucked my teeth, making a sound of
disgust. Segun laughed. Mira felt out of place among my friends
and me. She was more comfortable around Madja and the other
she-elves of the Remni. I wondered if that would all change once
she discovered her talent and had to start lessons at Shiloh. She
took her seat next to me. Mira was quite beautiful; I would even
go far enough to say she was fairer than I. Her light brown skin
and walnut- colored eyes were but the beginnings. Her hair was
long like mine but thin and airy, not anything like my course,
coiled texture.

After my friends and I scoffed down our food, we left for
school. It wasn't far. As soon as we entered the blue ring, it was
within sight. We walked in silence, exhausted from the night. No
one spoke about the girl named Nazda and our altercation and
somewhat reconciliation. I was too proud to tell Rayloh that I

wanted to see her again. Something about her intrigued me. I also wanted to know about the scars on her chest.

Due to our lagging, it took us longer than normal to get to school. Guards stood at the door and checked our papers, ensuring we were supposed to be there. I didn't know what elfling would want to infiltrate a school if they didn't have to go. We had just made it up the marble steps before we heard the call to order. We ran to the grand hall and took seats toward the back. The last three rows of benches in the grand hall were for the students in our rotation. There were three spaces at the beginning of the back row, so we didn't have to separate or step over anyone to be seated. Rayloh, Segun, and I were premieres, or first-year students. Although the three of us discovered our talents at different times, the school of talents started a new entry of students only once a year. If your birthing, or the discovery of your talent, occurred before this date, you would be entered as a premiere for the next rotation.

The school was named after Shiloh, the protector, who placed the veil over the city, keeping us safe from intruders. Even before my time, that's been the name, and the name, like the veil, has been there since the rifts between Dwala and Keldrock first began long ago. Or so I've heard. I don't know much about the city's past turmoil, but I do know it involved the betrayal of the Dwala people and the retreat of our elven clan within these walls. We used to reside in the forests, but now we hide within a keep of stone and mountain.

21

This was one of the few times during the school day I got to see my friends because the classes were separated by when one's birthing occurred and by gender. The classes weren't large. Each year brought on average twelve to fifteen new students, and normally it ran an equal amount of lads and misses, or close enough. This year there were two equal sets of six. Soon we were quieted for the call to order that happened right before our dismissal for lessons. We had to stand, raise our fist in the air, and pledge our allegiance to our great city. Translated:

> I vow my blood, my life, my talent, and my honor to the great nation of Keldrock. Whose gates of wood and iron guard my temple, my body, and my people from the evils of darkness and shadow. I pledge to the Great One, Olörun, the Courts, and our protector, by light, and our king, by blood, to abide by what is just in their eyes. For the law of the land is the sphere of the righteous and to break the orb is to unleash chaos. *Kina, kina, kina.*"

I hated this archaic tradition, and I didn't feel that I should have to pledge my allegiance to a nation who didn't even allow me to have a say in my life's course. At that moment we were dismissed and the grand hall began to empty. We had to wait in the adjoining holding chamber until our masters came to take us to our huts for lessons. I took this opportunity to ask Rayloh about the night before.

"So how do you know the Dwala children?" I asked. Rayloh looked uneasy. He took a moment, as if he were contemplating his response, then answered.

"Their parents were servants to my father when he was a sprite. The family was loyal to him, so he sends them tradable goods and food. I used to go with him to deliver them."

"But they're Dwala. Aren't they supposed to serve you loyally? Why send gifts when they were only doing for your father what they are paid to do?"

Rayloh's nose and eyes scrunched together like he had tasted a lemon. "I'm sure your father taught you that," he retorted.

I looked at him, confused. "What does that mean?"

"It means that you should offer a little more humility and understanding before speaking on such things you know nothing about. Hate is the very noose that holds the ignorant individual. That's what my father taught me."

Although I felt he and the girl named Nazda were a little more acquainted than a few sociable visits between families, I didn't question it, since his reaction was so tense. *What did he mean by that statement?* I felt that maybe I wasn't thinking clearly, and was acting like the mindless drones of elves that walked about the Remni and whom I resented so much. That I was nothing more than the breath, an echo of my father, whose ideals I wasn't too keen on myself, but I couldn't be wholly wrong in my thoughts. The Dwala were traitors. That was enough justification for resentment, even if Rayloh refused to acknowledge it.

23

I didn't have any more time to ponder this interaction before my master arrived. I and the other misses in my rotation rushed to greet her. We lined up and walked out the back of the grand hall to the third hut in the courtyard. I entered and sat, with crossed legs, in front of where my master would stand. There were fifteen huts lining the inner wall of the school. The misses used the marble huts because we weren't allowed to be trained in combat and didn't have use for the iron huts, which the lads used.

She-elves were not allowed to use their talents in combat, defense, or even in manufacturing, so they were not taught how to do so. We learned instead how to use our gifts to serve the households we would one day belong to. She-elves could hold certain other jobs as well. One of them was in the realm of entertainment. A lot of the misses wanted to join the Jalla, the dancers that performed at royal events, elite parties, and city rituals and festivals. The royal family was serviced by other talent-possessing members of the nation. She-elves were needed for these roles and a couple of other minor service jobs in the purple ring, but a great many were simply ladies of their houses.

My teacher walked in last and took her place at the front of the class. "Greetings, premieres." She always smiled and cupped her hands when she welcomed us.

Master Tali was striking. Her skin was smooth and rich, as if filled with starlight. Her hair was long and joined from each side by a braid that trailed down her back with the rest of her loose hair. When she walked, the ends of her auburn-brown strands

24

would play hide- and-seek with her ankles. Her cheekbones were strong and the angles of her face gave her an eccentric, feline-like look. Her eyes were big and brown. In the sun they glowed like amber encompassing the souls of those who dared to look upon her. My master had an interesting talent—she could command the actions of animals. I always believed that it was not her talent that manipulated the beasts to her will, but her splendor and grace. I wanted to be just like her. Like the animals she demonstrated her talents on, she was wild and only seemed tame while in the eye of the coordinator of Shiloh's school of talents or when walking the streets of the city. In our classes, she became a different person. Somehow I felt she was just like me and had the same thoughts I had of frustration and meaningless tradition. It didn't matter that I didn't connect with the misses in my rotation that dreamed of Jalla dancing, Keis, and courtship, because I'd found a friend in someone much greater. I made sure to always sit in the front of the class to stay close to Master Tali. By doing so, my talent progression was coming along at a faster pace than most.

"Today, we will practice using our talents to animate. As you all know, the specialization of our talents is drawn from our emotions. They operate by the way we feel and our thoughts. For this, you must be thoughtful, and draw from the innermost recesses of your mind. You must look within yourself, whether it is a memory or a person or a thing. Maybe it's your favorite dance." She began frolicking around, imitating a dance that misses performed at parties. She always poked fun at tradition and encouraged us to talk about things we normally felt too shy, uncomfortable, or were out of place to say.

My teacher was fully crafted, meaning she was a master of her talent, and no longer needed much to force it, other than her command. For the sake of the presentation, she took her time, allowing the misses to see the intricacies and the focus etched on her face.

Within a few blinks a dozen wild loricanaries, colorful birds with the voices of Sirens, flew into the room. According to what I've been taught, loricanaries were bred for the entertainment of the royal family and their guests, but when Shiloh's reign began, he felt anyone with eyes to see and ears to hear should be able to enjoy their stunning plumage and cherubic voices, so he released them to the wilds. Master Tali told us that smaller animals were a lot easier to control than larger ones because their will was easily broken and their minds weren't as great. This explained why she summoned such a large number of wild loricanaries.

I watched as the birds wove through the air. They looked like rainbows bouncing among the ceilings, walls, and floors. After a colorful display, each settled on the shoulder of one of the students, the remaining stationing themselves on small perches around the classroom, like archers at the ready. A pink, blue, and orange one landed on my shoulder, in my opinion the most gorgeous of the flock. They opened their beaks and began to sing a song I had heard only once before. I didn't recognize it at first but, as the glares around the room grew hard and cold, I recognized where I had heard it. It was a song of protest. The song of the banished Dwala.

Chapter Three

A few months ago, I had been playing with my sister Mira in the main corridor of the estate when I heard a soft voice humming a song. I stopped and listened. Mira stopped as well and we decided to find out where it was coming from. We followed the sound to the ladies' grooming quarters. My sister and I stood outside, on either side of the door frame, and listened. The door was cracked so the woman didn't notice our presence. A younger Dwala woman, named Canta, was kneeling on the floor scrubbing the mildew and mud someone had tracked in from outside, likely from Mira and me. She continued to hum this haunting melody. It was such an interesting tune. It was full of fear, loss, and regret, yet a powerful feeling of faith and triumph. As the song grew to its climax, I leaned forward, attempting to hear the full waves of sound that passed from the woman's lips. As I did, I slipped and pushed the door open, tripping into the room. The startled woman immediately began apologizing. My sister came into the room and offered our apologies, which I scolded her for doing.

"What was that you were singing?" Mira asked, helping the woman to her feet.

The woman dropped her head, looking to the ground. "I meant no disrespect, miss," she said.

"Let's go, Mira, she's clearly clouded and confused. Let the woman get back to work."

Mira didn't move. The woman looked up, set down her cleaning brush, and walked to the mirror, staring intently, as if debating whether to tell us the secret of this mystery song she was singing. Mira seemed absorbed. I, however, didn't want to express my interest, but I was intrigued as well. She told my sister and me the story. It was so profound and tragic and I wondered if it were true, so that night I asked my father. His eyes grew angry, but just as they had, they became gentle. He asked me who told me this nonsense. I told him of the young Dwala woman named Canta that cleaned the ladies' grooming quarters. I woke up the next day to tell the Dwala woman of her insolence and that whatever tale she had been told was wrong and that she had been misinformed. After searching for her, I asked the head of staff what happened to her. I was told that she had taken ill and had to resign. I was alarmed, because the day before, the young woman was a picture of health. I then realized that the tales of the Courts were true. That's the day I also realized my father was keen on keeping secrets. I can still recite the tale verbatim.

Almost nineteen years ago, a year after the last unveiling, a Dwala went to the purple ring, demanding to see the Courts. She was a middle-aged woman, who worked in the blue ring as a street cleaner but volunteered, on behalf of the Dwala people, to voice the opinions of her people to the Courts. The strategy was to send a woman because they were gentle in nature and calm under pressure. Of course, she wasn't allowed past the gate to the purple ring, which was guarded by the most elite members of the Guards of Candor. She stood there and instead of shouting obscene insults at the elven blockade or cursing the members of the Courts and the royal family, she simply sang a song.

She wanted rights for the Dwala, and not only rights for the Dwala, but also equality for all. Whether man or woman, Dwala or gifted, she sang this song for change. She came and sang every day, and every day the residents of the purple ring ignored her, not letting her pass. On the fifth day of protest, a kind guard insisted that she not come back and had her write down her requests, fearing her stubbornness and the wrath of the Courts, and promised he would give it to the Courts' secretary. She planned to meet him in five days to receive the Courts' answer.

After five days she returned, singing her song of protest as she walked. When she arrived at the entrance of the ring, she found to her surprise and great sorrow, the head of the guard on a wooden stake, with two pieces of parchment wedged between his teeth. She pulled one sealed piece of paper from his grit and unfolded it. Out fell her original request. She picked it up and tucked it in her sleeve. Then she opened the other piece of parchment, bearing the royal emblem, and began to read it. The notice read:

"The Courts, as well as the royal family, have been presented with your proposal. We have decided that your ideas for change, your recruitment of elven alliances, and your attempt to venture into the purple ring are revolutionary and should be met with punishment. For your treason, you are banished to the

edgewoods. The Courts as well as the royal family are just, and would not want you to venture into the wilderness alone. Therefore, every Dwala woman who has achieved the age of fourteen is banished as well. Kina, kina, kina."

That night, the Guards of Candor escorted the women from the city, never to return. They led the protester in front and read the declaration from the Courts over and over again, with one addition.

"Come now for exile. For those who are found in trespass after this exodus will be met with much harsher punishment."

The women began to cry as they were expelled from the city, leaving their husbands, fathers, brothers, and their few young daughters to raise their children and take care of the house. They filed behind a volunteer, some holding hands. That day, some girls were led to the streets with their mothers and sisters instead of having left over treats from their coming-of- age celebrations. As they walked, the volunteer who voiced the concerns of the Dwala felt great sorrow and began humming her song. More and more women gathered in the street to be exiled, and each joined in the song. As they passed through the silver-tipped gates, their sound grew louder, turning from quiet hums into a boisterous noise. Even as they crossed the bridge, and the last of them faded into the wilderness, the song could still be heard through the city.

The Guards of Candor then did a terrible thing. They set the edgewoods ablaze with fiery arrows and oil sacks. The women could be heard screaming as the wood cracked and the smoke rose

31

to the sky. Although less than half of the edgewoods burned, it was assumed that the women were either torched to death by the flames or devoured by some wild pack of animals.

Never again, after that day, had the city seen such an order of exile commanded by the Courts, and never again did any of the Dwala challenge the way life was to be within the walls of Keldrock.

A slight grip from the bird on my shoulder brought me back. I looked around at the other misses, who seemed to be in deep thought, as I was. The room was silent but for the chirping song of the birds. When the song ended, Master Tali relieved the birds of their duty by flying them, one by one, out of the hut's window. I could not believe that our teacher, a master of the city, placed in the school by the Courts, used a song of rebellion to demonstrate a specialization of "thoughtfulness." She stood for a minute with a smile on her face before saying anything. I could not help but wonder what was the true purpose of this demonstration.

"I know you all know the story and I'm sure the other masters dance around its details and origin when discussing the historical events of our nation. We all know about the banished women, the Dwala sisters, to never be seen again and set ablaze in the edgewoods. Today is the anniversary of their exile as well as the demise of the Dwala women. Today we will be using our specialization of thoughtfulness to remember these women and the legacy they left behind by expressing these honors through our talents."

"But Master Tali," a young sprite named Destili, whose father worked with my own under the Courts, raised her hand and without being called upon said, "They were *only* Dwala. I'm almost certain that the young they left behind can clean the streets and bring us our meals in the same, if not in a better manner, than they would have."

The room filled with squeals of laughter. Master Tali cringed.

"These women were fighting for something bigger, something more. And whether you know it or not, you are the lights that are going to see the tide of change."

Destili raised her hand and spoke in the same fashion.

"Isn't it perjury to speak of such things?" The class turned in unison to see the master's response.

Master Tali's face turned frigid. She smoothed out the wrinkles in her white silk robe. She then smiled and brought her hands to rest, folded at her waist. While staring daringly at Destili, she said, "Class . . . you're dismissed for midday meal."

We had been in class for a short while, not long enough for the lads to have begun their lessons, so I wasn't surprised to walk out into the courtyard and find all the other huts still in session. We were allotted a large amount of time for our midday meal, giving us plenty of time to return to our homes. On a normal day, we'd have specialization training before our midday meal,

and after, Keldrock history. I walked home alone today. I was
going to wait for Segun and Rayloh, but I thought it would be
great to go home and rest before midday meal since I was released
so early.

I made my way up the back steps of the Remni. I decided
to use the door of Coor instead of the main entrance, as I didn't
want Madja or one of the other ladies to see me coming in and ask
me to assist with meal preparations. Although the Dwala made the
meals and set them in their proper places in the main hall, the she-
elves of the Remni enjoyed picking flowers, gathering colorful
stones, and finding other beautiful elements in nature to
complement our dining experience. They foraged in the front of
the estate or the yellow gardens up the road for these things, so I
found it best to enter through the back.

I walked into the Remni and immediately took off my
shoes. The walk to the study wasn't long but I always loved the
feeling of having bare feet. It made me feel wild. Although the
study belonged to everyone that lived in the Remni, it was
understood that it was to be reserved for my band of brothers and
me. Even throughout the day, when we're at lessons, no one goes
in. I grabbed my favorite pillow from the lounge chair, roughed it
up a little bit for comfort, and lay down on the floor. After a few
moments, I was still restless. I wasn't going to sleep. I sat up and
thought of what I could do until it was time for midday meal.
Rayloh and Segun were probably still being slowly poisoned with
boredom at lessons, and my father, not that I would want to spend

this time with him, was in the purple ring serving the Courts, which left one "victim," Mira. I stood up and crept out of the study. I began to slowly tread down the corridor.

I went into the holding room next to the large front door, where we sat guests who were waiting to enter our main hall for a special dinner or stopping by to visit a resident. I peeked through the window to see the ladies of the estate in the garden with the Dwala. As I predicted, they were picking flowers and fruits, removing weeds, and gossiping as usual, it seemed. I didn't see my sister among them. I ran down the hall to our family quarters. I heard a voice coming from inside and thought it was my father. I didn't want to be bothered with having to explain why I got dismissed from lessons early, partly because I dreaded speaking to him, and also wishing to protect Master Tali from scrutiny. I didn't want her to take "ill" as well. I had never lied to my father, and the one time I attempted it he saw right through me. If I had something to hide, it was easier to just avoid him. I heard the rustling of the beads that hung from the first frame over the threshold.

I opened the small steel gate to the vent, where we put lit incense and candles that could run all day without worry of setting the estate ablaze. I didn't even look to see if anything was burning before crawling inside, but there was only a pile of ashes and a clay crucible. As I closed the steel gate, the door leading into my family quarters squeaked open. The tread was fast and harsh. My father was probably relieved early but anxious to return to work and was electing to miss midday meal. I jerked my leg to readjust myself and bumped the crucible. The footsteps stopped. I could hear him turn around and begin to approach the vent. I held my breath in the hopes that my father didn't open the door and pull me out by my hair for a reprimand as a pair of slippers I recognized to be his came into view through the slits in the vent.

I was as still as I could be. For a moment, I felt as if I had left my body and were floating next to my corpse. Madja told me multiple times to stop using the Remni as my own personal playground and that if I had the yearning to go on an "adventure" or act "uncivilized," the garden was but across the way. My father was harsh and never offered up such warnings. The slippers got closer and closer. I heard Madja and the other ladies singing and realized that they must be coming inside the Remni. My father turned back around and walked away, his slippers clapping down the corridor.

I sighed a breath of relief. I hopped out the vent as soon as the steps faded and ran into my family's quarters. I saw Mira lying on her cot. I wondered if this is what she did every day before midday meal. I sat at the end where her head rested, picked up a hair runner from atop her storage chest and ran the metal bristles through her hair. My younger sister brought out the softness in me, I had to admit. I could feel her body shuddering.

"Are you all right, Mira?" I put down the hair runner and began rubbing her back. "You seem tense."

My sister sat up, startled. She was sweaty and appeared to be in a daze. I nudged her to make her smile but she looked down, uninterested. She held her hand to her head as if something weighed heavily on her conscience. I thought joking might do well to ease.

"Heavens. You are quite swollen, sister. Someone has inhaled too many sugar cakes." I laughed and begin to reach for her stomach. Before I could touch her, she pushed my hand away and threw one of her small pillows at me. I threw it back at her as she retreated to the top corner of her cot, wedging her body in the crevice where the two walls met.

"Don't touch me! Never touch me!" she screamed. By this time, Madja had heard the commotion. I could hear the door open and it wasn't long before she came storming through the beads that hung from the second frame.

"What did you do, Alya?!" Madja shouted.

I was offended by her assumption. Before I could even address her allegations, Mira was up running past the both of us. We stood in shock. I thought it was odd behavior for her to be that dramatic over my pestering, and Madja, thinking she knew me well, assumed it had gotten out of hand.

"Sometimes, I ponder over you. You are my eldest. I shouldn't have to lecture you on how to behave like a proper lady. If I hadn't birthed you myself, I would assume you were born from some wild animal." I resented Madja when she made comments like this. It made me feel like I was less of what I was. I

37

made a point not to gossip and not to share my feelings with
Madja for fear that I would be judged or that something was
wrong with me.

"Madja, I—"

"Find your sister, Alya. It is almost time for midday meal.
I must go and help prepare the table."

Madja left. She was disappointed in me, and although my
intentions were to never be bothersome, I couldn't help but think
that I was not like the rest of my family. I wasn't conservative,
well mannered, or unopinionated. I was rebellious, and that was a
marker not associated with elven ladies, a fate that would be mine
sooner than later. I got off my sister's cot and went to find her. She
wasn't in the main hall, so I decided to look in the grooming
quarters. There she was, hunched over a basin. It smelled terrible.
I turned around and waited outside for fear of upsetting her again
and of losing my breakfast at the sight of her losing hers. I stood in
the hall, leaning against the door, propping it open.

"You know I was only jesting. I meant no offense, Mira."
I had a hard time apologizing at times, but this time I felt I had
done nothing wrong. Just thinking about the interaction and its
insignificance made my insides boil. I was just trying to make her
feel better.

I continued, harsher in tone. "You know, you would have
more friends if you had a mind of your own. It's a shame that
you'll bend to the will of everyone else but lose patience with the
one person who somewhat respects you."

"Go away, Alya," I heard her mutter from the basin. That made my even more angry.

I wouldn't be dismissed. My voice began to rise. "You're just like those brainless sprites in my rotation. You're an insignificant child. Madja is here for now, but remember, not even she can always protect you." Mira turned and sat back on her knees. "You're going to need me. And when you do, I won't be there."

"Get out!" The basin hit the wall adjacent to the door frame, and bodily excrements, along with broken shards, fell to the floor. Sickened by the sight, I scrunched my face in disgust. I decided my intentions of upsetting her were more than accomplished, so I left. But I had one more thing to say:

"You're common. That's all you'll ever be."

I let the door close and walked back to our family quarters, which were now empty. I took a moment to settle down. I had taken personal jabs. It was easier for me to take a vengeful tongue than to discuss the issue at hand, but even I had hoped that I had outgrown this feat of overreaction. I had gone too far and I knew it.

It was almost time for midday meal, and my friends would be back soon. In the meantime, I decided to practice the specialization I learned today, seeking to redirect the overwhelming emotions bubbling within me. I took out my parchment and jotted down a few memories strong enough for me to focus on, as Master Tali had instructed. After meditating on my memory and focusing on what I wanted to happen, I stood up. I closed my eyes and focused. I could feel energy flowing all around me, summoning something, in the same fashion Master Tali had ordered the loricanaries. After a few moments I opened my eyes and surprisingly found that I had done an exceptional job. Flower petals flowed in through our balcony doors from the garden. Petals of purple, blue, pink, and red flowed into our room. They began to form the silhouettes of young women. They danced in the room, a splendid whirl of color.

I didn't care for the Dwala people. Still, Master Tali's words resonated within me. She thought of them as more. Master Tali always made me question my beliefs when she thought differently because I was so infatuated with her. Why was that? Before I could ponder these thoughts any longer, there was a knock at the door. My trance was lost and the petals fell to the floor atop our patterned rugs. I opened the door to find my friends, eager and hungry.

I stepped out, closing the door behind me, and walked down the corridor with Rayloh and Segun. We went to the main hall, where our meals were waiting. Mira was already there except instead of sitting in her usual seat at the head of the table, next to me, she sat at the end, alone. Segun and Rayloh sensed that something was wrong, and to bring me to a lighter state, told me some news.

"Tonight, we're going to the base. We have some new interests," Rayloh said.

I smiled. We spoke in code often just to keep the adults and my sister off of our trail. Madja was already upset at the fact that I would slip out at night, but she would be even more furious to find that I was going outside of the city limits. I pondered the thought for a moment. I couldn't think of any of our associates from school who were brave enough and worthy of trusting to venture outside of the city's walls. Then it hit me. We were going to meet the Dwala children again.

My face changed. Although I was curious about the girl Nazda, I didn't want to be associated with the Dwala people, nor did I want to share our fort with them. I could hear my father's words in my head now: *They can't be trusted.* Still, if Rayloh found them worthy enough, then what was I to do but give them a chance? Especially since he's the one who discovered the fort in the first place. Besides, my father was barely around enough to know whether he liked me. How could he know for certain if all of the Dwala people couldn't be trusted? Master Tali would appreciate me keeping an open mind. I nodded at Rayloh to show my understanding and cooperation, which was what he and Segun were hoping for at the least.

We finished eating and headed back to Shiloh. The closing half of lessons was my favorite part, because I didn't have to leave Rayloh and Segun. We all gathered in one of the larger rooms in the main building for Keldrock history. Most of our historical records, the legends and great tales of battles won, were sacred and kept under restriction in the purple ring, or so I've been told.

The history we were taught was passed down to the masters from the coordinator given to him by the Courts. Master Tali and the lads' teacher, Master Roi, alternated teaching this class. Today Master Tali led the lecture, so I wanted to be as attentive as possible. As we walked into the hall, I took the lead as we searched for seats. I decided on the second row of benches. The lads wouldn't be as distracted and would pay more attention if we sat close to the front. Master Tali came in and stood before the class on a platform. She greeted the class and wished our midday meals blessed, and then began her lesson.

"Today we will be learning about the veil. As we have discussed before, the veil was placed over Keldrock by Shiloh, the Protector. In being the Protector and the holder of the light, he was able to shelter people, places, and things by cloaking a veil around them, among many other things. Shiloh hasn't been seen for years and no one knows how the veil remains, nor why at the beginning of the twentieth cold season, when the moon blocks the sun, it fades, leaving our great city unprotected. The Day of Unveiling."

The Day of Unveiling. This is what the sons of the city spent their lives preparing for. Becoming a member of the Guerr, the warriors of Keldrock, was a great honor. These elves were treated like kings, and for good reason. They lived in a separate quarter within the blue ring, and once initiated, could only return to their homes and their former lives after they fought in a Day of Unveiling. Their family became those elves that they would one day fight alongside. Once fully crafted in their talents and trained in the art of combat, these warriors were enlisted for the next Day of Unveiling. In the week leading up to it, they would spend days venturing to the border where the veil stands, deep into the forest, beyond the edgewoods, where no one has ever dared to venture. On the eve of the beginning of the twentieth cold season, the veil breaks when the moon encases the sun, and if anything seeks to enter while the veil is disposed, the Guerr are our first and most powerful line of defense.

The male premieres find out at the end of their first rotation whether or the courts will enlist their talents and if they will join the Guerr in protecting our great nation. They wouldn't be required to leave for training until they graduated from the School of Talents, but even then it would make every moment feel like a slowly trickling timer. Nothing could save my friends from this decision and I felt sympathy that like mine, their fate was decided for them. Only, while their battle was rewarded with honor and prestige, mine was rewarded with a life of servitude.

Chapter Four

"You're sleeping in your cot tonight, Alya Lightstar. I don't want to hear any more discussion concerning the matter." Madja had not forgotten about my slipping out the night before.

"Why can't I sleep in the study?" I dropped down on a love seat in the corner of our family quarters and put my face in my hands. I had only slept in our family quarters when I was a small sprite and on rare occasions when I argued with the lads and needed some time away from them, which lasted no more than a night usually.

"Since you don't appreciate the late hours as a time to rest but a time to roam the streets with your friends, I think it best you sleep in here with the rest of the family for a while." She picked up my swelk off the floor, folded it, and placed it neatly atop my storage chest.

I heard the door open and expected it to be my father. I hadn't seen him—well, heard him—since earlier today, when he rushed out of our family quarters. Madja hated when he missed midday meal and told me often that the reason I was so rebellious was because I lacked the discipline that only a father could give. I took my head out of my hands just to have it fall back down again. It was Mira who had entered. She brought the smell of pumpkin spice weeds in with her. She had been playing in the yellow gardens. Placed in her silky strands was her hair runner. It was a very pretty artifact passed down from Madja to us, and seeing that my hair was arranged in tight locks, it only made sense that Mira keep it. Besides, I found it pointless to share something so trifling.

"Madja, please. I hate sleeping in here. I—"

"That is enough, Alya. Now go wash up with your sister. She smells of the garden and you sound like a beggar, so I wouldn't be surprised if you smelled like one as well. It's almost time to eat. Like I said, I don't want to hear anything else concerning the matter." She turned and walked out of the room. Her very existence revolved around ensuring that each meal ran smoothly and that her daughters were prompt and presentable at all times. I rolled my eyes at Mira, and without inviting her to accompany me, walked out of the room for the ladies' quarters. She followed without speaking.

I washed, and had one of the Dwala braid my hair into one single, long entity that ran down my back. I walked into the main hall, leaving my sister to finish grooming herself. My father and mother were already seated with the other lords and ladies of the estate, along with some high-ranking officials they had invited as special guests. I went to them, standing between their chairs, and greeted them as a formality in front of our company.

"Greetings, Father. Greetings . . . Mother." I bowed and shot a disdainful look at her. I'd never addressed her as simply "Mother." I always called her Madja. My father's head snapped. His eyes were enraged.

"You're dismissed, Alya!" he said in a stern voice. Even Madja was startled that his tone was so aggressive. She quickly came to grips with the situation and backed him up obediently. I walked away holding my breath, which I did when I knew that the next words I uttered would land me in more trouble than I could handle. I took my seat. Mira took a seat next to me so I assumed she had forgiven our confrontation earlier. I, however, had not, and made no intention of starting a conversation with her.

I was hungry but took my time eating, seeing that I wasn't going anywhere but to sleep tonight after finishing. I played over my sweet mushrooms and pear. Mira ate her food in a hurry, gave her dishes to the servants, and scurried out of the room. I assumed she felt awkward and didn't want to prolong my company any longer than she had to. Even Rayloh, who always made it to second servings, hadn't finished his first plate before Mira had darted out. The crowd dwindled down and eventually everyone retired, even Segun and Rayloh. The main hall was empty except for Madja, of course, who was waiting for me to finish. I didn't bother to tell the lads that I couldn't stay in the study with them because I didn't want them to make me feel any worse about missing the new interests and any other adventure that I would be absent from tonight.

Madja got up, walked to my table, picked up my plate, and placed it in the basin outside the kitchen door. She knew that all I was doing was prolonging the inevitable. I pushed my seat back and stormed out of the hall. Madja followed close behind, ensuring that I headed to the family quarters.

"You know I don't need an escort."

She didn't respond. I entered our quarters, throwing the beads out of my path. If an adventure with my comrades was not an option, then sleep would be the only other option for me. I didn't care to wish my family a peaceful rest or to share details of the day's activities, and it didn't seem like they were expecting any of this anyhow. My father had already retired to his private chambers. I can't remember a time when Madja slept in the room with him. He was always busy with work, with the stacks of parchment and scrolls he brought home, so I assumed he didn't get much sleep anyway, their sleeping quarters transformed into his at-home study. Mira was already asleep in her cot when I entered. I decided to follow suit. I pulled the sheets back and got into my bed. Just as my eyes began to roll into the back of my head I felt something warm on the side of my leg. My gown grew damp, almost drenched. I hopped out of the bed in disgust, flipping back the sheets. Someone had urinated in my bed.

I sat up shrieking in disgust. My father rushed out of his chambers.

"What's the matter, Alya?!" he exclaimed.

"Someone . . . urinated in my cot."

At that very moment, Mira sat up, looking distraught. "I think I did in my bed *as well*," she said, clutching the front of her nightgown. "It must have been the pear juice."

47

She got out of her cot, hanging her head in embarrassment. My father, with angry haste, went back into his chambers. Madja rushed to my sister's side. Her nightgown was drenched, as well as her bed coverings. Mira looked at me and smiled. I sneered back. I watched Madja rush to take the sheets off her bed and put them on the balcony so the odor wouldn't fill the room. If I weren't so shocked at this incident, I would have laughed at the way Madja held the sheets gingerly to keep them from touching the floor as well as her body. After placing them on the balcony, she ran out of the room, returning shortly with wet rags. She began wiping my sister. My legs were sticky and I couldn't believe that Mira would urinate in both of our cots, reeking them of pear fruit juice. In fact, it smelled too much like pear juice.

"Did you urinate in your cot as well?" Mira asked in a caring voice as Madja walked back out onto the balcony.

Then it hit me. I sat in the wet patch on my bed, pushing the front of my gown between my legs so it could get wet as well. I put on my sobbing, meek voice and beckoned Madja. She was milk in my hands. She ran to me and helped me to undress, then took my cot coverings out to the balcony in the same way she had Mira's.

"Madja, I'm cold." Mira was a professional at bending Madja to her will, so it was no task for me to sit back and let her do what she did best.

"It's too late to take your cot coverings to the wash room. The Dwala have been given leave for the evening I'm sure. You and your sister will go down to the study to sleep. There are blankets and pillows down there."

Madja put her palm to her head, pushing her frazzled bangs to her temple. "I knew I shouldn't have requested the pear juice," she mumbled. I almost broke out in a fit of laughter but managed to contain myself.

My sister and I rushed out, carrying our gowns. I followed behind her, imitating her sorrowful expression. I could have skipped out of the room, doing cartwheels, since Mira was the one doing the deceiving. I had nothing to worry about. She and Madja had an unbreakable bond and Madja would curse all the nations of Keldrock before questioning my sister's honor. We waited until the door closed behind us in the grooming quarters before breaking our act. I turned immediately to Mira.

"Why are you helping me? I thought we weren't speaking."

"I know how much you like spending time with the lads so I thought I would do you this favor and maybe you'll do one for me in return."

We changed our gowns and walked to the study. We opened the doors to find Rayloh and Segun playing a board game. They were happily surprised to see me, and even more shockingly, Mira.

"What of this favor?" I asked her.

"I want to go with you and the lads tonight. I want to see the base."

"How do you know about the base?" I asked accusingly.

"I heard you guys whispering at midday meal. That's when I came up with the plan to pour pear fruit juice on the cots. That's why I finished my meal and went to the family quarters early." I never knew my sister had such deceitful wits about her.

I laughed sarcastically. I couldn't let her know where we were going.

"You're at the base. That's our name for the study. All you heard was Segun's imagination taking flight. You know how lads can be."

The lads glared at me. Rayloh sucked his lip.

"Then who are the new interests?" she asked.

"You know it's unbefitting for a lady to listen to conversations that she is not invited to partake in!" I mocked Madja's tone and words. I could see Segun smiling out of the corner of my eye.

"I wasn't partaking in an unwelcome conversation." Mira began walking about the room, one hand behind her back and one running along the shelved books on the wall as if she were a master addressing her pupils. "If *I* were discussing secrets that I didn't want others to partake in, I would be intelligent enough not to speak of the matter when the whole estate was present." This made the lads burst with laughter. I shot them a harsh glance, reminding them of where their allegiance lay.

"Okay, you snarky weasel. Let me speak with Rayloh and Segun in private to see if you're worthy enough to journey with us to the base." I gestured her in the direction of the door. She stepped out, leaving the door cracked. I followed behind and aggressively shut it to ensure our complete privacy.

"Much thanks, Segun. Now we have to bring her. If she finds out where we're going, she will tell Madja and I will never see the light of day again. She's not going to want to leave the city limits!" I dropped down on the love seat in frustration.

"She can't if she comes with us," Rayloh said.

"What do you mean?" I asked.

"If we bring her along. She'll be sneaking out as well, even though she won't know specifically where we are going. If we get to the wall and she doesn't want to go, she can turn around and come back. But she still won't feel inclined to tattle because she wouldn't want your mother to find out she went out as well."

"You are clever beyond your years, Lord Rayloh," Segun encouraged.

I smiled. Even I had to admit that the idea was quite clever. "Bring her in, Segun."

Segun walked to the door, opened it, and stepped aside to allow my sister passage into our chamber of ruling. She looked like a transgressor, coming before the sage to receive her verdict, with me being her judge.

"You can come, but you have to promise not to tell anyone where we go or what you see tonight," I said firmly.

Mira nodded her head and smiled. I turned to Rayloh.

"Do the new interests know where to meet us?" I asked.

"Yes. I told them when the sun is fully set that we will meet them at the tunnel so I think it best we leave soon."

We crept out of the door of Coor as usual. We were quiet, dodging guards making sure that we were not seen. There were a lot more guards in the blue ring than in the yellow ring, and in the black ring, the only ones that held posts were the ones that guarded the gate allowing entrance into and exit from the city. When we arrived in the black ring, we circled around on some side streets that allowed us to approach the tunnel, which was a couple of meters down from the main gate and the Guards of Candor that stood there at attention. They were always on their ground posts so there wasn't much worry about being spotted outside of the gate. They had no need to use the high posts atop the wall unless the city was being threatened, which never happened. We came around to the hole in the wall, the tunnel, and saw the Dwala children already there, waiting.

"Alya! It's good to see you again, my sister."

Nazda ran to embrace me and lifted me in the air. I didn't reciprocate the warm greeting. Partly because it had caught me off guard and partly because I was ashamed that Mira was there to see me hugging a Dwala. Unfazed by my less than mediocre reception, Nazda put me down and politely introduced herself to Mira. My sister didn't react the way I did. In fact, she was quite pleasant. She greeted Nazda with the utmost respect, as well as the other Dwala children. It didn't surprise me that she would have such a humble mind. It angered me how she could be so pleasant for the sake of appearance.

After everyone greeted one another, we discussed our plan of action. There were seven of us. Nazda bought with her two friends, two boys named Acar and Niegi. It was hard enough staying quiet with three people, so we had to be creative if we were to go out with seven. We decided that the best way was to sneak out in two groups. After a sour remark from Niegi, we decided to have a male group and a female group.

"Use your warrior instincts, Alya," Niegi snorted arrogantly, nudging Acar. I rolled my eyes. Although I didn't remember their faces from the night before, I sensed that they were the same boys from this snarky comment, or else Nazda had humored them with the story of our meeting. Rayloh interrupted, sensing the tension.

"We'll go first. Count to a hundred after you see us enter into the woods before you come."

Mira stood quietly. She seemed distant and uneasy. I could tell she was nervous. With the plans settled, the male group set off on their way. Rayloh led the way through the tunnel, followed by Acar, Niegi, and bringing up the rear, Segun. I crawled behind them, so I could see when they entered the woods but it was too dark. There was no way I could have seen them from the great distance. The moon was only a slit in the sky and it was too early for the stars to be out. I knew they hadn't made it

into the woods yet. I decided to count to two hundred instead
before crawling back into the tunnel.

"Ready?" I asked. Nazda nodded assuredly while my
sister just stood.

"Are you coming or not, Mira?"

She just stared blankly at me, her gaze fixed on the tunnel.
I sighed a breath of disappointment—even though this is what I
secretly wanted. I didn't want my sister to come, not just because
of her intruding on my friends and me, or even on account of her
young age, but also because I didn't want to have to deal with
Madja should anything happen to her.

"Go home, Mira! We can't wait any longer. I don't want
Rayloh and Segun to worry. Remember, you can't tell Madja!
You're just as guilty as we are. I have your word?"

"Yes, Alya. I promise."

"You remember how to get home?" She nodded.

I turned and began going through the tunnel, with Nazda
close behind. We ran, ducking into and out of the shadows. We
finally made it to the woods and followed our semitreaded trail to
the base. As we stalked the wild terrain, our eyes adjusted to the
darkness so it was much easier to make our way. After about a
couple of rounds and paces, the base finally came into view.
Nazda stared in amazement.

The base was a potbellied tree, named for its tremendous
trunk, that Rayloh found while we were playing. It had been
slightly hollowed out, probably by some large, burrowing animal.

Using some tools we borrowed from the yellow gardens, we dug out the remaining roots, dirt, and other debris that sat in the hole, and even expanded it. We were extremely proud once we completed our little project. We could fit about ten sprites, uncomfortably, into our base, but for the Segun, Rayloh and I, there was plenty of room. An old covering from Segun's family quarters was now being recycled as the curtain that hung as our wavering door. Above this sheet, inscribed on the tree, was our group's name: Au Magi. The Goodwills; we rarely, if ever, referred to ourselves as that. Still it hung.

I headed Nazda into the base. On the walls hung different pieces of parchment. A lot were Segun's paintings, while others kept records of who won Shadow Man or our many other games. I sat down next to Acar and readied myself to begin the initiation. For the new interests to join us at the base, they had to be sworn in, to maintain secrecy. I didn't think they were ready to join us as members of the Goodwills, especially since Segun and I didn't know them well enough, but Rayloh vouched for them. A compromise was reached that we would bring them, ask them to swear to secrecy, with which they happily complied, and let them decide to join later.

After the formalities and the pledge among Rayloh, Segun and me, they watching on, we organized a game of Plague. After we played the game, we'd hear their decision and then swear them into the Goodwills. Why go through the trouble if the edgewoods presented too much of an obstacle for them to want to return?

Rayloh explained the rules to them. A person would start off as the plagued one. As he or she caught more people, they would become plagued as well and continue hunting the able until everyone was ill. Once you were touched by the plague, you had to howl. That let everyone know that someone had been touched. The trick to the game was that you never knew who was sick and who wasn't. The last person remaining was the plague master. Normally we had to draw lots to see who would be the plagued, but Nazda volunteered before I could even make the suggestion. She counted to five, giving us a little headway before chasing us. We all went our separate ways.

Nazda was fast, but I was faster and familiar with the edgewoods. I jumped over roots and grounded branches I had seen many times before and glided swiftly through foliage and vines that hung from above. I ran for about ten rounds before stopping to take a breath. I heard footsteps, more than one pair, near me. I hadn't heard a howl so I didn't think anyone had been caught yet. I saw Segun's silhouette and whispered his name, hoping he would hear my voice and join me. I found that having one other with you was great in eliminating suspects and also having an easier target in case you're both discovered by the plagued. He was too far for my whispers to reach his ears and I didn't want to be any louder for fear of alerting Nazda. I wanted to win.

I crouched down in the bushes. Niegi was the source of the other footsteps I heard with Segun. I ran toward them, hoping to scare them into giving away their positions. Just as I was about to be upon them, we were attacked.

Chapter Five

It moved like a shadow. It was swift and I would have thought it to be a spirit had it not uprooted the trees with its rage and physical might. It was huge, greater than any beast I had heard about in any elf's tale. I could barely make out its yellow eyes in the night. I saw it coming sooner than Segun and Niegi did, but before I could warn them, it had Niegi within its grasp. It threw him in the air. I could hear his screams trailing off in the distance. The beast turned to retrieve its tossed victim, his screams still echoing through the forest. I wasn't sure if this was the way it killed its prey or if it was toying with its food, but I wasn't going to wait around and find out. I was certain there were others of its kind that were near.

"Segun!" I hissed, terrified.

He just stood there, in shock. I grabbed his hand and began running in the direction of the base. I wasn't sure specifically where it was but I could only hope that once inside the hollowed tree, we would be safe. We were too far from home and too close to the monster so it only made sense to take refuge in our wooden bunker. Segun had snapped out of his trance and was now running alongside me on his own accord. The canopy's foliage was blocking the little bit of light cast down from the half moon, so it was still hard to see where we were going. I almost tripped over a root, but my foot, in both haste and refusal to be stopped, tore it from the soil. My foot was aching, but my heart and the rest of my body wouldn't let me quit. I took in my surroundings as best I could as we ran, trying to spot anything familiar.

I soon came to accept that we were lost. I could hear rustling behind me. The beast was swift, but it was hard to believe that it had finished Niegi and had returned to finish us in such a short time, unless it truly wasn't alone. I heard it gaining on us. With all my might, I pushed myself to run harder and faster. Sweat rolled down my face. I had that feeling like I was falling to a certain death—no matter how much I flailed my arms, or prayed that I grow wings and fly, that I was going to hit the ground and die. I tripped and tumbled down in defeat. Segun kept running.

"Come on, Alya!"

But I couldn't run any longer. I heard the beast approaching. I shut my eyes and began praying to myself. All I could see as my eyes began to close was Segun running. I wanted him to make it. I wished I wanted to know my father. I wished I had listened to Madja. I wished that I had been kinder to Mira. So many thoughts ran through my mind in those few moments when death was almost upon me. Tears began streaming down my face. The anticipation was over. I could almost feel the beast's steps now. My breathing slowed as I tried my best to be at peace. It was over.

"Get up, Alya!"

I opened my eyes. Rayloh, Acar, and Nazda were running toward me. They moved like a pack of wolves. They were so in sync as they cut through the trees. I felt a jolt of adrenaline and

59

jumped up and started running alongside them. Rayloh led the way, and in a few moments the base was in sight. I only hoped that Segun found his way there, too. Rayloh reached the arch of the doorway first. He pulled back the covering and watched to ensure that we all made it inside—Acar, Nazda, then me. He pushed the piece of scrap wood from the potbellied tree that we used as a raft or in play to block the doorway.

Segun was already inside. I rushed to hug him. We held each other. Rayloh soon joined us in an embrace, we three friends in what could possibly be our last moments.

Nazda interrupted our reunion. "Where's Niegi?" I could hear the hurt in her voice. I wished I hadn't seen anything. I wished that I could say, *I don't know*, leaving her a glimmer of hope.

I turned and looked at her. Her eyes were full. Sweat and tears trailed down her face.

"Where is he?!" she yelled. She balled up her fist. I sighed and hung my head.

"He ran off without us. I'm not sure where he is now."

Her face softened. Maybe she knew I was lying, but her mind was put at ease, and that's all we needed for the moment. Just because we made it to the base didn't mean we were safe. That monster was still out there. I couldn't bear to look at Segun, but I hoped that the expression on his face hid the truth. The lads and I have had our encounters with wild animals, but this was no wild animal. This thing was intelligent, fast, and had purpose.

The base shook like something hard had hit it . . . or landed on it. Then we heard it. It was the call of the hunt. The call that beckoned the kin of this monster. The call that meant, "I've found them." We all gathered in the corner. Rayloh stood in front of us, with Acar and Segun slightly behind him. Rayloh picked up a faulty spear he had made to pierce fruit in the heights of the trees. He was never successful at spearing any with it and it was more of a game to him anyway, but I hoped for all of our sakes that tonight the spear would prove some worth in arms.

Before I knew it, I stood and aligned myself next to the lads. I didn't look at them, but I could feel their stares of surprise. That I wasn't shuddering in the corner afraid but that I was going to fight for my life and not be a burden to anyone. Nazda was still hysterical. She looked dazed and seemed like she had already given up and accepted her fate. The ground shook. I could feel the tree give out and release the hefty load it once held in its branches that the ground was now forced to support. The monster was panting heavily. I didn't know how I was going to fight this beast, but at that very moment fear left my body. My mind emptied every thought. Courage moved in where fear once was. I picked up a sharpened rock used to pin down the door covering and braced myself.

Suddenly, a flame appeared outside, seeping into our base. Was this thing human? To wield fire was nothing any animal to my knowledge had mastered. The light flickered underneath the scrap wood, passing shadows outside of our hideout. I could see

61

the outline of spears and hear the clashing of metal. We deciphered among the war cries something close to man or elf, and the wailing of a beast. Could it be our cavalry? Was someone sent here to save us? We waited, not moving. I was ready to run out when the sounds ceased and it was quiet for a moment. The shadows began to shrink, retreating to the bodies that were now approaching the entrance to our base. I looked at Rayloh. He nodded at me, and that's all the confirmation I needed to believe I was ready for whatever was out there.

A muscular figure kicked back the scrap wood with ease. It flew in sideways, knocking the lads and myself back into the wall. The figure was draped in plates of stone and metal sewn into a mixture of animal hides. Their face was covered with a helmet that only left their dark eyes visible. This was not one of our nation's warriors, let alone a citizen of Keldrock.

"Get up!" A husky voice commanded us. The mask and helmet made the voice muffled.

My comrades and I looked at each other, then all to Rayloh. He looked at the figure with distaste. The figure banged a large root against the wall with such force that the potbellied tree trembled, shaking lose the battle plans and paintings that hung from the walls. Nazda stood and we all followed, Rayloh bringing up the end as the figure led us outside. As we were escorted out, it tore down the covering that hung from the arch of our entrance. I could feel Rayloh tense at this blatant act of disrespect. Outside were three other figures. They wore helmets with masks as well.

The helmets were semibroken, missing the jaw hinge or revealing the forehead, but still shielded the majority of their faces. Their armor was also poorly crafted and outdated. I didn't stare at them long, for fear of upsetting them. The beast was nowhere in sight, so for the moment, I was content. At least our current oppressors were enemies of the beast. As we walked our semitreaded trail, I became almost certain that they were simply returning us to the city. Then, a few meters away from the end of the edgewoods, we stopped. The three trailing us moved around us like sheepdogs to livestock. By now the forest was beginning to lighten, but it was still too dark to make out these individuals.

"You're free to go, but you must never return to the edgewoods again," said one of the masked assailants.

We stood there in silence, not knowing what to say. All of us were too proud, or too cowardly, to agree or disagree with this command.

"We won't."

I looked at Rayloh. His voice faltered. He seemed discouraged, like a lion stripped of his territory, losing both his land and his pride to new arrivals.

"We have your word, then."

Within moments they disappeared into the shrubs. They moved quickly, maneuvering in the same direction but along different paths, like this was their home, a place they knew intimately. They had Rayloh's word that we wouldn't return to the edgewoods. My tongue, however, was held. I wasn't certain of a

lot of things. I wasn't even sure of the importance of his promise
and if I had any right to make one of my own. I wasn't even
certain that Niegi was gone. I was certain of one thing, however. I
wouldn't be defying these warriors by returning.

We didn't worry about breaking off into two separate groups on
our way back to the city. We just crept silently, trying our hardest
to reach the tunnel without being detected. Once on the other side
of the wall, we parted ways. Acar and Nazda headed to their
homes within the black ring and my friends and I made our way
back to the Remni. Even though I felt for their loss, I was relieved
that no harm had come to my comrades. I couldn't fathom losing
Rayloh or Segun, and if Nazda's relationship with Niegi was
anything close to what the lads and I had, then she was heavy with
grief.

"What happened to Niegi?" Rayloh asked when the Dwala
kids were gone. It was futile to keep the truth from him. We had
known each other for so long that we knew when something
wasn't right among us, and I didn't want to keep any secrets
between us anyhow.

"It got him. The . . . beast. It got him."

Rayloh bore down on his spear. It almost slipped my mind
that he still had it with him. I guess the masked woodsmen didn't
feel the need to make Rayloh surrender his weapon. In his hand,
the spear was consumed with flames, a wicked red. They devoured
the spear in seconds, leaving nothing behind, not even the

sharpened bone at the point. He must have learned this skill at lessons, or maybe it was fueled by his rage, but such raw power both amazed and startled me.

Back at the Remni, we went to the study, quickly and quietly closing the door behind us. We hadn't been gone for the entire night, so we had time to sleep. Mira was dozing on the love seat, her dark hair draped over the couch cushions, flowing like a river of darkness. The lads and I grabbed our blankets and pillows and each took our usual spots on the floor. Oddly enough, I went straight to sleep, but I can't say that my dreams left me at peace. All I could see was the great shadow and those yellow eyes.

Chapter Six

The woods were dark again. The moon was not out this night. It was tucked soundly behind the dense clouds floating overhead. All that remained alive in the night sky were faintly twinkling stars. I couldn't find anyone. I called out Rayloh and Segun's names in the darkness, to no avail. The torchlights were too far in the distance. I picked one that appeared to be closer than the rest and tried to chase it, but as soon as I got to where I could almost see the flames flickering, it went out.

Somehow, in my search, I stumbled upon the base, or what was left of it. The warriors in the woods had destroyed it. I knew that when they told us never to return that they would remove all evidence of us ever being in these woods. The paintings were probably burned along with the tallied parchment keeping score of our games. All I felt, all I could see around me, was death.

As a scream echoed through the air, a flame from a torch went out. I heard it. I'd stopped calling out the lad's names for fear that in their flight they would be discovered or I'd be caught myself. I carried no torch. If I were to die this night, no one would know where. I wouldn't be able to see my attacker. The only things I would be able to spot out would be those yellow eyes, but by that time, I'd be finished.

From the base, I run in the direction of the city. If I made it there, I could find help. I would return the very instance I made it through the gate, with guards, the Guerr, anyone that would prove formidable against this terrible agent. Yes, that's right. They were surely strong enough to avenge the smoldered lights. The clouds shifted and for a few moments I could see the moon. It offered no aid. The moon was but a sliver, forming the shape of a yeast-less crescent, so thin that no sustenance could be obtained. I stumbled upon a creek. I smiled. This was where my comrades and I rafted from time to time. My smile quickly faded when I realized that in finding the creek, I'd only run deeper into the edgewoods.

I don't let my mind begin to calculate how far I'd run in the wrong direction or how this had happened. It was like the world spun around or my memory was a mirage within itself, meant to fill me with false hope. I concluded that there was only one option. I picked a tree, one with a strong trunk, yet limbs that seemed to touch the heavens, and foliage enough to block my shadow. Being at any great height made me extremely nervous, but I couldn't let fear get the better of me. Not tonight. I climbed almost to the top, stopping on a sturdy branch that I hoped would be able to hold my body. I put my back to the tree and leaned my head against it to catch my breath. I closed my eyes. I felt the change in climate and could sense that I was way higher than I wanted to be.

With my eyes closed, my other senses became alive. I heard another victim experience the wrath of the monster, the beast tearing away at its prey. It was close. The unnerving sound of bones breaking and limbs being ripped apart sent chills down my spine. My mouth turned numb. I clenched my ears in an attempt to drown out these barbaric sounds of torture. Of being murdered, eaten, destroyed slowly. The last flame went out, as if the monster were signaling the company of the now deceased. That this whole time it was playing a game: how many lights can I make go out?

Part of me knew the monster wasn't killing for hunger or protection. If I survived, we'd return with others during the day to find strewn body parts, hardly eaten, skin and body innards still there, tossed about the edgewoods, the monster having had a killing spree for pleasure. Up until this point, this was child's play for the beast. Now it was presented a challenge. One had gotten away. Now it was ready to hunt.

This beast had intelligence. From our last encounter, I could tell that for sure. My stomach sank. That was the last torchlight! I mouthed it with my lips this time. I realized that there was no Segun. No Rayloh. Two tears, one for each of my companions, rolled from my eyes before I could stop them. I couldn't mourn them right now. I had to stay focused. The monster had ended them. There were five torches when we left the city, and I watched as each one was extinguished in the wilderness, some together, others alone. I didn't have a torch because I was supposed to stay with Segun and Rayloh. I couldn't believe I was the only one left. I sat in the heights of the tree hoping that if I made it to daybreak, the monster would retreat to its den to sleep until night fell again.

I took off my top shirt and then lay down flat on the branch. I balanced my body, wrapping my legs around the branch to stay steady. I took the long stretched sleeves of my top shirt and wrapped them around my body three or four times. The sleeves ended on my stomach, as I had hoped. I tied them tightly, two knots to be sure, to be as secure as I could possibly be in this tree.

I began to drift off to sleep. Although I tried to stay focused, sorrow was heavy in my spirit. I hadn't gotten much rest since the beast first crossed me. I hadn't felt safe, not even within the city limits. I think what made now different from other nights was the security in the fact that I had evaded the evil beast. Humility and gratitude were distracted by confidence and certainty within my dreamy thoughts. I, the only she-elf on the expedition, managed to stay alive. Oh, how Madja would feel when I returned home, thanking the stars that I wasn't some damsel waiting to be saved! But my pride was short-lived. I was too comfortable. I was too naïve.

My body jerked, sending my early dreams spiraling into the deep recesses of my mind. I didn't hesitate to question anything. I could only sit up slightly, wrapping my legs tighter around the underside of the branch to steady myself. I attempted to undo the first knot. The tree jerked and the vibrations were getting closer. The beast was climbing aggressively fast. I thought quickly. If I climbed higher, the tree wouldn't be able to support the beast. It would give up. It would go back to its home of bear bones and deer hides and rest, assuming I would still be in the tree when it awakened. I untied the knot.

    The vibrations were getting closer. Leaves and dead limbs started to fall past me from the top of the tree. The worst part of this situation was that I couldn't see my pursuer. All I could do was feel for it approaching me, which made me all the more anxious to break free. I quickly worked on the final knot. It wouldn't budge. It would take more time to pry it loose, time I didn't have.

    I could feel my branch being weighed down—so much weight that the branch yielded, splitting itself from the tree. I couldn't see anything in the darkness, but I could feel the rush and sensation of falling. I closed my eyes and held my breath. I didn't hit the ground. In fact, something was holding the branch that I was attached to. I sighed in relief and disbelief that I was still alive. This feeling didn't last any longer than it had before. Although my pride at evading the beast had left my body, my courage hadn't. The beast turned the branch. As the monster flipped the branch upright, I closed my eyes. I didn't want to see its face or those gruesome yellow eyes. On the branch, I resembled meat on a sharpened fire iron. Actually to the monster, I was meat. Savory, new, smart meat.

    I'd tightly tied the knot of my shirtsleeves, and I was part of that tree until either I untied the sleeves or the monster ripped me from its grip. I could feel its breath on my face and along my neck. I still refused to open my eyes. I didn't want the beast to have the satisfaction of seeing the fear in my eyes nor the pleasure of watching the light in my brown orbs fade away. With my final breath, I screamed. I awoke in a sweat. My heart was racing.

Almost a month had passed since our experience in the edgewoods. Segun, Rayloh, and I hadn't been out of the Remni except to go to lessons. We spent our nights now as they should have been spent: sleeping in the study. I could still see the yellow eyes in my head. I could still hear the trailing screams of the Dwala boy Niegi. It was hard accepting that something was living out there, roaming outside the city's limits, but I couldn't admit it to anyone.

My father had told me the edgewoods were once used as punishment for those who crossed the Courts. That we weren't to leave the city. Maybe he knew about this beast the whole time. Maybe there were others. The more I thought about it the more I wanted to seek counsel outside of Rayloh and Segun. Since this wasn't an option, I tried my best to quell the thoughts. The lads and I avoided the topic altogether, trying to wipe the incident from our memories.

My Kei was only seven days away. Had it not been for Madja reminding me of my ceremony, taking new measurements for the seamstress for my evening gown, and taking me to dance lessons, it would have slipped my mind. I found myself less worried about crossing the threshold and becoming a mistress because of the situation at hand. If the masked warriors hadn't saved us that night, I wouldn't be having a coming-of-age ceremony at all. Instead the estate would be cloaked in black and the only guests we would entertain were those coming to console my family after my death.

The lads were not in the study when I awoke. I was relieved they weren't. I assumed I screamed out loud, since I had in my dream. The lads had mentioned before that they could hear me crying and whining during the night. I didn't want to worry them. Especially since that night weighed heavily upon them as it did me.

I put on my sandals and walked to the grooming quarters. The bath maid helped me undress. She folded my clothes and sat them on a bench in the corner. As usual, she turned to leave the room.

"Did I dismiss you?" I shot at her.

"No, miss. I only assumed—"

"You assumed wrong. Have a seat."

She moved my clothes to the end of the bench and sat down. The truth was I didn't want to be alone. She probably had other duties to fulfill, but I wasn't in a place to be concerned with those things. She didn't try to summon an excuse to leave either. She just sat.

"I'm sorry for lashing out at you. I just don't want to be alone right now." I couldn't believe I was starting to have this conversation. She smiled and bowed her head in respect. "What's your name?" I asked.

"Kala. Kala Knark. Under the house of Demallo, my caretaker. She is a jeweler."

"What of your mother? Or your father? Is he not the head of your house?" Her eyes grew gray.

"My parents passed a long time ago. Now I live with Missus Demallo, at the edge of the black ring, just above the mines."

"My apologies, Kala. I meant no offense." I was sincere in that. "What mines do you speak of?" The confusion on my face was obvious to Kala.

She smirked with a giggle, brightening up once again. "You mean to tell me that you've never heard of the mines?" I could tell that she took my stare as a command for respect, so she retreated into her reserved state.

"The mines are in the black ring. That's where a vast amount of the Dwala men work. They dig for stone used to make the beautiful gold that accents our city as well as other precious stones and minerals. From what I have heard, it is dangerous work."

I couldn't believe I'd existed all this time and never heard anything about any mines. It would only make sense that the gold came from somewhere.

"Lord Fueto is over the mines. Such a great architect he is."

I thought of a gold necklace Rayloh's father had given me for my last birthday that was the pride of my jewelry box. Mira

73

had one as well. Mine was in the shape of a star, while Mira got a crescent moon. I liked mine better and convinced myself he had given me the more interesting and intricate of the two because I was special. Sometimes I'd dream that I was older, taller, and slender, like Master Tali. My hair would be so long in natural spirals down my back. Lord Fueto and I would live happily in a wonderful union.

I could see the girl's cheeks. Her light brown skin revealed red from her blushing. She likely fancied him just as I did.

"If you don't mind my asking, what is your father's occupation?" she inquired.

"He works for the Courts. A member of the Council." She stared as if expecting me to go on, as if I had left something out. Some detail. She persisted.

"I meant, what specifically are his workings?" I reared back my head at her inquiry.

"Nothing to concern yourself with" I snapped at her, before I had time to reconsider. "You're dismissed. I'd like to be left alone now."

"Yes, miss. I meant no offense." She exited without another word.

I wasn't offended. In fact, I was quite pleased to have had a conversation with Kala, the bath maid. I secretly loved that some of the workers in the Remni were my age. I could observe how young girls really interacted without feeling ridiculous for staring.

They were often innocent, and beautiful. The groundskeeper who employed them probably valued this a lot more than the residents who depended solely on the service of the Dwala and cared not for the attractiveness of these individuals. At least that was the assumption at the time. Some he-elves within the Remni had an appetite.

What caused me to dismiss Kala was her inquiry about my father and what work he did for the Courts. The truth is, even I didn't know. He would come home and lock himself in his study. He was an elf of mystery, but unlike most mysteries, I didn't care to solve his. He worked for the Courts that dealt harshly with transgressors, that dealt a heavy and swift hand over the Dwala clan. A sensation crept into me, sparked by Kala. This was the very itch that drove me to want to ask more questions. That familiar feeling of curiosity that was gaining on me.

The next time I saw Kala, I wanted to tell her all about what my father did. Maybe that would somehow validate for myself that he and I had a functional relationship. If I knew more, I'd understand more. I would understand why he had grown so cold. My father had somehow lost himself, and the only thing that kept him was his work. The one thing I knew so little about lay in his private quarters behind lock and key.

That ignited my first plan of action to come to fruition. The beast that lay on the other side of the wall retreated into a cave within the confines of my mind, ever so often peeking out to remind me that it was still alive. But now other questions bubbled and blurred those yellow eyes, like smoke and soot billowing from a vent.

I returned to my family quarters after playing a challenging game of collared throne with the lads in the study, where we stacked the most massive tomes there and threw smaller books as cannonballs, pretending we were destroying magnificent castles. I walked in with my nightgown on and sat down on my bed.

"Do you want me to unwind your hair?" I asked Mira.

She looked at me in confusion, as did Madja, who was out on the balcony, painting the night sky. I never knew Madja painted, but I figured it was one of her recently picked up "cultural" hobbies she used to distract herself from her marital problems. My sister picked up her hair runner and came toward me, bringing along a pillow to place her knees on. Madja taught us to place pillows under our knees so they wouldn't grow darker than the rest of our skin, but I rarely did as I was told. My knees were the darkest part of my body. Mira sat in front of my bed and I ran the hair runner through her long, beautiful hair. This wasn't the same hair runner. It was tense, and the teeth didn't wield easily. I didn't have long to ponder this odd trinket when my objective walked in. My father took off his Council robe, and after doing so, pulled from his pocket a key that he used to unlock his chambers. Then he placed the key back into his robe pocket.

As I combed through Mira's hair, I thought about the next objective. Now that I had discovered where he kept the key, all I

76

had to do was find the right time to take it. If done too soon, it would be obvious that the key disappearing the first night I willingly slept in my family quarters would be the same as writing a sign saying that I did it in bright red. So I was going to wait. I thought of a night when everyone would be so busy and so worked up about the goings on of life that they wouldn't have any time to worry about a key. My Kei was in seven days. I smiled to myself, peering down at Mira, who was by now relaxing as I looped this strange new hair runner through her hair.

Chapter Seven

Over the next couple of days, I came up with all sorts of theories concerning what my father could be up to in his chambers. Perhaps he knew about the affairs outside of the city's limits. I'd seen him come in with a vast number of scrolls and parchment. I never saw Rayloh's father come home from work with such a load. Segun told me that his father, at times, came home with reports that he kept under lock and key, but considering that he was an elite medic, I would assume those were records of patients with ailments that should be kept in such a manner. Maybe my father received reports from the Guerr, informing him of their progress. Maybe when the warriors left the city in segments for training, they were really tracking down the last of these beasts, relaying the news to my father, the liaison for the Courts. How many warriors were lost, and how many beasts remained?

Perhaps these beasts have always been part of our existence. Living within the city walls, there were no adversaries. It only made sense that in a mostly peaceful world, there was some unseen evil. The whining of privileged citizens was the only negativity that filled the streets of the city—at least it was so in the two middle rings. I was concealed from the concerns of the purple ring, and I cared not for the troubles of the black ring because they didn't apply to me. Either way, my world was pacific.

I pondered these thoughts as I walked with Madja to have the final fitting of my gown for my Kei. I always found the appearance of these gowns to be overly detailed, and they looked highly uncomfortable. There was so much material to keep up with. The tail seemed to get in the way of doing things normally, such as dancing, eating, or walking, even breathing. I just wished I could come to my Kei in a warrior's garb, which is what I requested for my coming-of-age present. I begged Madja. Under normal circumstances she would have said no, but she got so caught up in the excitement of planning my special event that she answered "possibly." That was enough for me to believe that she would get it for me, and I prayed every day since that my wish would come true.

Madja chose a servant to come along with us, just as an extra set of hands. Madja listened to my father, as did I, about keeping our distance and not befriending the Dwala, but she made no effort to degrade them. She was kind, but not too kind, ensuring that the divide in class was still evident. To my surprise, she had picked Kala. I wasn't expecting to see her since I had yet to find out the details about my father's duties in the purple ring. When I found out, I wanted to naturally bring it up, maybe somehow loop her into asking about his occupation again, which probably wouldn't happen since I addressed her so coldly for even mildly prying into my father's affairs.

Kala greeted me formally. "Greetings, miss." She lowered her head, giving a slight bow.

"Greetings . . . Kala."

There was a slight hesitation. I never addressed any of the servants directly, mostly because I didn't take the time to get to know any of their names. I would just beckon them. Any slight movement or twitch of my mouth or eyes would have one of the many Dwala at my side, waiting for an order of assistance. Madja thought nothing of this. She continued on about the gown and how truly spectacular it was. As she spoke, she walked, us following, making our way to the blue ring. Kala, however, had noticed my kinder demeanor—that I wasn't trying to pretend our conversation in the grooming quarters had never happened. I wasn't ashamed of our interaction and she understood that. Even though she seemed pleasantly surprised, she kept her composure. She'd seen many forget their place and forced to find work elsewhere. Some even paid the ultimate price.

One instance came to mind. It was a story that I had come to know from Segun. A young woman who served in the kitchen was caught in an affair with Lord Bitoni, one of the commanders of the Guards of Candor, who used to reside in the Remni a couple of years ago, before retiring. At this time, Segun's mother was pregnant with child, so a house nurse was needed. This girl was faithful and diligent in her work, so Segun's father hired her. It was rewarding because she was enlisted as a special resource instead of a simple servant and was compensated a little more for this task. Still, it was a cheap hire for Segun's family. She was just someone to fetch rags, respond to the endless wants of Segun's mother, and assist Segun's father when it was time for the baby's arrival.

One night, Segun's mother began having pains. These were the kind of pains that only happen when the birth was nearing. Madja told me that bearing offspring was painful because anything worth having comes at a price. Segun's father was up tending to his wife and required the assistance of the house nurse, who was allowed to sleep in the family quarters to be nearby should anything happen. He saw that she was not in her cot and went looking for her. The baby was coming.

He assumed she was in the grooming quarters, since she wasn't in her cot, and he, needing wet rags, peeked his head in the bathing room to alert her of his needs without entering. What he saw was a he-elf, with his trousers down, breathing heavily, hushed grunts echoing in the quiet quarters. Startled, Segun's father burst in on what he thought to be some form of assault only to find the he-elf was not some common slug, but Lord Bitoni. Lord Bitoni pulled his trousers up as he witnessed his startled house nurse rushing to adjust her undergarments and work dress. Segun's father led her by her hair to the streets and dismissed her from his service and ensured that she would have no place in the Remni come morn.

When he returned to the grooming quarters, he didn't find Lord Bitoni, only the rags he himself had dropped in his anger and haste. He wet them and returned to his family quarters. By this time, it was too late. The child had slipped in its entrance into the world, only to leave it. In his absence, the baby passed in its few seconds of life, in wait for its deliverer and nurse. The next day she hung from the gallows, Lord Bitoni heading the charge. A year later he left the Remni, probably paranoid from the constant glares he received from Segun's father and the other residents whose ears had caught rumors of what had transpired. Every year they hold a memorial for the lost elfling. Segun's little brother.

Not to insinuate that Kala would ever fall mistress to anyone, but ever since this instance, and others, the groundskeeper surely put in her mind, as well as that of the other servants, that no relationships with the lords and misses of the estates were to be formed and none would be tolerated. The promiscuity of the house nurse served as the prime example. Not that the Dwala were to remain separate or even that they weren't appreciated, but that they were all replaceable. Those words echoed in my head. The same that made Master Tali cringe and now made my heart weary. They were *only* Dwala.

Once in the blue ring, we turned down a side street that led to a small plaza where most of the marketers were. There were jewelers, spice merchants, ironsmiths, artisans, and other craftsmen and specialty makers. I used to love coming to the market in my younger years. Madja always let my sister and me buy treats, as many as we wanted. My mouth watered at the thought of sweet taffies, and my nostrils flared from the wonderful aromas of miniature cakes. It was a moment of nostalgia and peace of mind.

The goods in the market were mostly purchased by those with luxurious tastes in the yellow and blue rings. Wealthy mothers and daughters, aristocratic families, and flashy dignitaries were their regulars. Even government officials would make their way on occasion to dilly-dally and soak up the cultural life of the city. The black ring had a market as well; although I was certain that it didn't contain as many variations and detailed work as this one, I felt that it was probably an interesting sight.

Mistress Colar's cottage was at the end of the street. The sounds of the hustle and bustle of sales and trade seemed to clear into concise and orderly conversation once we reached her place of business. Her keep was made of fine wood, and hanging from walls, the ceiling, even circling the columns, were dresses. While she and Madja made small talk at the entrance, I wandered around inside, marveling at the sights. The dresses were like angels, hovering about, their radiance shining. Some were small, like cherubs, giggling, fluttering on the railing of the upstairs balcony. These were probably for baby dedications and first birthdays. Some were elaborate, with trains long enough to almost kiss the floor. The breathtaking gowns had sashes and bows, and elaborately designed veils. They hung from the ceiling along the stairs leading up to her workroom. These dresses were most certainly the seraphs, guiding saved souls to the afterlife.

Tucked behind the spiraling staircase was what the seraphs kept at bay. Hell raged along the back walls, where no lantern hung to lighten the darkness. The seraph's trains streamed down, protecting the keep as well as shoppers and traders from its evil aura. Along the back wall were black dresses, dark and sinister. These dresses had no fancy cuts; stones and gems; or long, elaborate detailing. Although they ranged in size, they all looked the same—sorrowful and dreary. The material floated on the air like a lost spirit, ghostlike in movement. I ran my hands along a sheer black dress, barely catching it as it dodged and swirled in an attempt to evade my touch. I had never owned such a dress, although I had once seen one like it—when Segun's mother lost her youngest son.

"Miss?" I turned to see Kala, appearing timid as she interrupted my trance. I let the fabric ease from my grip, slipping through my pressed fingers gradually. "Mistress Vesti is ready for you. She and Lady Alyawan are in wait outside." My heart warmed to hear someone call Madja by her name. I smiled, knowing that our names were so similar and yet we were so different, something that she likely hadn't projected when naming me. I walked back to the front door, where, just outside, she and Mistress Vesti stood.

"There you are, Alya. Taking your time, I see. Keeping us waiting." She shot me a look of disdain, less at the fact that she had been kept waiting, but that in her mind, Mistress Vesti would think that she didn't have a hold on her daughters. Madja was always a stickler for public appearances and took the judgments of her associates to heart.

"Shall we?" Mistress Vesti held her arm out, gesturing Madja toward the inside of her keep.

She led us to an assortment of dresses on a shelving rod, which held a mixture of current projects and completed orders waiting to be picked up. From the far end of the rod, she pulled out a dark green gown. It reminded me of the wild vines and shrubs that flourished, undisturbed, in the depths of the edgewoods, just as I had described. The bodice was a lighter shimmering emerald, with silver lace holding the back to keep the shape of the wearer. It had a shoulder strap on the right that stemmed from the bodice, giving it a uniquely exotic look. Along the collar of the dress was a mixture of jade and silver-colored crystals that sparkled magnificently. The sleeves were ironic—that same thin, grim black material that created such distaste in me before, in silver, was like a breath of fresh air, pleasing to the senses. This gown, although in the eyes of anyone else was just as beautiful as the ones flying gracefully about the keep, was the fairest to me. This amazing piece was like me, creative and uncommon. Madja had done it. She had illustrated the perfect dress. I couldn't hold back my smile any longer.

"The color is great but there are some much-needed changes," Madja said. My smile faded just as quickly as it had appeared. I almost took more offense than Mistress Vesti, who, after receiving this comment, tensed. She remained poised, however, not forgetting that we were her clients whose business she wanted.

"Alterations? I assumed the only alterations to be had were for her height and weight. What exactly about the dress are you not fond of?" I could tell that within her, a battle for control of her emotions was occurring. Madja only made the situation worse.

"I feel it's a little . . . I don't know . . . daring. Yes, daring would be kind. Alya wants something more standard. I expected the green to be lighter, a little more pleasantly flamboyant. She is to be a lady. I understand it's extremely late notice with her party being two days away, so we will pay whatever price necessary. Maybe a dress with some sort of floral pattern, in bright pinks or oranges to add, will do."

Madja walked to the middle of the keep and began shuffling through a few dresses that appeared to be my size. The green dress to me was something marvelous, something wonderful. The very idea of changing it was blasphemous to the very being that blessed Mistress Vesti with the inspiration, and in turn, this amazing talent. I couldn't hold my words.

"Mother . . . I want this dress. It's fine just the way it is! It would be foolish to even suggest anything be changed." A twitch from the corner of her mouth showed that she noticed I hadn't called her Madja.

Madja stared at me in wonder, as did Kala and Mistress Vesti. I stared right back, not flinching. I held Madja's gaze and felt her thoughts rushing through my eyes, her feelings of embarrassment, of disrespect, but there was something else I sensed. Some realization. Her eyes were slowly softening. It was a feeling so familiar, yet from her, so foreign. She grinned.

"You're not my little Alya anymore. This is your Kei and your decision, and I might be a little more involved than I should be. You're quite right." She turned to face Mistress Vesti. "The gown is acceptable as it is." The feeling wasn't passive, or polite. It was a genuine emotion. It was *acceptance*. She accepted my opinion, my desire, and allowed my freedom to flourish, even though it was likely due to the fact that I was expressing some interest in my upcoming celebration. Although this situation was minute, I could feel her slowly letting go, letting me make my own way. I walked proudly out of Mistress Vesti's keep. With our purchase, she added a pair of silver-laced sandals for no charge. She didn't do it because she appreciated our business or even because I shifted Madja's disdain to blissfulness. It was because she felt appreciated. *Her* ideas, *her* visions, were appreciated.

We headed to the line of side shops and mobile carts to find accessories to accent my dress. Kala carried the gown, holding both arms out, letting the dress drape over them. She was so considerate of its intricacy, even though it was encased in cloth, because she didn't want to be the one responsible should something go wrong and the dress, in its radiance, be damaged. I dived in and out of the shops and between carts with Madja while Kala waited patiently on a wooden crate, outside the thicket of sellers and buyers.

Suddenly I was just as enthusiastic about my Kei as Madja. Madja sensed this energy, which made her rants even longer and more detailed. We both agreed that earrings and a necklace would be the only accents I would need. She said that at home, she had a bracelet that would be perfect to wear for this occasion; I told her I would consider it. That made her smile. I willingly tried on anything and everything Madja picked up, but everything she thought would accent perfectly, I thought was too flashy, or had excess colors that were too bright or exuberant. I really wasn't focused on the other details of the Kei. All I could imagine was the dress, it enveloping my body, sending a message to all the new lords and lads, even my own comrades, that I was now a worthy candidate for courting. Still, I hadn't forgotten my priority that night, nor had I forgotten the conversation I had with Kala. My disapproval of the trinkets in the blue market gave me an idea to inquire about something that would take all of my power of persuasion to be granted.

"Madja, I'm not finding anything here. None of these will do." I was so convincing that she rushed to my side, pulling from her side pouch a silk cloth to wipe my cheeks, even though no tears fell. If Mira were here, she'd be proud. I continued, "I just want my Kei to be wonderful."

"We'll find something, Alya. You aren't giving anything a chance."

"I want to see the black market." Madja's nose scrunched and her eyes searched for reasoning, so I continued. "The dress is really unique, and I want everything to be perfect from my crown to my heel. I just want to . . . feel special."

I almost burst into tears—tears of laughter, that is. Madja crossed her arms and studied my face. I dared not look up. I wasn't a good liar. I sweated nervously. She stood for a few moments in thought, which seemed like many moons, then reached into her side pouch and pulled out three markels.

"I won't be seen walking into that filthy nest of poverty, but if you feel there's something down there that you'd like, then by all means take the maid and go. Three markels should be more than enough for you to find something...decent. I'll meet you back at the Remni for dinner."

By this time, Kala had seen us conversing and was a few steps away, waiting for our next call to action. Madja took the dress away from her, and draping it over her arm, began making her way out of the market in the direction of the Remni.

"Will we not be accompanying her?"

"No. I still need some earrings, a necklace . . . and to see the mines."

Kala's face froze. "The mines? Why the mines?"

"That's what I wish to see. This is to stay between us. Do I have your word?" Kala smiled and shook her head in agreement, her mission only to please. With that, we began making our way to the black ring.

The roads began to change as we entered the black ring. It was something that I never really noticed until now, being that I'd only walked these streets at night. As we progressed away from the upper rings, the roads of fine stone slab cuts that glistened pure and white in the sunlight and showed in the darkest of nights were suddenly transformed into a mixture of rough cobblestones. Every so often, I'd see a fine brick that was like an oasis in a desert of poorly kept streets. At night, this difference between the upper rings and the black ring seemed so small, but during the day, the tide and the shore were obviously separate. We went to the black market first, careful to keep track of time. The day had been half spent and the markets would be closing soon.

"Do you know where I can find earring and necklace jewelry sets?" I asked Kala.

"What materials for the pieces did you have in mind, miss?"

I thought about this for a moment, never making a point to coordinate the metal used in my jewelry with the color of my dresses at other formal assemblies. Madja normally would lay out what she wanted me to wear, and because I gave little thought to such trifles, my neck and ears were usually bare. I pictured how my new dress looked. "Silver. Something silver would go best. What are your thoughts?"

"I concur, miss. The silver would be most pleasant. If you don't mind my suggesting, my caretaker, Demallo, makes intricate pieces that I believe will be to your liking. I can take you to our home."

I smiled, remembering that her home was close to the mines. "That would be lovely."

I followed her into the black market. The garb I wore, although nothing above the norm in the upper rings, spoke to the traders and buyers within the black ring. As we walked, I attempted to greet fellow civilians with a gesture or a smile to not appear out of place, but as we passed, they hung their heads, avoiding eye contact. From a distance, I could feel their stares burning into my skin.

The black market was a different sight than the markets I was accustomed to. There weren't any carts, or fine keeps. There was a simple shed, old and worn, some parts newer than others, probably the sad attempt of an untrained carpenter to heal the damages that poor construction and nature's wrath inflicted on the building. To get to Kala's house from the path we were coming from, we had to walk through the market shack. There was no door on either end, just two gaping holes that were uneven, like someone had hacked into the wood with an ax to create them. Along the lengthy walls were merchants with rugs, and on these rugs, their goods for purchasing.

I walked along the thin path between the rugs. Sellers smiled, sending flirty eyes and welcoming gestures in an attempt to catch our attention. I stopped at one cart belonging to a craftsman of sorts, to look at a set of wooden sparring equipment I thought Segun, Rayloh, and I could play with. The old man, neglecting his other shoppers, tended to every need and want that we had. He even went so far as to entertain us by telling us of his family, and how he learned to create different things from wood.

"It doesn't sell as much for the use of actual sparring, but the children love it. It's a little fun for them before they have to start work."

I decided to get the sparring equipment, quite enjoying the man's efforts and his passion for his craft.

"How much do I owe you?"

The man scratched his chin. Small flakes fell from his beard and glistened in the fading sun as they floated around like glitter in the air.

"Normally it would be a dozen kons for a full set, but for you, my lady, since you listened to my banter and lived, just seven kons." He chuckled, as did I. I pulled out a markel and handed it to him.

"For the equipment and for entertaining two young misses with such care, will a markel do?"

He smiled, wiping his brow in both pleasure and disbelief. "Twenty Kons! You are too kind, my lady. May blessings and great fortune follow you and your household."

Kala grabbed the sparring set without my having to ask and we were on our way. Seeing as none of the jewelry at the black market caught my eye, my hopes solely rested in Kala's caretaker.

"My home is just around the break in the road."

Kala lived at the end of a round, where the road met mountainous rock. Although none of the houses, huts, and shacks we passed looked extraordinary, Kala's home had character that made it stand out from the rest. It was made of wood, like most of the homes in these parts, but carved in the wood were quotes, names, and shapes that were filled with dyed saps of pink, turquoise, and lavender that dried and made the writing shine like ancient hieroglyphics. Outside hung crystals with glittered rope that tinkled as the wind blew. Although it wasn't particularly my taste, I appreciated the art. Meeting Kala's caretaker would be interesting, for a woman so creative had to be somewhat eccentric.

Kala entered first, and since they hadn't a porch or a holding room for me to be seated until the host of the house welcomed me in, I stood inside right by the door. I heard whispers and the sounds of items being pushed into cupboards and crates being closed and stacked. I could hear Kala being scolded for not sending her warning of my inquiries, and her caretaker instructed Kala in assisting her in organizing her jewelry pieces so it would be easier for me to browse. Kala came back to the door to see that I had not moved.

"Won't you follow me, miss? I apologize for the wait, but I can guarantee it will be worth this small inconvenience." I sat my purchases by the door and followed her.

She led me to a room full of trinkets, ranging from rings, broaches, and bracelets to hair ornaments, armbands, and nail gems. Her caretaker greeted me, bowing her head as if in the

93

presence of royalty, and led me to their dining table, where her earring and necklace sets lay in wait. Demallo's frazzled red hair and thin body gave her the look of a mad- woman. Age and late nights showed through the wrinkles on her face and the dots of her eyes. She seemed scattered, as if she were plotting and keeping marks on many different thoughts and ideas at once.

Kala left me for a moment while I browsed Demallo's collection, looking at the many spectacles that shimmered on the table. I saw an intricate piece slipping from under a folded corner of the tablemat that looked promising, but after releasing the fold back to its rightful place, to my disappointment, I discovered that a tacky red jewel was attached to it. Just as I was about to give up in defeat, I saw something interesting in the corner, in a crystal snifter, barely catching the flash of green reflected in the light from the lantern that hung on the walls.

"May I see that?" I asked, pointing at the snifter.

"That snifter?" she asked as if she couldn't believe my words.

"Yes, ma'am. I see some hint of green and would love to examine it and see if it could add to the emerald in my dress."

"Well, of course, miss." Her eyes began to water. "I must warn you, these were one of the first sets I mastered and I am very proud to say it is one of my favorites, but no one has had the want to purchase it. So if you're disappointed, don't worry about sparing my feelings."

She picked up the snifter and brought it to the table. She carefully poured the contents onto the table and adjusted them neatly in front of me, bringing closer the candlelight so I could revel in the fullness of her craftsmanship.

This was it. I put it on immediately to confirm my decision and ran to a dirty mirror that hung above the unlit fireplace. I wiped it with the sleeve of my top shirt and peered into the glass. The necklace was sterling silver. It was in the shape of an inquisitive snake, with its body coiling around my neck while its head and neck slithered toward my chest, stopping right before entering the crevices of my bosom. Engraved in the silver was crosshatching that mimicked the detail of the scaly skin snakes possess. In place of the eyes were two tiny green stones, cut to protrude out of the snake's head. Its tail ended quite close to the head. I would have thought that it continued into something else but instead had been broken, leaving the piece cleft. For other than this, it was more than intricate.

I remembered seeing on the table a pair of earrings similar to the necklace. They were silver spheres with emerald squares in the center and would do brilliantly in accenting the necklace, which I was falling deeper and deeper in love with the longer I stared at it.

"This will suit me perfectly. Name your price." I stared at her with enthusiasm, willing to bargain until the end to her liking. She smiled.

95

"It would be wrong of me to take the money of the miss whose estate provides my Kala with sustenance through labor. Take it as a gift for your house, ensuring that she stays in your care."

Kala's caretaker must be familiar with the process of the estate, I thought. Selection, promotion, even dismissal within the servant order is up to the discretion of the residents, and if none were specifically requested, the task then fell to the keeper of the estate. After giving her my word and still pleading with her to give me a price as well, Kala and I left, for we still had business. Before leaving, I assisted her in removing the items from the table so she could prepare dinner. I picked up the snifter and returned it to its original position in the corner. Since it bestowed upon me this heavenly trinket, I paid it my two remaining markels, hoping that Demallo would discover them. Then, with great anticipation, as she emerged from the folds of her home, and with my selections in hand, Kala led me to the mines.

Chapter Eight

As we walked deeper and deeper into the outskirts of the black ring, Kala told me more about herself, her friends, and her caretaker. Night was starting to creep through the city and I assumed the workday would have ended or be nearing an end by now. We cut through streets and alleys until I no longer recognized where I was. The scenery changed to nothing more than cobblestones and wild plants along the path. I never knew how big the black ring was, considering my friends and I only knew the paths that led to the wall, which were short and direct.

I began to see small fissures as we crept over what was now just the earth of the mountainous cliff our city sat atop. I could tell Kala was familiar with the route and must have visited the mines on her own because she knew where to step without hesitation, so I took solace knowing that everything would be all right if I followed her steps. She fluttered like a graceful bird, hopping from perch to perch. I tried my hardest to imitate her movements, and although I landed every step, it didn't translate nearly as gracefully as Kala. Torchlight flickered through the crevices. The mines were right below us. My interest grew exceedingly.

There had to be an opening, big enough for a large group of men. The fissures we passed were nothing more than little cracks that even for our smaller size were too tiny for any person to pass. In the distance I could see a greater amount of light. Kala stopped abruptly.

"This is as far as I've ever been."

"Why have you not gone farther? Have you known danger to lie ahead?" I received no answer. I craned my neck higher, standing on my toes to gain a better vantage, and realized that the light was coming from a cluster of torches that lit a gigantic hole in the ground about a quarter mile from where we stood. We were far from it but still close enough to see the shadows dancing on the walls. People were still down there.

"Shouldn't their duties be completed for the day?" I asked. There were laws regarding labor, set in place so that workers would have time for their own personal tasks and familial obligations.

"Rules differ in the mines than on the surface. No one knows what goes on down there. I'm almost certain that we shouldn't even be this close to them, not to mention the dangers it holds without proper precautions. Still, the pay is good, I've heard."

"How many men work in the mines?" I asked her, still watching the shadows on the wall.

"I've no clue. I'd assume a great deal, though. Most of the men that I was accustomed to seeing are gone and I assumed took up work there. The only times I see them are on holidays, which happen every other month for five days. All the families and the mineworkers meet in the black square along with the elven heads of their charge, the head of their legion being Rayloh's father. They say it's because they want the chance to meet their families and friends. Hear about their lives." She surveyed her surroundings before continuing. Even though we were alone, she leaned close. "I think they just want to monitor the conversation and ensure that whatever secret happenings that are going on in the mines, stay secret."

I paused, my throat going dry. I saw my father every day, and even when he was home, the Courts still held possession over his being. Maybe in the mines, the men had changed and she didn't want to accept it, or perhaps there was something more. Perhaps the answer to this too lay behind the locked door in my family quarters.

The day had run short. Stars were slowing starting to peek from behind the clouds that were, inversely, fading into the darkness. I wanted badly to continue on to the entrance of the mines. I wanted to see what treasures were held beneath the mountainous surface of our city, even though I wouldn't be able to see much, considering it would most likely be deemed too dangerous for a miss of my age and class to be taken into the deep pit. Still, my curiosity always stemmed simply from having restrictions. In fact, I don't even think I would have cared to pass the city's limits into the edgewoods if there wasn't a decree finding it unlawful. Still, it was late and Madja was likely already worrying. My curiosity would have to be fulfilled another day.

"Will you escort me to the main road? I know my way from there." Kala nodded, turned, and began even more cautiously, since there was less light from the sky to guide us.

It seemed like a much longer tread back to the estate, probably because I was eager to match my dress with my newly discovered accents as well as show the lads our new sparring gear. Kala escorted me longer than she needed, which wasn't a bad thing because I enjoyed her company, but I secretly knew the main parts of the black ring from my visits to the edgewoods. She walked me all the way back to the blue ring's market, where we first departed from Madja. By now the market was closed and the last of the traders were locking their goods away in their carts or comparing sales for the day with other vendors in front of their keeps. The moon had nearly reached its peak in the sky, so dinner was likely being served. I was late. After thanking Kala for her kindness, I ran, with my purchases in hand, all the way to the Remni. I didn't want to miss dinner entirely. My stomach would never forgive me.

When I arrived at the Remni, I slipped into the grooming quarters to freshen up. I wiped my face with a cold, damp rag, tucked my sparring set under a pile of large bath towels that sat on the windowsill, and headed to the main hall with my jewelry in hand. It was not in my nature to obsess over trinkets, but something about the necklace made me want to keep it close to me. If Madja didn't favor them, I could talk her into keeping them at least to wear on a separate occasion rather than trying to convince her about the sparring set, which she wouldn't be pleased about me buying with the money she gave me.

In the main hall, mostly everyone had gone except for Rayloh's father and a couple of his guests, fond friends I assumed by the way they laughed with each other. At my table, there was no one other than Madja. I'd assumed the lads had gone to the study by now and were about to turn in for the night. She sat at the head of the table, her back to the entrance of the hall. Food, cutlery, and the rest of the dinnerware sat in my usual place, undisturbed. I braced myself as I continued toward her, preparing to be lectured about punctuality and presentation, qualities she believed a young miss like myself should possess. I placed my purchases on the table next to her. Surprisingly, she wasn't upset. She was anxious for my return to the estate but not for worry of my whereabouts but to see what items I bought to complement my dress.

"I was planning on having you try it on tonight so myself and the other she-elves could see you in it. However, I understand how your Kei can make you want to spend all your time in the market," she said as she stood up. "We'll see you in it tomorrow. Just think: soon my little miss will be a young lady." I cringed at these words.

She kissed my forehead and left. My stomach was growling by now so I was happy to see sweet berries and foxtrits on my dinner plate. I sat down and ate, mulling over my accessories that I had failed to send up to the family quarters with

Madja. I was both relieved and disappointed at her departure. Madja and I were bonding, and I would be a liar if I said I wasn't appreciating the time we were spending together.

As I ate, I found myself mulling over the mines. *What could be that precious in the earth to keep these men away from their homes?* Then it hit me. Rayloh's father, Lord Fueto, was in direct charge of the mines. I looked up to see the table where he and his company sat; it was now completely empty. A chair pulled out next to me. I jumped. But I was calmed when I saw that the very disturbance that had come to join me was the very person who had just abruptly entered my thoughts.

"I didn't startle you, did I?" He smiled. "Of course I did, or you wouldn't have jumped six leagues into the air."

I laughed. Rayloh's father was very humorous, and if I had a choice between the easiness of his father and mine, I felt Lord Fueto was without a doubt the kinder one. As I took a sip of my melon juice, he prodded the jewelry I bought. At first I thought it meaningless, him poking at the accents like a dog at an unfamiliar insect. Then I remembered he worked as our city's chief architect and concluded that he was just examining the metal's intricate detailing. He finally stirred as I emptied the remnants of my cup.

"Now tell me, where did you find this beautiful specimen?" he asked as he mulled over the necklace. "The artisans in the blue market couldn't possibly possess such vision."

"I didn't find these in the blue market. I went to the—"

"Oh, I figured as much," he belted, interrupting my response. "You must have found it in the black market. It's interesting you picked these pieces. They have a lot more character than the lackluster, overpriced unoriginality in the blue market."

"Yes. The bath servant suggested it would be a great place to find an intricate piece to wear at my Kei." I felt it odd calling Kala simply a bath servant, since she had proven herself as a kind acquaintance, but I still felt tentative about our relationship. "Wait until you see my dress."

"I'm sure it's lovely."

I blushed. The older, handsome he-elf undoubtedly made all the she-elves of the Remni squeal, wedded or not. After a few more courtesies of each other's day's activities, I moved on to my inquiries.

"While in the black ring, I heard in the midst of the market, gossip . . . concerning the mines."

His expression didn't waiver. "Ah, yes, the mines. The workers and superiors are a small segment under my charge. What of them?"

"Is that where all the gold that crests the buildings in Keldrock come from?" He paused and then rose from his seat and walked back to the table where he once sat with his company, returning with their flagon and his goblet.

"It looks like you need refreshment." He poured us both the remainder of the contents from the flagon. The smell of pungent wines rushed into my nostrils, making my eyes spark with sensation and my mouth water with anticipation. "Promise me you won't let your mother know of this. She would have my ears if she found out I gave you wine to drink before your Kei, but only a breath lies between then and now. Which reminds me, have you thought about what you want as a gift?"

He seemed to have had no aim with his change of subject other than good conversation. Still, I had other questions and maybe he could be the one to answer them.

"I haven't thought about it." I paused for a moment. "I would love a broach to match the necklace you got me on my last birthday."

He scrunched his face jokingly, slowing scratching his chin, making a face as if debating if he could accomplish such a feat. "I think that can be managed."

I giggled more flirtatiously than what would be deemed acceptable. To ease my embarrassment, I quickly continued, slightly shifting the direction. "I wonder what my father is going to get me. I've been trying to figure it out for a fortnight now. He's always so busy, the lord of my house."

"Agreed, miss, as are all the lords of this estate. Our work can be consuming. He hasn't spoken to me, however, about what he's getting you, and if he had, I'm most certain he wouldn't want me to reveal his plans."

"Of course, and I wouldn't want you to. It's just . . . I know you all work so hard. I mean you probably spend a great deal of time with him."

"Actually, I rarely speak to your father when it comes to matters of career. He works more closely with officials deep in the purple ring, under the direction of the Courts. His work is kept quite private as well. I would not know much about it but I'd assume he deals closely with city politics and possible . . . conspiracies."

Conspiracies. What conspiracies could be happening within Keldrock? And for that matter, why? Our nation was at peace. Even the Dwala weren't horribly disgruntled in my opinion to start a war or a siege, nor would they have the strength to do so.

"Well, I don't want these things to weigh heavily on a little elfling who should be finalizing the plans for her Kei." He stood up and patted me on the head like I was some toddler, and exited the main hall.

I sat for a moment in defeat. Even Lord Fueto didn't know what my father's work specifically dealt with and hadn't answered any of my inquiries concerning the mines. That made the key, the door, and what lay behind it even more important. I stood and pushed my chair in, positioning it neatly under the table. I picked up my plate and sat it in the bin next to the kitchen door. I took my necklace and earrings and went to the grooming quarters to retrieve my sparring set. It was exactly where I had left it. I gathered the set, being careful to balance the jewelry on top of the

cloth-wrapped wood carvings. I lightly tapped the door of the
study with my foot. Segun opened the door, his eyes taking in the
load I maneuvered on my forearms and kindly eased the purchases
out of my hands. Once he had them, I took the jewelry and placed
them atop a desk that sat under a lantern against the wall next to
the door.

Segun eyed what I had in hand but quickly lost interest
and turned his attention to what was wrapped in the cloth sheet.
He sat the heap on a large oak chest and began prying at the strips
of leather that held the rolled cloth together. Rayloh, disturbed
from the book he was reading, reached under his pillow and pulled
out a small knife. He cut the leather strips with ease, a feat that a
small dagger in the hands of an elfling of average strength could
not accomplish. He returned the blade back to the underside of his
pillow and lay back down, continuing in his book as if he had
never stopped.

I removed the leather strips and began releasing the folds
of the thin cloth that held the wood carvings. Segun's eyes grew
with excitement and I was pleased, especially since they weren't
the most finely crafted specimens. Rayloh seemed more concerned
with his book. He didn't even look up when Segun gasped
excitedly, pulling out the cloth's contents. The set came with two
swords, so I asked for an extra one so no one would have to sit
out. There were also two small spears. They didn't interest me as
much as the swords, so I didn't bother to purchase a third. There
were two flags, I assumed for the use of an organized game, if we

were to come up with one. Segun picked up one of the swords and attempted to surprise Rayloh by tossing it on him, but Rayloh's reflexes were too quick. It had just left Segun's hand when Rayloh reached up and snatched it out of the air. He set down his book, stood, and began fencing with Segun. I was almost certain that Rayloh and his father bonded over impromptu sparring lessons in their family quarters. His movements seemed natural and unrehearsed, as if he'd had years of practice.

I turned back to the wood carvings on the table. I reached to grab the third sword when I noticed something else in the cloth wrapping. The sheet had a pocket sewn at the edge. No leather strips bound this pocket, only sewn string that could easily be torn away. Segun and Rayloh didn't notice my absence in play and I didn't want them to. It was good to see them acting like their normal selves. I haven't seen this side of the lads since our ventures into the edgewoods. While they fenced, I tore the pocket's stitching apart.

Inside, to my surprise, were a bow, string, and a quiver full of arrows. These pieces, however, didn't resemble the sparring set. The bow and arrows were made of a beautiful brown wood. They had been sanded, removed of all blemishes and knots, with shiny metal ends. The quiver was of fine leather that I had never seen, a dark, rich black. In the quiver were arrows, at least a dozen or so. I pulled one halfway out of the quiver, admiring the quality of work. *Who could have made such a thing?* A growing desire began to burn in me. I wanted to keep the arrows and bow, but returning them was the honorable thing to do. Yet I had paid the man for the sparring set an amount far more than what he asked. Maybe he gave the bow and arrows as a gift for my kindness, just as Mistress Vesti gave me the silver- laced sandals.

"Will you be joining us, Warrior Alya? Or are you no longer worthy of the title?" Rayloh teased. I could hear him and Segun panting heavily, briefly resting after taking many blows from each other's swords. My back was turned to them,, and for good reason. My eyes were watering, and for the first time in weeks, I felt we were elflings again without a care in the world.

I quickly wiped my eyes and whirled around, sword readied. The vibrations of wood colliding were the only sounds heard as Segun's sword met mine. He confidently held his stance and I was pleased my surprise attack hadn't caught him off guard. We swung away at each other. Sometimes, because Rayloh was more natural at it, we'd gang up on him. He indulged in the challenge and fought us confidently. By the time we had finished, we were bruised and tired, lying strewn out on the floor like logs in the forest.

"Are you ready?" I asked. "For tomorrow, that is."

"I believe so. From what Master Roi has told us, it's going to be a grand celebration, and I look forward to seeing who is selected to join the Guerr." Segun grimaced. I could tell that he wasn't looking forward to this news. Rayloh sensed his concern and comforted him. "I'm sure you'll better serve our nation behind the wall. Maybe as a medic."

Segun eased but retorted defiantly, "If chosen, I will serve alongside my brothers on the Day of Unveiling."

It soon quieted and everyone drifted into sleep. My mind began to roam. I thought of tomorrow and the possibility of seeing one or two of my comrades receive the news of their fates. Both Rayloh and I sensed that Segun didn't want to join the Guerr. He was timid by nature, even more passive and squeamish than I. He was a beautiful elfling with an even more beautiful soul, and gentle he was as well. The Guerr would prove too much for one of his character. I, however, dreamed of combat and the bonds made in battle. I would prefer that over dancing alongside my sisters in the Jalla or the bores of keeping a home.

Although I thoroughly enjoyed the sword, my interests weighed heavier toward archery. I had never taken to the skill, but now I had the chance. I was enticed by statues raised throughout our city of mighty he-elves with great bows and arrows that even in blunt stone seemed sharp enough to pierce the hide of a mighty beast. My mind wandered to the bow and arrows and the restlessness that filled my spirit. *A few practice shots wouldn't hurt. Everyone is asleep.*

I rose, careful not to make any noise and disturb the lads. I had no idea how to string the bow. Still, I felt it would be fairly simple; at least I hoped so. The equipment was still wrapped atop the oak chest. I picked up the long bundle and slowly unwound the thin cloth, feeling for the bow and the quiver of arrows. I ran my finger along the shaped wood. My eyes began making sense of the

object I held, but something was different about the bow. As my
fingers ran up the upper limb, toward the nock, I felt something
adding pressure, straining the ends of the bow. I moved along the
string groove, and to my surprise, found the bow was already
strung, the string tight and secure. The lads couldn't have done it
without my noticing. In fact, ever since first discovering the bow
and arrows, we hadn't left each other's company.

  This had to be some magic or some spell of the mind. I
picked up the bow and the quiver and crept outside, into the full
moon's light. My eyes had not deceived me. The bow showed
even more beautifully than before. The string, silver in color,
brought a touch of modernity to the rustic appearance of the bow. I
dumped the arrows on the ground and picked up one, placing its
nock on the string. I thought to go to the yellow gardens but the
Guards of Candor would be patrolling and a young miss shooting
arrows at night might raise suspicion, probably more for the fear
of her sanity than any actual danger posed. So I stayed in the
grassy yard behind the Remni. There were a few trees, none of
them taller than a full-grown elf. Much like elves, they were
slender. With an untrained arm and at even a slight distance, I
could never dream to hit these targets, but I tried anyway. I shot a
couple of times, each of the arrows piloting to the ground, digging
deep into the grass. I reached for one of my two last arrows from
beside the empty quiver. The others I'd shot were scattered around
the yard like grave markers. One lay right at the foot of a tree,
where the grass turned to a small, round patch of dirt. I carefully

put the nock of the arrow on the string and drew it back, pinning my mark on the tree. I held it steady and shot. Just as I let it go, the tree disappeared from sight in a mist that had suddenly drifted in from the east.

The fog was thick and damp, and the whole estate seemed to disappear, just as the tree had. I picked up the quiver, returned my last arrow to it, and threw the bow over my shoulder. I searched for the scattered arrows, relying heavily on memory. I could feel myself moving deeper into the mist, but I didn't want to leave the arrows out for someone else to discover. Something shifted in the mist, interrupting my search. I pulled the bow off of my shoulder and drew the arrow. I didn't suspect it was anyone but the lads having woken up in the night. Still, the night when the beast attacked was not forgotten. I stood quietly, hearing the quick movements. Something brushed my leg and I reacted. My reflexes were quick. Drawing the bow back, I pointed the arrow at the figure. One flinch and it would be released.

My reflexes could also be altered at a moment's notice, and for that I was also proud because what stood in my path was not a horrible beast, or even the lads, but something resembling a fox.

It was white, almost the same color as the dense fog. It looked mysterious and cunning staring at me, its eyes aglow in the night. I had never seen one in the city before and definitely not one like this. Other than the domestic animals, the birds that flew about, and the rodents that hunted their eggs, there were no other wild animals that regularly appeared in the city, let alone made it to the yellow ring. The only time I'd ever seen a fox in person was with Rayloh. It was drinking from a small puddle after a hard rain while we roamed the edgewoods. Even then it was at such a great distance that all I could make out was its orange coat. I had never seen one this color. Still, we were taught that a fox was a good omen, it even being the symbol of the royal family, so I convinced myself that this rare occurrence was fate and that the creature meant no harm.

It felt like a lifetime had passed. We remained at a standstill, waiting for the other to move. I eased my hold on the string and placed the arrow back in my quiver. After surrendering my weapon, the creature moved like an apparition, turning its body fully around. Its tail flowed in the mist, cutting its way through like the mast of a ship. The fox lifted its paw and stood still, from its nose to its tail, imitating a compass pointing me in the direction it apparently wanted me to go. As I crept forward, it did, too. As I followed it, the fog grew denser and the only thing I could see was the white fox, the fog yielding to its noble form. Soon, a gazebo came into view. It was white as well, resembling clouds shaped together. It all seemed like a dream. The mist floated together, forming a delicate veil that draped around the structure like a canopy, parting only in one space for entry. The fox settled itself there by the steps, circling around as dogs do, before tucking its paws beneath its body and sitting down, its tail swishing on the ground behind it. For a minute it stared at me, waiting for my decision.

I had forgotten about recovering the arrows. My curiosity drove me to take that first step. Distant whispers rode the air. I took another step, the fox's tail swishing even more eagerly. Another step. The mist started gripping me, edging me forward toward the gazebo. A voice coasted the wind, causing me to come to a high alert. I turned around to see if I was followed. I hopped up the steps. My hair floated behind me, as if I were fluttering about the clouds unburdened by gravity. A door stood at the back of the gazebo, its frame filled with stars and lights. The fox growled behind me, peering off into the mist. The voice came louder. I made it out this time, knowing exactly what I heard. The voice was telling me to stop. From the doorway came a loud hiss, and I began backing away. The fox turned, its ears flattened against its head, snarling, saliva dripping from its sharp teeth. Its hair stood on end and its tail curled at the end in fury. From the door shot a snake, its head stopping just short of my nose. Then everything went black.

I looked up. It was still night. What seemed like an eternity hadn't been that long. I felt drained. I sat up, my eyes adjusting to the darkness once again. I wasn't outside anymore. I wasn't in the gazebo. The familiar smells of the Remni filled my nostrils. *How did I get back inside?* I wasn't in my family quarters or in the study or the main hall. I was in a place I had never entered, or cared to, for that matter. I lay at the back entrance of Lord Calo and his sister's quarters. I couldn't come up with an explanation for it. I might have fallen asleep in the yard and sleepwalked. I couldn't ponder these thoughts for long. The arrows remained scattered in the yard.

I stood quickly, anxious to retrieve the arrows, the quiver and bow still resting on my shoulder. I ran to the door of Coor and out into the yard. No mist remained. In fact, the grass was dry, as was the air, as if the fog had never been. My arrows were still positioned in various directions and angles from the tree. I counted as I picked them up. Some were deeper than others. One even landed in an anthill. By the time I got to the thirteenth, I was exhausted and was happy that it was easy to remove, considering it had landed in the soft soil surrounding the tree. I sat back on my knees, searching the ground for my final arrow. The moon shed light on all the green in the yard, so it wasn't hard to see the ground. No arrow. I leaned against the tree, putting my weight on its limbs as I pulled myself up. As I did, my cheek brushed the soft feathers of what I knew to be the fletching of my arrow. I stepped back, marveling at my achievement. There, stapled in the bark of the tree, was my final arrow. I had hit my mark. I studied it proudly. With only a few tries, I had succeeded.

My nose twitched with anticipation and sadness at the thought of having to return the bow and arrow to the craftsman, since I wasn't sure if it was a gift. Still, there was something else I could do. In the morning, after lessons, I would tell Madja that I needed to purchase some other things for my Kei. She would be more than willing to allow that. The man wouldn't deny me this purchase, especially after my display of kindness. I smiled at my plan and the revelation of my new skill. I was a natural. I didn't think that even the guards of our city could hit a target so narrow, although they weren't skilled at much of anything. I plucked the arrow from the tree and shoved it snuggly among its kin in the quiver, then ran back to the door of Coor.

I entered the study to find the lads hadn't moved from where we had collapsed. I placed the spears, swords, and the wrapped cloth in the oak chest beneath some blankets and pillows. Then I laid down on the love seat, tucking my quiver and bow beneath it. Within seconds, sleep consumed me.

Chapter Nine

I woke up the next morning with new energy. Madja was surprised to walk into the study and find that I was already gone before the call of the mornowl. I even beat Mira to the grooming quarters, which rarely happened. I went through my usual routine, having my hair braided and putting on my swelk. Today would be a long one. We would get to see if Rayloh and Segun were chosen to join the Guerr, I had to make any final plans for my Kei, and I was going to haggle with the old craftsman over the bow and arrows.

I walked into the main hall, finding no one there except Segun's mother. I was surprised that Lady Kailowan wasn't with the other she-elves and servant women out in the garden. She sat alone at the lord and ladies' table. She looked like she hadn't slept all night. There were bags under her eyes, and her hair, normally combed and falling beautifully down to her lower back, was messily braided, frizzled bits and untamed pieces strewn about her scalp. As I walked past her to the table where the sprites sat, the strong, pungent smell of spirits curled my senses. I could taste vomit but I kept it down, careful not to draw attention to myself. Lady Kailowan stared off at the wall, and other than the occasional blink of her eyelids, she didn't move. I poured myself a chalice of goat's milk. It was awkward for a moment until I realized that she wasn't here. She was in another world. I had seen her like this only once—when Segun's brother passed at birth. Madja explained to me the damage of spirits and how people drank them excessively in times of hardship. I drank my milk in silence. After finishing her glass, Lady Kailowan got up, tucked in her chair, and left.

Just as soon as she had exited, the room began to fill with the residents of the Remni. Trays of fruit, mushrooms, greens, spices, and an assortment of breads were brought out by the Dwala and placed on a buffet table against the wall, in celebration of the Guerr selection. I readied my plate and selected from the various items, some fresh fruit and a slice of bread, then returned to my seat. The lads hadn't come in yet. The servants and the ladies of the estate brought in their fresh flowers, placing them in the scattered vases among the tables. Today was a beautiful mixture of oranges and bright yellow sun lilies. I had finished my plate and even had a second slice of bread and still Rayloh and Segun had not appeared. We had to be at lessons soon and they were nowhere to be found. Mira sat down at the head of the table with her plate full of mushrooms and greens.

"Will you be leaving soon?" She picked up a mushroom, digging her fork into its gills, and then gracefully placing it into her mouth.

"I'm waiting for the lads. I wonder what is keeping them." I popped a sun grape in my mouth, letting its thick juices revel on my tongue.

"I heard them leaving early this morning. Lord Fueto escorted them on his way to the purple ring. I believe they are to arrive early for their placements."

I was an imbecile. Of course they would have to be present at the school earlier than I. That would only make the most sense. Without formally ending the conversation with Mira, or depositing my plate in the bin with the other dishes by the kitchen door, I scurried out, my satchel banging against my side. It was cooler than normal outside, due to the shift in seasons starting to take place. I arrived at school, my school papers already prepared for entry.

"You are to report to the blue ring's square. There you will receive further instructions," I received from the guard once I arrived at the school. I didn't bother asking the guard why. But confusion blanketed my face.

I began running. My delay this morning in wait of Segun and Rayloh barely allowed me enough time to make it to Shiloh without being tardy, but the blue ring's square was an altogether different trip. I rounded the streets, cutting through the blue market. I passed Mistress Vesti as she rummaged outside, removing from the front of her keep withered flowers and weeds from summer. When I finally arrived at the square, nothing had taken place yet. Everyone sat in the sunken platform surrounded by stairs on every side except one, where performers would stand to be seen by everyone. The misses' legs were crossed, hands gracefully atop their knees. The lads were seated at the front. They didn't wear their swelks today. In their place instead were white robes falling just short of their ankles, where their breeches and slippers met. A grip ensnared my upper arm, and as I tensed, it released me, only to grab my two shoulders, turning me fully around.

"You're late, sprite. Have a seat."

This guard, tall and serious, nudged me in the direction where the misses sat. My rotation was lined in the back, eagerly awaiting the ceremony to start. It seemed like we were the only ones who were excited to see this day come. Other sprites in attendance wore blank expressions. A horn's bellow came from the main road leading into the square. Six guards carrying the purple flags of our nation emerged over the crest of the hill. Two others rode atop brown bucks. Behind them, a band of elves carried a golden litter adorned with jewels and ornaments and veiled with black sheets. Five cloaked figures followed behind on foot. Trailing them were two more guards riding bucks and six carrying flags, only these flags bore the crest of the royal family. The golden crest was the head of a fox, its nose narrow and its ears arched.

The litter came to rest at an incline. The guards carrying flags surrounded the square, standing in equidistant spots on the stairs. The band of elves carefully set the litter down. The square was quiet; not even the bucks trotted in place or grunted. Two of the elves from the group that carried the litter stepped forward and parted the black sheets to reveal the litter's contents.

119

Out stepped a he-elf, not fully mature, but not a sprite either. He was tall and stiff, his skin the darkest I've seen. His hair was pure black. On his head rested a gold crown forged in the liking of leaves and vines intertwined. The ends of his hair held gold beads, and his ears, gold hoops. His eyes were a piercing blue, both light in color and hauntingly dark at the same time. He stepped forward not in fine robes but adorned in war garments. His silver breastplate, gauntlets, and greaves were embellished in gold atop his silver ringed mail shirt. He was a sight to behold, in both beauty and might. The sprites in my rotation sighed at his presence. I held my composure. The cloaked figures standing behind him let their hoods fall to their backs. One I recognized, Master Roi, the lad's teacher. I had never seen the other before, not even among the other masters that taught at Shiloh. The crowned elf began.

"Greetings, Keldronians. I am your prince and heir, Alag. Today is a glorious day for our nation. Olörun, The Great One, shines down upon you with grace as we welcome those fortunate individuals into the Guerr. I, the Courts, as well as your instructor, Master Roi, have come to a decision. Through his guidance and expertise, we are proud to announce that all of this year's premieres will be joining the Guerr."

Shock rushed through the crowd, and then quickly turned into cheers. If I could see Rayloh at this moment, he probably was smiling, while Segun forcibly made peace with this announcement.

"We know this is the first time in history this has happened, but Master Roi has assured us that they are by far the most skilled rotation this nation has ever spawned. Also, for that, we have more great news. These new inductees, as well as those in other rotations who have been extended an invitation, will have the opportunity to venture outside these walls and participate in the upcoming unveiling."

Whispers coasted among my peers. Guards glared at them, causing them to cease.

"I know this news is troubling; they are still sprites, after all. However, as I stated, Master Roi is confident in their abilities, and with the proper training they will assist in defending the border when the veil breaks and continue to keep our great nation safe." Applause broke free after this passionate assurance. "Now rise, descendants of the nymphs, so that I may give you each my blessing."

The lads stood, walking up the left trail of stairs and lining up to the right of the prince. One of the four other robed elves, which I now understood to be the members of the Courts, pulled from his sleeve a censer and placed himself to the left of the prince. He was older than most of the elves I had seen. His face showed his age, as well as the gray of his beard, and having lived longer than most, he appeared wiser and more aware. The censer wasn't lit, but inside was blue oil that shimmered like topaz crystals in water. The other three carried medals that were to be placed on the new initiates.

Master Roi stood next to the old he-elf. He started calling the lads' names one by one. They stepped forward as they were called, each swearing in loyalty to fight and defend against the "dangers of the edgewoods and beyond." After a sprite swore his oath, the prince dipped his thumb into the blue oil and marked the lad on his forehead. Then he would walk toward the other members of the Courts and receive a medal. Once all six of the lads were sworn in, they lined themselves next to the prince, the robed officials stepping back to allow the front.

"Rise now and welcome your brothers to the Guerr!" We stood in applause. The lads looked serious and distinguished, their faces holding back, for some their tacky smiles and for others their discernment. The crowd quieted, and the prince spoke again. "In your honor, on this glorious day, we will light the gold censer, Calantine." The prince but glanced at the censer and it lit, sending blue smoke into the air. The oil on the lads' foreheads glowed blue and then ascended into the air as a puff of blue smoke as well, burning away as if it had never been placed.

The prince held his right palm to us; then, with a swift turn, he returned to the litter. One of the guards on the buck commanded our attention, initiating us to rise and begin our nation's pledge:

"I vow my blood, my life, my talent, and my honor to the great nation of Keldrock. Whose gates of wood and iron guard my temple, my body, my people, from the evils of darkness and shadow. I pledge to The Great One, the Courts, and our Protector

122

to abide by what is just in their eyes. For the law of the land is the sphere of the righteous and to break the orb is to unleash chaos. *Kina, kina, kina.*"

When the last praise escaped our lips, the recession began, with the flag guards and guards atop bucks leading the way. When the party was out of sight, we were dismissed. Since it was the final day of lessons, we didn't have to worry about returning to Shiloh's School of Talents. I wanted to wait for Rayloh and Segun before heading back to the Remni, but they were engulfed with congratulators, ranging from masters that taught at the school to the ditsy sprites in my class. Even some of the city guards came down from their posts to congratulate the lads. I waited for some time before leaving, assuring my conscience that they wouldn't be offended if I displayed my felicitations in the comforts of the Remni. I had other pressing matters to attend to.

I walked home, wondering how things would change now that Rayloh and Segun were both part of the Guerr. In my mind, I had found subconscious reliance in the almost certain fact that Segun would not be selected and that we would spend our days writing Rayloh while he trained in the barracks, exchanging secrets in code. Even though Rayloh would be a hard person to depart from, I took comfort knowing that Segun would be there to help me through it and that I wouldn't be alone. My eyes began to water but they didn't run. The cold air outside nearly made that impossible.

Back at the Remni, residents seemed to be going about their day per usual. My first order of business was to find Madja. I needed enough money to convince the old craftsman to sell me the bow and arrow set. I didn't want to waste any time and I didn't want to risk being invited to pick flowers or pretty stones for decoration, so I tried the main hall first. To my elation, Madja was there, with Lady Kalawan. I'm sure by now she had heard the news about Segun. She was in a much worse state than when I had first seen her early this morning. Her eyes were puffy, like rain clouds. Her hair remained a mess, and she still wore her nightgown. I inched toward the table, unsure of whether I should interrupt this moment of obvious distress. Still, I had my own plans to attend to. So with careful words I requested the money, alluding heavily to final details concerning my Kei. Madja pulled from her purse three markels, warning me to spend them wisely. I put the markels in my satchel and left without another word, careful not to give her any suspicions.

I peeked into the study to ensure that no one was inside, and as usual, it was empty. Bringing my palms to the floor, to retrieve my bow and quiver I crawled to the love seat. I lay on my stomach to get a better look under it. In the night, I had tossed the items all the way back to the wall so they would be out of sight, and I was grateful that I was still small enough to fit my upper body under the love seat because I didn't want to have the hassle of moving it. Once the bow and quiver were in my possession, I grabbed a blanket and wrapped them in it so that when I walked through the city, I wouldn't draw any unwarranted attention.

I stepped out and decided to cut through the back streets and through the blue market before entering back onto the main road. While there were different streets that led into and out of the yellow and blue rings, only one led into and out of the black ring, and only one led into and out of the purple ring. Once inside the black ring, I moved through the streets, trying my hardest to remember how to get to the market. When I finally found it, mainly due to the high traffic, it was extremely busy. People were crowded in the shed, talking loudly among each other. I worked through them, trying to get to where I remembered the man and his trading section were located. After much maneuvering, I found him standing over his rug, bargaining with a man concerning some hooks and clamps. As I approached, he caught sight of me and gestured that he would be able to talk to me in a few moments. After a few more exchanges of barter, the old craftsmen yielded, giving in to the customer's offer.

"What can I help you with?" he asked me as he placed his revenue from the purchase in his purse. "Was something wrong with the sparring set?"

I inched closer, nervous to start, and definitely not wanting our conversation to be overheard. "No, the sparring set is wonderful. My comrades and I quite enjoy it. It's just, in the bundle was a . . ." I paused, gathering myself, searching for the right words. "I just want to assure you I didn't pilfer them, but in

125

the bundle, I believe you accidentally included a bow and arrows set." He squinted his eyes in confusion, not sure what to make of this situation. To ease his mind, I peeled back the blanket, revealing the bow and arrows.

His eyes grew wide as he ran his fingers over the exquisitely shaped brown wood of the bow. I stared at him, waiting for an acknowledgment. He responded, "I wish I could claim such a beauty as my own, but Olörun would strike me right now if I promoted such falsehood. I also cannot say that I gave you this." I folded the flaps of the blanket in relief. "But for what it's worth, I wouldn't mind alleviating you from its care. I could probably sell it for a handsome price. We could even split the profit."

"No, thank you. All my questions have been answered." I turned, heading for the exit. I could feel the man's eyes cutting into the back of me, wondering about my hasty retreat and about the mysterious bow and arrows.

I emerged from the shack, taking in the fresh air. *How in all the skies could I have gotten a bow and a quiver of arrows if not from here?* As I walked, I considered other possible reasoning behind it. *What if Kala or her mother placed it in my possession?* The idea was a stretch. but it would be an affectionate gesture, considering the bonding and kindness between Kala and me. I decided I might as well stop by and inquire, since I was in the black ring anyway. I didn't want to deprive my mind of any plausible answer, and the hunger in my stomach could be satisfied

126

a little later. I wished I had waited until after midday meal before leaving, but urgency and secrecy were more important.

I bumped through the streets looking for anything familiar that would steer me in the right direction. I passed huts and shacks that I thought I recognized but looked no different from the others I passed. As I strode, the smells of freshly baked breads and sweet pastries filled my nostrils, making my mouth water with desire. My stomach growled in desperation, so I decided to quell its whining. I followed the aromas to an old wooden shack, where fumes rose from the chimney into the air. Inside, people sat at long tables, eating bread and pastries. I wandered to the reception area, where the baker stood taking orders and overseeing his domain. As he saw me approaching, he tucked his shirt into his trousers, attempting to seem more presentable.

"How may I help you, dearie?" he asked, wiping flour shamefully from his brow. He was a heavier man, stereotypical for a baker. His gut barely held under his recently tucked shirt. His head was bare and pale, shining in the light like a viper's egg, his face rough with stubble. He pointed to a hulking shred of parchment on the wall with harsh scribbles written with black ink. "Anything from the menu, beautiful?" I stood staring for a few long moments. He had everything from nut and seed mesh, to layered cakes topped with dried cream and syrups. "Well, ma'am?" he politely inquired, urgent to assist me so he could help the others in line behind me.

"She'll have the raspberry jam cake with lemon petals on top, the same as I." I turned to see who was bold enough to order for me. Nazda, about three places behind me, emerged from the line. I beamed at seeing her face. The girl I so much admired had somehow found me in an old bakery in the middle of the black ring. I nodded at the baker for confirmation, handing him four kons.

I embraced Nazda, this time ungrudgingly. I hadn't seen her in weeks, ever since the night in the edgewoods.

"It's great to see you, Nazda." Her facial expression remained poised, but I could tell that she was happy to see me as well.

"Come. Let us sit. Saleem will bring our orders to our table when they are prepared."

We picked a small table in the corner. I stood the bundle upright on the floor, letting it rest between my thighs. It wasn't long after we sat down that Saleem, the baker, came with our cakes. They were decorated with a steady hand. The petals seemed to dance on the pastries, like yellow lilies on the lake. It was a true pity to have to disrupt such beauty, but my stomach would not allow my eyes the only satisfaction. Nazda and I tore into the cakes. The cream dissolved in my mouth, sending waves of flavor through my taste buds. The center of the pastry, which you couldn't see from the outside, was filled with chocolate. It spilled out like oil spiked in the ground, drizzling over the remnants of my pastry and onto my plate. The lemon layer was both pungent and sweet, with little pieces of apple-nut and hardened citrus syrup bits piloting through its tart goodness. This cake was one of the best I'd ever tasted, but I saw in Nazda's eyes that things concerned her that even a delicious cake couldn't quell. I made a notion toward averting her mind from such troubles.

"I'm looking for a house. That's why I'm here, you see, in case you were wondering. The house belongs to a woman who makes jewelry. Her name is Knark. Demallo Knark. Could you escort me to her? I've lost my way and only stopped at this bakery for fear my stomach would consume my innards if I didn't find nourishment soon."

Nazda giggled and I was pleased that my joke amused her. "Of course. It would be extremely distasteful if I were to let you roam the streets when they have given me so much. My helping you will be a debt paid to Olörun for my well-being." We finished our plates and left, careful not to tarry, since more customers were coming in. "I've never met this woman, let alone knew she cared for a girl, but I do know where she lives."

Nazda's mood slowly began to lighten, as my attempts at distracting her thoughts grew more creative. I made sure not to allude to the edgewoods, Rayloh, or even the band of Dwala children, to evade the thought of Niegi. We mainly spoke of hobbies, likings, and family. We had a lot in common. She, like me, loved adventure and wasn't typical in her beliefs. She was strong-minded and had the will of an ox, even more than myself. Nazda had been orphaned a couple of years ago. She didn't go into

129

much detail, only stating that her father died and her mother was taken from her.

Soon the buildings began to look familiar. I saw the windy, rural road that led to the end of the road where Kala's home stood. The décor on the outside shined bright in the middle of the day.

"This is where I must leave you. I have work to do if I want to eat again. If you're ever around, I work in the barn a hill's crest away from the bakery. If you get lost, just follow the smell of dung heaps and animal musk." Nazda laughed as she turned and trotted away, waving over her shoulder.

I walked up the small path to the jeweler's door. I knocked a couple of times, receiving no answer. After all of the trouble I had been through to come back to the black ring and locate her home, I wasn't going to give up because of a few unheard knocks. Not without being sure no one was home. I pushed on the door. It creaked open. *Someone has to be home. Why else would the door be left unlocked?* I convinced myself.

I eased my way inside, listening for sounds of movement. I saw a candle flickering in the kitchen and heard the low hum of a woman's voice vibrating through the air, so low that I could feel its rhythm through my feet. I turned the corner, expecting to find an outlay of jewelry. But there were no beautiful gem-crested necklaces, or finely charmed bracelets. In their place were glass containers, ranging in shapes, filled with powders and fluids, in an array of densities. A cauldron sat in the middle of the floor,

130

emitting a flurry of pops and crackles from bubbles bursting, rippling the air, echoing off the walls. Incense burned in the corner, sending tiny currents of smoke into the air, mixing with the cauldron's fumes.

In the middle of the kitchen stood Mistress Demallo. She looked even wilder than before. Her face was thin, and bags hung heavily from her cheeks. A red bird perched on her shoulder, its head every so often twitching, as if the poor animal were drugged. I watched them intently, intrigued and frightened at the same time. The hum still echoed in her throat. She didn't move. Finally I ended up right in front of her, close enough to see her eyes in the windowless kitchen. Her pupils were gone. Her eyes seemed clouded, glistening like dewdrops at the break of dawn. It was as if she were in a trance. I waved my hand in front of her face, trying to make out this weird scene. As my hand swept across her face, her hand caught mine, like a snake snapping at a rodent. I tried to wiggle free but her grip was firm and unyielding. Such might for an old woman. Without moving, her eyes now emboldened with her returned pupils, she spoke.

"What is it you seek, young elf?" she asked, her gaze still aloof.

"I found, in my purchases from the last time I visited, a bow and a quiver of arrows. I thought maybe you or Kala placed them by mistake." Mistress Demallo's head snapped to the left, where the bird sat. It looked as if it returned her glare with calm.

A giant breath clawed its way from Mistress Demallo's mouth, sending the smoke from the room. Almost immediately her face was healthy, almost youthful. The wrinkles that once weighed heavily on her face were now smooth and relaxed. The gray in her hair lightened, revealing the fiery red, making her even more appealing. Her dark skin brightened with a natural glow, not needing the rays of the sun for its full beauty to be revealed.

She turned and giggled as a new energy seemed to move within her. The bird flew from her shoulders, leaving she and I alone. "Wild mushrooms, my child. If you start, you won't ever stop." She laughed obnoxiously. I cracked a nervous smirk, unsure of what I had just experienced. I, however, wasn't an imbecile, and if she thought that her simply alluding to wild mushrooms was going to convince me of her normalcy, she was highly mistaken, but for the moment I'd play along.

She nudged the cauldron with her foot, sliding it with godlike strength and precision to the corner of the room. "Kaladria will see you out now that your question has been answered." It hadn't, but in some weird way, it had.

"Ready, miss?" Kala entered the room, wearing her servant's robes. "I will be working the night shift so I will have the pleasure of walking you home." I bid farewell to Mistress Demallo, and with that, Kala and I left.

As we walked, I began to pry, targeting my questions tactfully.

"Your full name is Kaladria. That's beautiful, might I say."

Kala giggled. "Thank you. I much prefer Kala, though. It's more appropriate for this age."

What an odd thing for a young woman to say. As if she had experienced many ages other than *this* age. We walked in silence for a moment, the sweeping sounds of our sandals the only things heard as we traveled the cobblestone streets. Eventually she broke the quiet.

"So, do you like your bow and arrows? I've been keeping them until the right person came along."

"You speak as if you're much older than you appear. What of that? And I know those weren't 'shrooms in the cauldron. And I thought your mistress sold jewelry." My attempts at tact and waiting for the right time were futile. I regretted my words as soon as they left my lips.

"Demallo sells many things. Depending on what you seek. Before, you sought jewelry, so jewelry was what she had." Her answers were well structured, her voice steady. She sounded extremely experienced, not like the young servant girl I had come to know. "However, in that snifter was something only a special someone could have, just like the bow and arrows. I assure you, you wouldn't have seen them if you weren't meant to."

By this time I was beyond befuddled. The corks and screws of my mind were grinding together, trying to piece together this riddle. She might just be odd, I concluded as a resolve to the pounding in my head. As we approached the entrance of the Remni, one more thing occurred to me.

"The bird," I muttered. Then with confidence, "There was a bird; a little red one. Perched on Demallo's shoulder. A weird creature of sorts, wavering as Demallo had." I wanted to see her explain out of this one. I wanted to see the screws and corks in her mind burn from exhaustion. To my disappointment, I received no such reaction. She smoothed the wrinkles in her servant's garb, smiling as she did.

"Wild mushrooms. They're powerful things, they are. Once you start them, you can't stop." She winked and walked into the Remni.

I sat down on the small steps at the front entrance, feeling heavy from all I had experienced of late. All of these strange occurrences, from the mist, to the odd red bird, to Mistress Demallo's odd behavior, filled my head. The Dwala didn't have talents. Demallo couldn't summon birds in the way Master Tali could. Perhaps the bird was something more.

"There you are. What a shame that Segun and I return home to find our greatest friend gone." I stood up and embraced him, holding him tight.

"Congratulations, Rayloh. I knew you'd be selected."

His faced reddened a little, and he cracked a smile. "I haven't seen Segun since the ceremony. His mother was quite upset."

"She's been that way since I first saw her this morning. I wonder what weighs upon her so heavily." I looked past Rayloh, along the corridor behind him. Mira and Lord Calo were having a conversation—odd, since I didn't think they were even remotely aware of each other, let alone well enough to have anything to argue about.

"Alya!" My conscious relayed back to reality.

"I apologize. I just thought . . . never mind. It isn't anything to worry about. What were you saying?"

"I was saying that Segun and I have some news for you." My eyes and mind battled between the aggression exchanged between Mira and Lord Calo and the conversation I was having with Rayloh. Finally they dispersed, Mira going into the main hall and Lord Calo turning down another hall, leading to the west end of the Remni.

"I will have to hear it at dinner. I have to go."

I slipped past Rayloh before he could object, cutting the corner just as Lord Calo cut another one, slipping into a windowless corridor with nothing but an exit at the end. As I readied to turn the corner, I heard a door slam shut behind him. I followed closely, pressing my ear against the door to ensure that his footsteps were far enough away before continuing. I braced myself, unsure if I should be trailing him after he had a heated discussion with my sister. Perhaps she had crossed him or injured his pride. I hoped that whatever they were arguing about could be discovered if I followed him.

I lifted the latch, and gripping the door tightly, pulled it open. I poked my head out of the archway. Lord Calo strode from the side of the building, stopping about halfway down. He peered around, and I, to ensure that I was not seen, ducked back into the archway. I peeked back out just in time to see him pull from his robe a small book, no bigger than a pamphlet. Suddenly I heard the creak of footsteps in the long hall behind me. Startled, I turned to see if someone was coming. The creaks stopped, and after holding my gaze into the darkness, I turned to make sense of Lord Calo and his secret business. But when I peeped outside again, no one was there. It was odd. We elves are naturally light on our feet, but it didn't make sense. I closed my eyes, hanging my head in frustration.

When I opened my eyes, I saw a familiar being. At my feet, its head perched back and its eyes wide, was the fox-like creature. It appeared transparent; the light from the sun seemed to pass right through it, as if it were some apparition. It wasn't frightening at all. It seemed more heavenly than lost and vengeful. Master Tali, with her love of nature, had mentioned animal guides, shape shifters, even something strange called a familiar, that clung to a host and were neither good nor bad, but powerful all the same. I had hoped to encounter one, and with the other oddities, I wouldn't be surprised if this pleasant being was something special. We stared at each other, its eyes captivating me with its beauty.

"There you are, Alya."

M.C. Ray

The creaks had to have been Madja, searching the halls for me. Rayloh must have told her the way I was headed. I assured her that I would be there in a few moments. I turned to find the white fox gone, as if it had never been. I sighed, disappointed. There was no one I could tell—I didn't want to cause concern for my sanity. But these walls carried so many secrets, and it was high time that I found some answers. I closed the door, letting the latch fall, and trudged back down the hall, where Madja stood waiting.

137

Chapter Ten

"Ah, Alya. The last day I get to see my beautiful daughter as an innocent elfling. Mistress Alya. So profound." Madja's eyes grew warm as she said my name alongside this new title.

I followed behind her to the family quarters. The room smelled of pumpkin and maple. Orange and red leaves had settled on our balcony, giving a festive look as the beginnings of fall layered our world. My gown was laid across my bed, as if it were a being in slumber. My jewelry lay next to it. Obviously Madja had been into the study and felt that my necklace would better keep in the family quarters.

"Why don't you try on your dress one more time. Just for us."

I nodded and beamed. I had somehow lost the urgency I had before to try on my gown. The feeling soon returned seeing it again on my bed, glimmering just as beautiful as the first grass of spring pushing through the last of winter's snow. I began unstrapping my swelk, letting it fall to my ankles, leaving me in my undergarments. I turned to look at the large mirror that hung next to my bed. My body wasn't how I remembered it. From my once girlish figure sprouted hips, and from my chest, breast buds. Abs had surfaced beneath them. Hanging from tree branches and running through the edgewoods had trimmed my body. I unwrapped my mallimare, revealing my bare chest. I stared for a moment, forgetting Madja was there.

"You're stunning, Alya. A stunning she-elf indeed." I smiled at her in my reflection, now moving my eyes to the masterpiece settled on my bed.

I carefully turned over the dress, bringing the back of the gown to the light. There was a single silver button on the back, with a thick emerald-colored material used as the noose to hold it in place. I unbuttoned the dress. I picked it up, letting the folds that were once confined by the button and its noose fall freely, welcoming my body as I slipped my legs, one by one, through its open center. I pulled the bodice over my hips, careful not to stretch out the fabric. One I had the dress on, Madja buttoned it up for me. I turned to face the mirror, closing my eyes so I could take it all in at once.

I opened my eyes to find not a young wild sprite that rummaged the edgewoods, throwing rocks at ground rodents, and sparring with lads. I felt attractive. My hair flowed wildly, unraveled from the braid it was used to being confined to. I tucked a few strands behind my ears, bringing angles to my face. My cheekbones that made my mouth grit and seem masculine now gave me an alien appearance that seemed distinguished. I smiled at myself, noticing these subtle changes. I had become so complacent and assumed that I was untamed.

When I was little, Madja used to take my sister and me to a pond where a bevy of swans lived. I used to marvel at how these creatures, in their youth, were so different from their graceful parents. Where their feathers were supposed to be were patches of hair, giving them the appearance of large and dingy cotton balls. Madja used to say that every miss becomes a swan. I took her words for babble, but Mira feasted on them like manna from heaven. For the longest time, Mira ran about the house pretending she was a swan, flapping her arms as if she were flying with mighty wings, bending the air with belligerent strokes. I resented her, and in time, expressed my annoyance. After that, I didn't hear any more about swans; in fact, I didn't even care to go to the pond again. Yet years later, as I looked in the mirror, I stared at my body, my face, my very being, loving every bit of what I had become. Mira and Madja were right. Every miss does become a swan, and I don't believe it happens when one is on the brink of maturity, or even when she is courted or engaged. I believe it happens when that first spark of realization, of acceptance breaks into her soul; from her dawning reflection she realizes that she was a swan all along.

"I love it." I breathed in deeply in an attempt to keep myself from tearing up.

"You look beautiful." This time when she said it, I believed her. She stood behind me, adjusting the dress to perfect alignment, then with both hands, moved all of the locks of my hair to my back. She went to reach for the necklace, unbuckling its latch as she spoke. "I wish the other ladies could see you now, but they're busy with the farewell dinner." She placed the necklace around my neck, latching it securely in place.

"Farewell dinner for whom?" I ran my fingers down the body of the snake all the way to the head. I couldn't have been more satisfied with my purchase.

"For Segun and Rayloh. They leave for the warriors' barracks tomorrow."

A lump grew in my throat and the troubles of the world returned to me yet again. My comrades would have to leave for the barracks sooner than later, considering the prince had decreed that all are required to fight in this year's unveiling. Still, I figured I would have time to grow accustomed to their absence, training myself by gradually withdrawing from their company or finding an outlet that would make it easier for me to cope. But their time to leave was now unexpectedly arriving.

"Can you unbutton my dress?" Madja sensed my grief and released the silver button from its noose.

"Please understand, Alya, that—"

"And the necklace" I interrupted her, throwing my hair over my right shoulder so she could get to the latch with ease. She let it fall into her hand, then laid it on the mantel.

"I'll see you at dinner." She left the room, leaving me standing bare, still looking into the mirror. I reached for my nightgown, which hung from a hook on the wall.

I wandered to the balcony, pushing open the glass doors. A rush of fresh air chilled my body, making me shudder until I grew accustomed. I stood over the stone railing, peering at the open skies, and the wide array of people wandering about the city. The skies were most stunning at this time of day. The sun was just about to dive behind the tops of the trees, far beyond in the edgewoods. The clouds and sky showed an assortment and mixture of pinks, yellows, oranges, and blues, all flowing into and out of each other. As many times as I've seen the setting sun and its effects on the heavens, I always attempted to see where the colors started and ended. And every time, I concluded that there was no way to tell.

I breathed in deeply. Aromas filled the air. I could smell pine needles in the Remni's yard, covering the beds of dirt where the trees were planted. The pleasant scents of peas, rice, and corn fritters lifted high into the atmosphere. I could even smell the fumes from chimneys in the lower rings, billowing to the skies and joining together into one huge mass. I took it all in, calming my body and mind. Somehow it made it easier, observing the simple things in life. The moment you smell the warm scents of autumn, play in the first snows of winter, witness the burst of new saplings leading the rest of the world into spring. It was a never-ending cycle, and if the seasons could accept that in life things changed and you have to keep living and growing, then maybe I would be fine when Rayloh and Segun left.

I wasn't relieved of sadness, but for the moment I was content. The knot in my stomach quenched any thirst and hunger that I had before and was replaced with grogginess and fatigue. I decided I should turn in for the day, not wanting to interact with anyone else. I laid down on my cot, resting my head on my pillow, my tears dampening the linen casing.

As I slept, I felt cold and empty, as if all the heat had been stripped from my body, leaving nothing more than hollow organs, the inevitable loss still pounding away at my heart. Segun and Rayloh were probably worried about me. It wasn't like me to miss a meal. I slept for what seemed to be days. When I felt the sun warm my forehead, I snuggled even more under my blanket, pulling the ends up to my chin. I didn't want to get up. If I opened my eyes it would be the day my friends left, but in some strange way, I had convinced myself that the day wouldn't start if I didn't open my eyes. But I finally accepted the inevitable and sat up in my bed.

My family was already up, Mira's bed neatly made. It was still early. The sun was low in the sky and the air was still cool. I stood and stretched. My back, knees, and shoulders popped. The glass doors to the balcony were open. I stood out on the terrace, letting the early sun kiss my nose as I watched the business of the day unfold below. Today was my Kei, and although I wanted no hand in the decisions concerning decorations, food, and entertainment, I was sure that Madja had taken it upon herself to make this celebration overly extravagant. After all, I was her first daughter, and I had already accepted that she was going to enjoy this event way more than I would.

I peered down at the path trailing away from the Remni at all the people coming in and out. Some I recognized from the market, while others I didn't recognize at all. They waddled around like ants in an anthill, using their talents where Madja saw fit. One she-elf, whom I especially enjoyed, made blooms through the cold ground, tulips and roses, varying in shades of green, no doubt encouraged by Madja to match my gown. The flowers blossomed, their petals full and vibrant. As she pulled these flowers from the earth, two figures caught my attention, urgently striding away from the Remni. It was Segun and Rayloh. They were headed toward the blue ring, dressed in fine red shirts without collars. I watched them until I couldn't see them anymore. *I can't believe they left without bidding me a proper farewell. I thought they were allowed to stay for my Kei.*

I felt disrespected and betrayed but surprised at the same time. I know I didn't go to their farewell dinner, but I didn't expect them to leave the day of my Kei, let alone without saying good-bye. I turned my back from the balcony in anger and plummeted into my bed. Burying my face into my pillow, I screamed. For a while I laid there, noisily sucking air through the corners of my mouth, refusing to lift my head.

My stomach growled noisily during my fit of pity. Midday meal was a couple of hours away, but my stomach refused to let me sit in self-loathing. I stopped by the grooming quarters to make myself look somewhat presentable. While I didn't feel the need to change out of my nightgown, I did feel obligated, because we had guests in the agency, to not look as if I had just awoken. I splashed water on my face, washing away any residual sleep and depression.

The main hall was cluttered with crates and barrels. Workers clung to the walls like bees in the hive, marking where decorations would be hung. I passed in a hurry, not wanting anyone to notice my presence, especially since today was already going to be all about me. I went into the kitchen. No one was there. Plates and cutlery were stacked high on the large worktable, looking like mighty mountains on a small island. I snooped around, hoping to find some leftover bread, or some fruit from breakfast. There wasn't much. After going through a cupboard, I found a bag of dried berries. They would have to do. I was starving and would eat about anything right then. I scurried from the kitchen, past the workers, and back to the family quarters.

I closed the door behind me, sighing in relief. Madja had hung my dress neatly from the shelf. I pulled from under my bed an arrow from the quiver. I ran my fingers along its spine, while with my other hand I traced Segun's scar, which had become a habit of mine. I didn't want to leave the room, but I definitely didn't want to sit in boredom until my party. I shoved dried fruit into my mouth, ravaging like an animal at a carcass. Having satisfied my hunger, I felt more comfortable. My mind slipped out of reality, bringing back that feeling of fatigue. I shoved under my pillow the almost empty bag of dried fruit and drifted back into sleep.

When I awoke again, a silver tray with fresh fruit and warm bread sat atop my dresser. I had missed midday meal. I looked outside. The sun was beginning to set and it looked as if the time for my Kei was fast approaching. I hadn't even begun to get ready, not that I planned on doing much more than bathing for this "momentous" occasion. I stood, shoved a few berries and a slice of bread into my mouth, and sat on my bed, mentally gathering myself.

I had yet to plan what I was to do about my father's private chamber. His robe was already here, hanging on one of the hooks on the wall next to his door. I got up and felt his pockets for the key. It was there. *Why don't you just do it now?* I thought. I hustled to the balcony and peered over. The front yard had returned to its normal state, quiet and uninhabited except for the voluptuous bushes of green flowers and plants that graced the walkway and the front of the estate. It was too quiet. With my father being home so early for tonight's events, I didn't want to risk being discovered by him when there's no other place for him to be. I reached my hand into the pocket and slid my slender fingers around the cold medal.

Just as I began to remove it from the robe's pouch, the knob to my father's chamber door twitched. I removed my hand, spinning to my right, where Mira's trinkets were located. The door opened and out stepped my father, already dressed in his formal eveningwear. He had on a collarless shirt, much like the red shirts

146

the lads were wearing. It was a rich green, a little lighter than the emerald I would be wearing, most likely Madja's doing. A single gold button rested at the top of the shirt, trailing from it a gold stream running all the way down to the hem. His breeches were a tan color, with a gold lacy pattern down the sides. He wore black velvet slippers, on the tip of his shoe a gold triangle, matching the gold lace on his pants and shirt. I brushed around Mira's things, pretending to search for something I had lost. I could feel his body growing near.

"Happy birthday, Alya." His voice had no emotion.

I didn't respond right away, surprised somewhat by his kind remark. Without turning around, I said, "Thank you."

He placed his hand on my shoulder, then left. I shook in relief, my nerves finally settling from the shock. I would have to wait.

I decided to go ahead and get ready. Kala greeted me warmly upon my arrival in the grooming quarters. She sat in her usual place, thumbing her fingers and humming. After preparing my towels, bath, and dry clothes for me to wear, she was allowed to leave. Today I felt like a change was in order and I didn't pick the maple flower petals and cinnapine stem sap to go into my bath. Instead, I chose a rose petal and honey sap combination. Together they smelled uniquely pleasant. I ran the fragrance over my body multiple times. I wanted to smell exceedingly good, so I was thorough, wiping and rinsing in every nook and crevice.

After bathing, I dried myself and put on my undergarments and a dry gown. I headed back to the family quarters, where during my bath, Madja had a servant prepare my items for the evening. She sat in the corner, awaiting directions. She seemed annoyed, probably because she had to wait on a "spoiled sprite." I smoothed peach oil on my body, bringing back to life my pruned-up skin from the bath. I slipped on my dress and adjusted myself in the mirror. Madja wasn't around to ensure that I looked perfect, so I tried my best to make corrections with my most keen eye. The young servant latched the snake necklace around my neck. I reached back to ensure that the latch was secure. I picked up a bowl of ruby grapes from the platter on my dresser, and sat down on a stool so the woman could fix my hair while I plucked the fruit rhythmically into my mouth. She grouped the long strands of black together, forming a bun by using one single lock, wrapping it around a couple of times, and then drawing it through the bundle. When she had finished, she retreated to the corner and sat down, annoyance still etched on her face.

I stood to look in the mirror. My head was heavier since all the weight of my hair was centered in one place but I held my posture, tightening unused muscles in my neck as to not appear lazy or uncomfortable. I walked to the mirror. The dress still held its effect on me and the necklace fit perfectly, its gem eyes peering into the glass, sending a reflection of green back at me. The bun made me look older, revealing the angles of my face—my chiseled cheekbones, my slender eyelids, my light brown eyes. I felt that a lip stain would be appropriate, so I spread a deep red color made from beeswax and a hibiscus plant. My lips appeared more full and luscious, and my teeth showed alluringly white against the cardinal tone.

The door flew open. Madja rushed in, already dressed as well. She sported a simple gown, of the same color as my father's. It hugged her hips, showing the youthful form that most elves of her age had lost a long time ago. Her hair fell down her back in a shower of curls. She covered her mouth dramatically, her eyes swelling, trying to hold back the floods that at any moment would burst from their dams. She cradled me gently, careful to not smudge my lips or unleash the bundled mass atop my crown. She dismissed the servant, who looked relieved as she gathered the spare towels and half-eaten platter of food and let herself out.

"Here, we can't forget the bracelet I promised you, can we?" She went to her bureau, pulling from one of the drawers a small wooden box.

"Oh, Madja, you don't have to" I said modestly, even though I was excited to see what artfully crafted, relatively expensive trinket she would bestow upon me trustingly for the night. Even Mira would be denied constantly when she would beg Madja for her most idly worn of possessions, some even sitting in a tangled mess on top of Madja's dresser. I would be the first to flaunt something from her gorgeous jewelry collection. She opened the wooden box, revealing a silver bracelet with a gold

149

half sphere that linked the two parts of the bracelet together. She placed it on my wrist gently. It fit just right, not loosely sliding from my wrist to my upper arm and not tight enough to leave a mark on my flesh. It just crested firmly against the sheer material of my sleeve. If the gold half sphere weren't embossed on the silver ring, it would have looked like a complete set, along with the silver earrings fastened to my ears.

"Shall we, *mistress?*" Madja angled herself sideways, as if to usher me to the door. I clutched the front of my gown, carefully letting the material catch the hold of my fingers.

Each step was a new moon. As I drew closer to the main hall, I could hear more voices, the strokes of music growing louder, the smells of exotic dishes and spiced wines. All of this and my nerves made my senses rejoice in exuberance. We strode the corridor together, Madja and I, and I was happy that she was with me, although I didn't show it.

I could hear the usher making a few announcements of the arrival of guests before I came into view. Then a trumpet blared, sending chills through my body. Madja had really put a dramatic touch on this ceremony.

"Introducing the honor of this evening, Mistress Alya Lightstar, from the House of Meoltan."

As the usher stepped out of the walkway to the left side of the door frame, Madja stepped to my right, where my father stood, waiting to receive me. I gracefully fluttered in, taking in the splendor of the main hall that had been transformed to a heavenly dream. Gold accents rained from above in the forms of crystal chandeliers, the largest hanging from the skylight. Sheer ribbons of silver and gold sprung like a fountain from these chandeliers like multiple springs, connecting them together. From the ceiling hung aerial fabric that the Jalla dancers now rested on as I entered, shimmering in their leotards of sparkling green and silver. Servants lined the walls, balancing platters of sweetbreads, rich cheeses, fruits, vegetables, and desserts, while others brought from the kitchen kegs of spiced wines, warm ciders, and fruit juices in flagons. Fireflies danced around the ceiling, imitating stars, lights favored by my people.

There were many guests, too many to number. Some I had never spoken to greeted me familiarly all the same. They were dressed in their finest of robes, tailored dresses, and gowns, some similar to the ones that floated in Mistress Vesti's keep. The entirety of my class was present, even Destili, whom I had never taken a liking to, and she knew that. She and the rest of my rotation greeted me warmly, I being one of the first to have her Kei. I looked around for Segun and Rayloh, hoping that they would return to celebrate my birthday with me. After all, this transition wouldn't be anything without my two most loyal comrades. I scanned the numerous faces, some grinning aggressively if I made eye contact, hoping for a chance to wish happy tidings on my special day.

I had almost given up the hope when I saw Master Tali from about halfway across the hall, among the multiple heads and necks of elves grouping together, socializing. She turned to see me coming, her radiance a sight as always, and began making her way to me. I pushed through countless elites, cordially smiling. I even passed Destili, who stopped me in my course to wish me congratulations. She reached out for an embrace, which I accepted with a lukewarm response. After being released, I smiled wryly at her, and continued on my way. Just as I came to a clearing, where a chandelier glistened and no one stood, I heard the blaring of a trumpet. Distracted, I turned to see who it could be. The horn was only sounded when the guest of honor entered an affair. The only reason the horn would be sounded is if royalty, themselves, made an appearance at this common and generally insignificant event, which I found to be unlikely.

"Introducing the Honorable Alag, the heir to the throne of Keldrock, sons of sons of Shiloh, from the House of Estrellar. Prince of the Elves."

All over, guests bowed. I began to lower into a curtsy when I saw two blotches of bright red appear, aligning themselves on either side of the prince. Segun and Rayloh had returned. My eyes watered from the overwhelming excitement. A flood of emotions suddenly ran through me, as all at once I wanted to kick myself for even doubting them. The prince held his palm to the ceiling, greeting his subjects. I didn't mind the attention being taken from me. The lads' eyes met mine as I glided toward them through giggling misses and stately elves. Just as I was about to embrace Segun, they hung their heads, allowing the prince passage to speak with me.

I looked up to see his black hair flowing down past his shoulders, stopping just short of his lower back. He wore a darker green, almost identical to mine. In fact, his entire ensemble was weirdly similar to mine. The sheer material that wrapped my arms hung from the ends of his shirt at the cuffs. His breeches were a lighter emerald green, the color of my bodice. A silver crown in the form of a snake wrapped around his head, as if resting on a rock in a coiled slumber. Its tail clenched the back of his head, and arched on his forehead was the head of a cobra ready to strike, the same eyes of emerald that rested on the small triangle head beneath my chin on my chest.

I scowled with wide eyes at Madja. This was no innocent coincidence or even a rare gracing for his people. This was a tacky attempt at courtship. Obviously I had been watched, desired, and selected. This day was just a part of the plan, and suddenly Madja's anxiousness, the lending of her valued bracelet, the overindulgence in planning of this Kei. Nothing seemed genuine, and a great anger swelled within me. Thoughts scurried like rats through my mind, and I wanted to run away. My world was crashing in, and just as it peeled me apart, I entered a new one where betrothals, households, and the politics of society would be my sport. For the moment I held my calm, bowing my head.

"Good evening, Prince Alag, from the House of Estrellar."

"Good evening, Mistress Alya. Happy birthday. You look quite beautiful tonight." I blushed. If I didn't believe anything else about this night, I believed that his opinion held true.

"Thank you, my lordship." My eyes slid to the lads. Segun smirked, still the little sprite that I had come to love. Rayloh held his gaze on the party, ignoring whatever flirtation was happening between the prince and myself. I returned to the prince. His lips pursed perfectly. His top lip was slightly darker than the lower. When he bit his bottom lip seductively, I could see all the blood rush to the spot where his teeth grooved his skin. He had low stubble, the hair of maturity beginning to grow on his face. We stood in silence for a minute.

"Your speech yesterday was very inspirational," I said. "The sprites in my rotation responded well. They couldn't stop their jaws from dropping." He smiled, leaning his head back in a confident chuckle, the hair that gathered at his shoulders moving to his back.

"That's great to know. Well, they'll be disappointed to find that someone else has caught my attention and I have plans of staying intrigued. Hopefully their lost hopes won't lead them through too much despair." He winked at me. He was seemingly suave for his age. He was mature, yet beautifully rebellious and egotistical at the same time. I liked and disliked him all in the same breath. I continued, engaging the best way I knew how.

"Who is this lady that intrigues you?" I asked.

"My prince." He peered over my shoulder at an official who stood a few steps from us. "Sir. Your people wait. There are some very important officials and dignitaries awaiting to address your lordship." The prince nodded to his attendant before turning back to me.

"She will know in due time." He tightened his posture, transforming back to his stately position. He bowed, and I returned with a curtsy. He gestured toward the lads before walking away. "I will leave you to your comrades. We will speak again before the night ends, Mistress Alya."

He walked off, his head erect, as if he were some graceful bird, gliding across the dance floor. I sighed, then turned to face the lads. Segun looked slender, retaining his cerebral appearance. The barracks would most likely change that. Rayloh looked highly comfortable in the uniform, his orange curls tucked tightly to his head. He filled out the shirt, his biceps widening the sleeves and his chest sticking out without him trying. In this moment I realized the same things about Rayloh that I had recently realized about myself. He was truly handsome. All the things I admired about his father were reflected doubly in his form. I subconsciously looked him over in admiration before snapping back to reality. He didn't notice. He just stared off into the sea of guests, eyebrows furrowed.

Of course, I was excited to see them, but a part of me felt betrayed. At what moment were they going to tell me they were leaving the Remni for the Guerr barracks? Segun smiled and began.

"Happy birthday, Miss—I mean Mistress—Alya." I wryly wrinkled my cheeks, making a frowned expression, pushing out my lips.

"You guys look quite portly. It appears you're too august to even let your lowly friend know you were leaving for the barracks. I had to find out from my mother."

Rayloh let out a gust of air before speaking. "Figures as much. I should have known you weren't ill or fatigued when you weren't at our farewell dinner. I tried to tell you yesterday outside of the Remni. Before you ran off." I recalled the instance. He was right, but I felt more effort should have been used and rolled my eyes, insinuating that I didn't remember. He folded his arms in response. "Besides, it seems we'll be forgotten soon enough. The prince is quite an outlet to take up, from what I've seen." His face reddened, and Segun stared in disbelief at Rayloh's comment, which was blatantly disrespectful toward his royal highness. If I hadn't known any better, I would think Rayloh was jealous.

Segun chimed in. "The prince knew of your Kei before we requested an extension and just summoned us to the barracks as a formality. We knew we were to return, so there was no reason to say our good-byes just yet." He placed his hand on Rayloh's shoulder. "We wouldn't miss this day for the skies." I let out a sigh and decided I wouldn't let this tainted blood brew any longer. I needed their help.

"We have one more mission before our time together comes to a recess. I have many questions that need answering, and I feel that my father is deep enough in the political circle to possess this information. They won't be leaving the hall, especially since we're entertaining guests, but they wouldn't want me out of their sights, seeing as I'm the guest of honor. I need to be allowed to search his private chambers without being discovered."

"You want us to help you leave casually, without them searching for you if you're gone. You want us to help with a distraction," Rayloh inserted, he now thoroughly intrigued, forgetting his distaste.

"Exactly, or something of the sort. Just to buy me a little time."

"What exactly are you searching for?" Segun timidly inquired.

"There are strange occurrences, recent findings that I for my sanity and yours can't be said. Not to mention the ceremony where it was announced that you all are being 'awarded' the privilege to fight in the upcoming unveiling with so little knowledge of anything concerning battle. Then there's the . . . beast."

I had just uttered the word when the party coordinator who orchestrated this evening's agenda tapped me on the shoulder, interrupting our conversation. I turned in alarm.

"The night's first dances are to commence now. I'm sure the prince would be delighted to share in this tradition with you." He put his palm to my shoulder to lead me away, but I didn't budge.

"Actually," I said, "I'd like to share my first dance with my comrade." The party coordinator stared in awe so I decided to explain further, so as not to ruffle feathers and put him in any kind of awkward place. "He is my most loyal of friends, and he departs for the barracks at the closing of this event, and it would be most appropriate that I share this dance with him. It would mean so much to me." I turned to Rayloh, who stared at me with glowing eyes, smiling oddly, the same way the prince did. Rayloh was a great actor.

"That's a fine reasoning. I'm sure the prince will be obliged." He bowed his head cheerfully in exit, and wandered off to the center of the floor, readying his breath and voice for his announcement. "Good evening, lords and ladies, and elfkin alike. We have reached the first dance of the evening." He stretched his arm, the tip of his fingers hailing toward me. His arm parted the cluster of people, creating a passage between him and myself like a sliver of land atop the seas, connecting an island to the mainland. "Introducing Lord Rayloh and Mistress Alya."

We both knew how to dance formally. We had been taught at a young age, as all sprites were, and I'd even had many opportunities to practice these skills at elite parties when asked for my hand in dance by young lads interested in putting on a show of maturity. I would always accept, taking it as the one time to undermine Segun and Rayloh, who thought I wasn't even remotely interested in creating bonds with anyone outside of them. Still, I couldn't help but be nervous now. All eyes were on me tonight. The main hall was stone quiet. Then the harpist began.

As custom would have it, Rayloh was to pick the dance. To my surprise he chose a mating march, which released giggles and sighs from immature misses and easily amused wives. We raised our hands, placing our palms together, gliding in a gentle circle. Rayloh looked majestic as he pranced around me. I admired his movements, the way his uniform made him look more dignified than his actual personality normally allowed. He made me work even harder to fully animate the movements. After our first round, people began to join, but I was lost in this special moment between two friends who realized that this would be their last time spent together for a while. So we lingered one more round, not wanting it to end. When I saw my father and Madja join hands and venture onto the dance floor, I decided it was time to make our move. I bowed out, displaying a dramatic act of exhaustion.

Rayloh and I joined with Segun, and we exited the hall. We seemed natural, since everyone would understand this event was bittersweet for my comrades and myself and nothing suspicious would be suspected. We were almost down the corridor when the party coordinator bowed graciously but then grabbed my arm, inquiring about my destination. He seemed agitated but he was sure to keep a façade of calmness and cheer. I told him we were going for some peace, to rest after the dance, and to share a few moments of quiet.

"Oh, of course, Mistress Alya. It's just that in a few moments we were hoping to begin presenting your gifts, and I don't want to keep your guests in wait." I nodded at his concern and expressed in all artificial sincerity that I would return in a few breaths.

"We were just going to discuss a few things in the cool of the night outside." I was evidently becoming better at lying, and even worse, I was comfortable doing it, or perhaps it was because the coordinator didn't know me to point out my falsehoods. He bowed graciously again and returned to the main hall.

We turned almost immediately after he had crossed the threshold into the main hall, darting down the corridor to my family's quarters. Before entering, I had Rayloh stand outside, instructing him that if he saw anyone making their way to our chambers to knock three times and then stall casually to give us enough time to lock my father's study and situate ourselves to appear like we weren't doing anything criminal. Rayloh's sharpness would be put to better use that way, and Segun was clever and his father had a similar chamber so he'd be more cautious in keeping things in place than Rayloh I'd hope.

I opened the door and headed straight for my father's robe. It was lighter than before and I automatically assumed he had taken the key with him to the party. The Remni was full of elven families from all over the city. He may have taken the key for safekeeping just in case a nosy guest or curious relation made their way to our family quarters and stumbled upon a locked door that they just had to open. I turned in half dismay and half relief, both wanting to know what lay on the other side of the door and also not wanting to know for fear of regret after my discovery. Segun walked toward me to assist when his foot tapped something metal, sending it skidding under Madja's cot. I saw it just in time as it went under the bed frame. The key. Segun got down on to his belly, squirming like a snake in a rabbit's hole. He resurfaced successful, the key in hand. It was a rusty iron key; most likely the door was the same from when the Remni was first built. I plucked it from his thin fingers, sticking it firmly through the keyhole. I turned it with a quick flick of the wrist but it didn't budge. I tried two more times, each time shaking the handle. Still nothing. I kicked the door in frustration, leaving the key in the hole, walking away for a moment to stretch my wrist before giving it another go. I heard the click of the knob and the door opened.

"It's old. I pulled the knob in before turning it, and it worked." An egotistical smirk pressed Segun's lips. Where brute strength failed, intellect reigned supreme. Segun was good for that much.

We slipped into the room. It was dark, so I retrieved a lantern from the post on the wall next to my bed. The chamber was lined with volumes. Some were in the form of pictures, something we were taught at lessons were called hieroglyphics. There were

161

maps of lands, some that I'd never known to exist. I knew a world lay beyond the veil, that we couldn't be the only beings, and that there was a reason that we stayed secluded—but I imagined this knowledge from the outside world had been lost. Now I feared that it was being kept.

I picked up a book with a blue cover, with a body of water and a setting sun on the front and began flipping through its pages. I loved reading and wished I had the time to skim all of these books, but we had a job to do this night. After poking around for a few moments at the detailed maps and intricate paintings of oceans and stars, we refocused our energies on finding anything bearing the crest of the Courts. On my father's desk were many pieces of parchment. I turned the heat up in the lamp, making the flame brighter as we sorted through papers. Most were updates and personal notes until we came to a stack clipped together with a pin. My teeth gritted with anxiousness and my body twitched. It was all of the Council's agendas. I looked at the most recent. It read as follows:

9th of October

Call to order

New Business

- The New Recruits
- Day of Unveiling

Threat

R: 1

L: 13

- New tactics

  (Below this was illegible scribbling, highly detailed and looked of little importance, just notes my father jotted.)

Reports

The Courts

(Members were listed.)

The Royal Family

(Prince Alag was the only name listed.)

The Council: EW devision

(Listedc were a few names, including Sr. Meoltan, my father.)

Conclusion

Dismissal

Threat? Was this "threat" the beast from the edgewoods? I flipped through piece after piece of parchment, all of them nearly the same. Most of them had few additions, probably meetings held more out of habit than for new business. I flipped and flipped. The number next to "R" suddenly began to grow about eight sheets in. There were three, then seven. There were ten, then fourteen. I kept flipping, the anticipation filling my insides. I had the sense I was getting close to an answer or at least an inkling that would help lead me in the right direction. I almost forgot to breathe. Segun was panting on my neck, just as intrigued as I was. Months passed, then years. Then:

13th of December

Call to order

New Business

- Famine (apportionments and allocations)
- Day of Unveiling (strategy Improvement)
- New Threat (Mongrowls)
- New tactics

  (These were the beginnings of highly detailed traps and confrontations my father jotted as reliable suggestions.)

Reports

The Courts

The Royal Family

The EW division: Volunteers

(This was underlined, my father having been intrigued by this new opportunity.)

Conclusion

Dismissal

My eyebrow twitched. This was the page. The page that was different from all the others, but it held a lot of random subheadings and initials that I wouldn't have the faintest idea of their meaning. There were three sharp knocks on the family quarters door. I snagged the page of parchment and returned the rest of the stack to its original position. I grabbed the lantern, and Segun closed the door behind us. I placed the lantern back on its post and headed for the door, brushing swiftly past the beads that shimmered like coils on a rattler that hung from the second threshold before the door. A hard knocking shook the door—in anger or urgency I couldn't tell. but I prayed it wasn't Madja or my father. Hopefully it was just Rayloh, hurrying us along. Segun alone with me in the family quarters didn't spell out a great situation for a young mistress and an assumedly eager lad. I shoved Segun the piece of parchment and flicked my index finger to the wall where my cot sat, hidden from the door, indicating for him to step out of view. I unhooked the latch and opened the door to find the party coordinator. When I discovered it was he, I opened it wide, grinning as if there were nothing to hide.

"Mistress, it is time. We have been searching for you for quite a while now. Your friend said you were checking your garments for perspiration. We haven't time for such trifles. You are summoned. It's time for you to open your gifts."

His forehead was sweaty and his veins pulsed, protruding above his eyebrows and along the side of his face, running adjacent to his sideburns. He took my hand gently but offered no choice in the matter and led me back to the main hall. As I passed Rayloh, I narrowed my eyes at him. *The best excuse you could come up with was "perspiration"?* was the message I attempted to convey. I heard the door behind us creak open, likely Segun slipping out, and for a minute I thought the party coordinator was going to turn around and investigate, but he was stressed and the expression on his face was focused on navigating through the hallways back to his current project that he didn't notice. My Kei.

Before we reached the archway's main hall, he released me. He adjusted my gown, dabbing my face with his long cuffs. I hadn't realized how eccentrically dressed he was. His robe was gold and flowed behind him like the train of a wedding gown. His sleeves were rose pink and looked like the wings of butterflies, fluttering as he swung his arms. Thickly wound gold thread, a slightly darker tint than his robe, made flowery patterns on his turquoise collarless shirt. His hair flowed freely but stayed layered and untangled. I walked in first, and my father, standing on a platform, received me. People applauded as if he had just given a speech and I was right on time for its conclusion.

"And we couldn't be more proud of Alya." He was, in fact, giving a speech. As he finished, I took his place on the platform, we not exchanging anything but the glare of his silent rage at my absence as he descended the stairs, taking up host next to Madja.

Then it began. The guests presented gifts, having the Dwala bring them to me, showcasing them one at a time to the other attendees, who seemed only concerned that their gift wasn't on the bottom rung as far as appeal and luxuriousness. One family, whose daughter was rather quiet and to whom I had spoken only when we had group assignments or needed partners for talent practice, brought me an entire array of fine silk robes, five total, each a different color, flowing together like a rainbow. Mira's jaw dropped when she saw this wonderful present. I could see the desire in her eyes and realized I wasn't going to be the only one to

166

don these new garments. More and more gifts were shown to me, the servants each aligning and the party coordinator announcing them one by one and from whom they were being gifted. Madja's brother, Aole, brought me scented candles, ranging from the simplest of scents to the most expensive distilled essences and mixtures of sweet oils. Every birthday after my eighth, he would bring me a candle, which I had expressed strong interest in after visiting him one day and after spending the entire visit watching the candle, its flame flickering wildly and inhaling the sweet scent of pines and pumpkins. Aole was a master at crafting them, and the candle produced tantalizing smells; I loved how the wax tamed the fire, its slow melting keeping the flame calm. It was a sacrifice for a sacrifice, a partnered dance. Everything from fine gowns to hair accessories were brought before me, and I felt, in this moment, like a queen in front of her subjects, trying to remain attentive while they tried to appease my desires. I was grateful for all of my gifts, and while some were more trifling than others, I kept my manners.

After the last gift had been shown, I thanked the party and went immediately to Madja's side and hugged her. It wasn't customary for the parents of the honorary to present gifts in the presence of the entire party, but now was my opportunity to see if my greatest wish had been granted.

"So when should I expect my warrior's garb?" Madja pulled out of my embrace, still keeping on a smile for those who might be looking.

"I found the sparring gear tucked away in the chest in the study," she said in a whisper. "I feel this has gone too far, Alya. You have a responsibility, and people have been gossiping about you. I just think it best that you go for something more . . . traditional. Your father and I bought you a dozen dresses to make up for your disappointment, which I hope will suffice. Please understand, it's because we love you."

"No. You love what I could be," I snapped, louder than expected. Even though the hall rang with excitement and laughter, those within a ten-foot radius turned in confusion; some looked directly at us, while others propped their noses, searching with sharp eyes to see the conflict. Madja didn't lose her composure.

"You're not a warrior, Alya. You never will be. Your friends are gone and now you have more pressing things to worry about. You're to be a lady soon. It's time you start acting like one." Those words stung. I had a fate already decided, and no matter what I did, it would come to pass. With that she turned and walked away, and I stood there, beneath the skylight and the grand chandelier.

Despite my high-strung emotions, the rest of the night went on smashingly, helping to distract briefly from my disappointment. I had a few refreshments and even got to dance with the prince before it was time for him and the lads to depart. I assumed he would go to the purple ring and the lads to the barracks. Before he and I said our farewells, we walked outside to the front yard, the lads and the prince's guards standing a good length from us, where they were within sight but could not hear our whispers. We flirted, I laughing at a few of his jokes and enduring a few of his rants kindly. My eyes shifted to Rayloh and Segun, who looked more mature in their training uniforms. My smile couldn't help but fade into longing. Things wouldn't be the same.

"You favor them, don't you?" The prince reached toward my face, removing a lock of hair from my cheek and placing the hair behind my ear.

"Yes. We grew up together, you see. They are like my kin. I don't know what I am to do without them." I turned to find his eyes staring back into mine. I could feel his high infatuation, and from that, not out of kindness toward the lads, came his next gesture.

"I will make them my personal aides. They will train as warriors, for I will be joining the recruits in the barracks, but their privileges and duties will fall alongside my own will, according to the duties of my agenda." I wanted to reach out and hug him. Because of him, maybe I would see them on occasion, even if they weren't personal visits. And if they were his personal attendants, they would likely survive. They would stay alive. The Day of Unveiling was approaching, and there were no guarantees. A part of me wanted them home, but even more of me wanted to be in the barracks, preparing to fight alongside them.

The prince nodded, and I curtseyed and they departed. The lads didn't look my way. They followed in their places on either

169

side of the prince. I went back inside to say farewell to the rest of my guests. Back in my family's quarters, I undressed, laying the gown at the edge of my bed. I pulled back the sheets to find the folded parchment and the old rusty key. I placed it without delay into the pocket of my father's robe. Sighing a breath of relief, I climbed into bed, placing the folded parchment safely in my pillow casing, and thanked Olörun for the cleverness of Segun and the bravery of Rayloh. I drifted off as tears rolled down my face, a bittersweet night coming to an end.

Chapter Eleven

- New Threat (Mongrowls)

I had gotten my answer. Assuming that the predatory beast from the edgewoods was one of these so-called mongrowls, the Courts had known about them for some time now. Four days after my Kei and the discovery of this agenda, I was still pondering what all this could mean. The Courts knew, but they allowed the citizens to remain ignorant of this threat. Then again, there wouldn't be a need to make anyone aware other than the Guerr, who were likely attempting to combat these beasts. The law was that everyone else was to remain within the city limits.

A boy had gone missing, and this monster was his abductor. I had seen with my own eyes his body being flung into the air, and the monster, with godlike speed, fetching him. He could be dead, but if I let my father or some other authority know about that night, I could put all of us in danger. Although my father held a high position, I'm almost certain that the hand of justice wouldn't be spared upon my brow just for his sake. I contemplated many courses of action, all of them leading to a dead end. What about Nazda? She deserved answers. She couldn't get them now, especially with a beast roaming violently in the edgewoods. Still, I knew more than I had revealed to her. That much I could change. That much I *would* change. This was a mission that I was to complete, a duty to myself and to my friend. A duty to Rayloh, whom I missed dearly.

I walked into the study to grab my satchel, to find Madja and Master Tali sitting on the love seat, sipping tea and eating doughy snacks together. It had been less than a week since Segun and Rayloh left, and the lads' and my sanctuary had already been defiled and put to some other use. A tearoom.

"Ah, here she is. Didn't even have to fetch her. I'll leave you two." Madja stood up, winking at me as she left. I half smiled, wondering what this meeting could be about. The school was out on holiday, and although I enjoyed any time spent with Master Tali, I was ignorant as to why she would be visiting me.

"Pleasant morning, Alya. I'm sorry I had to leave your Kei early. There were complications that I had to address."

I truthfully hadn't noticed. Among the search of my father's office, the prince, and dodging the party coordinator, I had forgotten to mingle with some of my favorite guests. But I reacted as one of proper manner would, pretending that I had indeed noticed her absence and wished that we had spoken and all the other mannerly things one says in these instances.

"I have a proposition that is quite a special gift, if you look at it from the right angles. We are on holiday, I know, but you're one of my brightest and most promising students. During this hiatus, I wouldn't want you to lose your drive. I was hoping you would train with me. It's time for you to become better acquainted with your skills." From the expression on my face, Master Tali knew my answer.

"I would love that. I mean . . . I would be honored." I lowered my head, giving her a slight bow.

"Very good," she said, standing and smoothing her attire. "We'll start first thing in the morning. Be at the school's courtyard before the sun kisses the hills. And please keep this to yourself. I wouldn't want the other students to grow envious. I have your word?" I nodded. She let herself out. Before closing the door behind her, she said, "Speak with your mother. I've given her something for you. Wear it tomorrow. You're going to need it."

I had no intent of following her out. I wanted to wait until she was far away from our estate. I hadn't forgotten about Nazda and the conversation I owed her. What Master Tali had given me would have to wait. After a few stretched moments to ensure that Master Tali was long gone, I left the study and moved swiftly toward the front of the Remni. Neighbors had been attentive to my needs and my lonesomeness lately. I didn't want anyone latching on to me thinking that I needed amusement, and diverting my plans. No. I had to be elusive. The hardest part would be leaving the blue ring. I had no more excuses of shopping for my Kei. My parents couldn't know about this visit. They couldn't know about Nazda. They couldn't know about *that night.*

I grabbed a shawl on the way out, one brought in by one of the women working the day shift. Even if I didn't return before she was relieved of her duties, I'm sure it wouldn't cause much of an uproar. It was shabby and worn but smelled sweet, like peppermint. I pulled the hood up. I didn't look as odd as I'd anticipated. It was cold, so most people in the streets had their hoods up. I walked steadily but hurriedly. I was almost about to begin the slender path down into the black ring when I bumped into someone. I kept my head down, careful not to look up, but saw those familiar slippers. The same ones I had seen while hiding in the vent; the same that belonged to my father. It couldn't be my father. What would he be doing down here? The hood hid my face, and I, in keeping with my disguise, recoiled as if I were a weak and feeble beggar.

"Sorry, sir. I meant no harm."

"Oh, you're quite all right, miss. You sound young." A friendly laugh wavered from above my covered head. My father's voice wasn't coming from the figure. I saw his body tense at the waist, as if he were about to bend down to peek under my hood, but I caught his movements just in time, turning to the right and pinching the holds on either side of the hood together, close around my face. "I'm sure you're beautiful as well. Probably just tasting the fruit of womanhood. That's when you'd be the *ripest*."

Something about this situation didn't feel right, and that last word this stranger said made me cringe, as it appeared familiar in some way. The bustling in the streets seemed to slow behind me. I felt like an angel-winged cricket caught in the web of a spider. I could see the man's shadow on the thick ground of stone, his arm wavering toward my hood, his outstretched fingers like daggers, ready to slice away whatever stood in their way. My confidence shrunk and I thought for certain I would be revealed.

"I think I should be going." I shifted to the left this time, but he moved with light feet, blocking my way. A hush grew— whether in my mind or in fact, I could not tell. It didn't matter. The silence was clear.

"There's no need for you to go. You seem to have been relieved of your duties for the day. There's work I can give you. Dreams I can make come true. A young girl like you shouldn't wander these streets alone." His hand crept up my neck to my chin, gripping it softly between his bony fingers. I realized then that the shawl did what I had wanted it to do, in fact it did it too well—I wasn't Mistress Alya, daughter of Lord Meoltan and Lady Alyawan. I was now a helpless servant girl, disposable in his eyes. I didn't want to see the stranger's face. I closed my eyes.

A voice rang out from behind me, and with that, the hustle and bustle of the city came back to life. I barely made out the name that was called, but with it I could hear everything now. My chin was free of his hold. I still clutched the ends of my hood around my face, drawing a quick step back from the mysterious figure just to be sure I wouldn't be revealed. I watched the slippers sidestep away at a fast pace. I followed them with my eyes as they moved farther and farther away from me. I finally got the courage to look up, feeling that his gaze was not still upon me. There he was, his bald head shimmering in the light of the sun. I heard his addresser say it, and it was almost as if an echo rang from when I first heard him call out.

"It's good to see you, Lord Calo," I hissed through gritted teeth, realization rushing over me.

Chapter Twelve

I stood there for a moment, unsure if I was allowed to move again. To him, right now, I wasn't a high-ranking elf's daughter but a Dwala peasant girl, assumedly fragile, weak, and worthless. I began taking steps down the path, the stone slabs turning to cobblestones and old weathered pieces of brick as I crossed into the black ring. I turned down a side street and disappeared among the crowd. I looked back to see if I was being followed. Lord Calo remained where he was, but although his conversation continued with the he-elf, I saw his eyes pierce my gaze, and with that I turned, pulling my hood farther down around my face. A pit swelled in my stomach. Had he been the one I saw in my family quarters? No, it was my father. He had the same slippers. I knew he did. I thought he did. It was preposterous, this idea that was warping my brain. I had to write it off. I had no basis. I couldn't believe it. I would restrain the thought until I found out for sure. I would know.

I worked my way back to the black market as an ongoing war went on in spirit. Even in my disguise, people knew I wasn't who I was pretending to be. The glances of surprise and wonder that once made me nervous were no longer there. Now it was of dissonance and suspicion. Within the market, few people were perusing the different vendors. Traders mostly conversed with each other or were making fresh crafts and trinkets to add to their collection for sale, making good use of this slow hour. I saw the old man I bought the sparring set from. He was whittling away at a little figure, a wooden statue. It was of a boy and a dog, standing next to each other. The boy was smiling and the dog's tongue hung from the side of its jaw, as if it were panting, trying to catch its breath after a game of catch or a run through the meadow. The old man didn't look up when I passed. I didn't want him to see me anyway. I reached the other end of the building and turned, trying to remember where I had found the bakery. I moved about the streets and alleys solely on instinct, and soon I made it to the front of the old bakery. The smells were wonderful, but this time a little different. Scents of pumpkin filled the open air, a seasonal flavoring favored by the locals, even apparently among the Dwala.

I began up the road, remembering Nazda saying that the barn was but a hill up from the bakery. The air shifted, almost darkening, as I grew closer to the barn. In fact, if it weren't so close to the bakery, masked by its sweet aromas, I would probably smell it from the black market's alley. It sat on the crest of a hill, just as Nazda said. Parts of the building looked charred, as if it had been rebuilt from the remnants of a burned-down structure. Its shutters were a rose-colored red, vibrant against the dark brown wood of the barn. The house that corresponded with the barn was of the same variety, its wood not charred but aged, as if it had been an heirloom to the owners, inherited and passed down continuously through the generations. I knocked on the front door of the house, rattling the thin piece of scrap wood. It reminded me of the base and the wood piece that Rayloh used to prop up against the opening of the potbellied tree.

A portly man waddled to the door. He scanned me with bloodshot eyes. He wore an apron and a thin shirt, stretched beyond its suggested size. Despite his plump figure, his arms were buff and his shoulders broad, adding to his intimidating features. He leaned forward, the smell of hard ale on his breath, slapping me in the face. He tried to peer under my hood, but I turned away.

"Nazda." Between the stench of the barn and the stale smell of cheap beer, I refused to let my nose inhale. The cold air filled my lungs as I sucked in air through my mouth, making them ache from the chill. I labored between breathing and speaking, but I finally made out the words. "I'm looking for . . ." Breath. "Nazda. She told me . . ." Breath. "That she lived here." Breath. "Can you . . ."

"That little runt doesn't live here," he shot at me, spraying my face with saliva. I could taste the bitter brew on my tongue, and I had to swallow a couple of times to keep from vomiting. He continued, "Her and her band of runts stay in the barn. I feed those vermin and they do the bitter work 'round the house 'n' barn. They're done for the day so you've struck some luck." He hacked up some mucus and spit it into an old can on the stoop. "Don't cause no trouble, missy, and if she's caused any herself, know she's no duty to me. Now be on your way and next time just go straight to the barn 'n' leave me to my business." With that he turned, the door slamming behind him.

I exhaled, finding the smell of animal waste and musk-filled hides far more tolerable after dealing with this pungent, intoxicated man. I walked around to the front of the barn. The door was ajar. I slid in like a rodent from its safe haven, venturing out to find food. As I advanced, silent eyes watched me, belonging to half a dozen pigs; two cows, including a sickly one; and chickens, too scattered to take count of. A mare brayed mightily as I passed by. I looked around. There was no sign of Nazda. A mare seemed to be beckoning me, its head reaching over its stall gate, its neck extended and its lips flicking. She was beautiful. Her coat was a beige color, her hide freshly washed and brushed. Her nose, around her eyes, and her lower legs near her hooves were a creamy white. She was a muscular spectacle, but even under her coat, I could tell she wasn't fed as often as she should. I picked up a handful of hay, her pink underlip acting like fingertips, pulling the hay into her gaping mouth from my hands.

"Nazda says we're not supposed to feed any extra. That hay has to last her the whole month. What's your business?" The voice came from above. I looked up to see a girl staring over the side of a hatch of sorts in the ceiling floor. Black curls surrounded a pale face, her color beginning to turn red from leaning upside down.

"That's who I'm looking for." I pulled back my hood. Her eyes widened, and her kind smile turned to fright.

"An elf!" Her head ducked away out of sight and I could hear the patter of feet, growing softer as they trailed away from the hatch.

"Wait!" I lunged toward a beam that hung right above the stall, and as if I were in the tree branches of the edgewoods, flung myself to the hatch's edge. I pulled myself up, anxious to catch up with the little girl before she disappeared. I squatted after making it over the ledge, ready to shoot up into the space above and continue in the direction of the small footsteps, when a gleaming mass of metal stopped me. Two boys blocked my way, one with a shovel and the other with a blunt hoe.

"We've done nothing wrong. Did Mister Harmon send you?"

"No. I'm looking for Nazda." They brought the tools closer, the cold of the metal on my face, just a nick from touching my brow. "She's not here."

I wasn't afraid. Their weapons were nothing more than rusted, worn field tools, but I needed to convince the children that I was a friend. I recognized neither of them from when Nazda and I had our awkward introduction. They were much too young; the older one couldn't have been more than twelve.

"Please," I pleaded. "I need to speak with her about something important. I sighed. "I'm a friend. I promise." The girl I saw initially peeked from behind the shorter boy. Her stout structure and voluminous curls covering rosy cheeks gave her the appearance of a porcelain doll. They looked at each other as if pondering if there was any truth in my statement. Finally the taller and assumedly the older spoke.

"She's gone to the baker's to fetch us a meal. You can wait here if you'd like but if this is a trick or some sprite's game—"

"I assure you I'm a friend. You're right to be distrustful of strangers, but I'm not here to harm you." The taller boy nodded to the shorter.

The shorter boy laid the hoe gently to the side of him and helped me up into their loft through the hatch. The taller still kept the shovel, but these children weren't fighters. Even with their tools, they were scared, and I didn't want them to feel any wariness if I could help it. I sat on a bean sack against a wall. The children sat across from me, against the opposite wall, the shorter boy retrieving the hoe and positioning himself between the older boy and the girl. We sat in silence. The loft was dirty. They were children living on their own, after all, and considering their appearance, they probably had a lot more to worry about than cleaning a barn loft. A beam of sunlight came through the loft window, particles of dust dancing in its rays. I broke the silence after the silence became piercing.

"What are your names? If you don't mind my asking." The shorter boy and the girl looked to the tallest. His head didn't shift at all. He just stared back at me.

"My name is Rose . . . like the flower." Pointing to the others, she said, "And that's Meca and Cadon." Cadon, the taller, shot her a look.

"We should have waited until Nazda returned. We're not even sure if we can trust her." Cadon turned, looking at me, frowning his mouth into a scowl.

"Alya Lightstar is my name." The girl smiled. The shorter boy, Meca, just fiddled with the hoe, unsure of what to do but seemingly trusting my words. It was a good measure for me to reveal myself without being asked.

"How do you know Nazda?" Rose crawled in my direction, sitting on her legs, tucking them beneath her bottom, the beam of sunlight giving her curls the effect of a halo on an angel's crown. "She's told us about a he-elf but she didn't tell me she knew an elf-miss. You're very pretty." The girl, like most of the youth, was innocent in speaking and stated, without shame or couth, how she felt. I was happy that her opinion was kind.

"I met her through my friend Rayloh."

"That's the he-elf's name. Rayloh Emberstone," Meca said without looking up. Relaxation was in his voice so I figured he was just quiet and not as nervous as I had assumed. Rayloh was clearly favored by him.

"Yes. That is he," I responded. Cadon still sat against the wall, glowering. I had given my name and the name of a friend that he was familiar with, and he still would not yield. "How did you all come to know Nazda? Is she your sister?" Nazda spoke vaguely of her mother and father but never mentioned siblings.

"That again is none of your business." Cadon stood up, the shovel in hand, and walked slowly to the wall that faced the path. He peeked through a crack in the wall, big enough for his eye to peer out of. "She's cresting the hill. Until she arrives, I suggest you keep to yourself."

A few moments later, I heard the bracing of the beam beneath the floor and soon Nazda emerged through the hatch. In her hand, wrapped like a newborn infant, was a tiny loaf of bread.

"She says she knows you," Cadon pressed on Nazda, not giving her any time to take stock of what was going on. I stood up and Nazda greeted me. Cadon grunted. I suspected in the back of his mind that he had wanted me to be some enemy or even an unwanted guest so he could have the satisfaction of using that terrible excuse of a shovel.

"I hope they haven't treated you too improperly. I've told them to protect themselves and to be distrustful of everyone. Especially those who know of my whereabouts." She turned to Cadon and tossed him the wrapped loaf. "That is to last you all until tomorrow. Understand?" He nodded, unwrapped the bread, and handed a slice to each of his loftmates. "Come, let us go somewhere private."

We walked out into the cold autumn air to the back of the barn and rested on a bundle of wooden crates. "A moment, please. I must eat as well. I'll be right back." Nazda got up and went into the barn, returning with a chicken, its neck already snapped, its legs slightly twitching. She sat on her crate and plucked a small knife from her side pocket. The ivory blade was overused and probably rarely sharpened. The handle, however, was a sight, especially for an orphaned girl to possess. Like the blade it was ivory, slightly stained from relentless use. However, that wasn't its most intriguing attribute. Engraved in the ivory was a woman. Her body was extraordinarily detailed, from the creases of her frame to the strands of her hair, which were delicately etched. After Nazda drew the knife, she immediately cut the chicken's head from the body. It rolled to her feet alongside the crate. Almost immediately a rat darted from a pile of rubble, and gripping the head in its jaws, darted back to its hiding place, a routine it seemed to be familiar with.

"We used to have a problem with a raccoon picking off the chickens, but I solved that problem permanently by sealing all the cracks and weak planks of wood in the lower level of the barn. Still, if one bird goes missing every once in a while, it's easy to just blame it on the black-eyed burglars." She laughed.

I couldn't even enjoy her sense of humor because I was fighting nausea at the sight of her hacking away at a chicken while trying to have a conversation, especially one as serious as I was about to have, as if this were just a usual event for her. She turned the poultry upside down, letting the blood drip down into the dark soil. Then she took the knife and began skinning it, starting at the neck and working her way down. I stared, surprised that a young woman had learned such a skill. I had not the stomach for such lessons.

"So what is it you have to talk to me about? By the way, your other half came to visit me the other day." She smirked, her eyes still on the chicken.

"Who?" I asked.

She continued without answering my question. "He told me your Kei went well and that he is to join the Guerr."

I couldn't hold back my laugh. "Rayloh! No. He's my best friend. He's like a brother to me." She smirked, still keeping her eyes on the half-skinned chicken. I continued in an attempt to divert the attention from Rayloh and mine's imagined romance. "I hope they'll be trained well enough to fight whatever may lie on the other side of the veil at this year's unveiling."

Nazda stopped, the chicken and the knife plummeting to the ground, landing in the pool of blood and wet soil. Her eyes were still downcast, but her face possessed no smirk now.

"What do you mean? He's fighting in this year's unveiling?" Her words came out harsh but concerned, as if some horrible fate had befallen them.

"Yes. He and the other sprites in our rotation and the ones above that were selected to fight were pulled before graduating from the School of Talents and sent to the soldier barracks. The prince said they would be needed." I swallowed hard, not sure how she would react. Her face was hard, and her mind, I could tell, was racing, the vein above her eyebrows pulsing, whether in anger or a great spell of emotion and realization, I wasn't sure.

"I have to go." She picked up the chicken, hurling it to the rubble, from where a colony of rats emerged. She tucked her knife in her pocket and jetted off down the side street before I could even raise myself from my crate. I called after her, but she did not stop.

I heaved in frustration that she was troubled and that I would have to carry this secret even longer. I couldn't keep making these fruitless trips to the black ring. People would grow suspicious and I wouldn't want any unwarranted attention brought upon my family and myself. All I could hear above my own thoughts were the squeaks and shrills of the rats. I looked over to the pile of rubble to find the bird already stripped of its meat. A pile of feathers and a few large bones were all that remained, while a few kin in the colony fought over a scrawny leg. Even the rats here were impoverished. This was a side of Keldrock I had never seen or maybe never cared to see. I pulled up my hood and made my way up the road, burdened by a heavy heart.

The estate seemed empty and busy at the same time, probably because now that I had no one to roam with, I felt lonely and distant, like a stranger at a party. With the lads gone and Shiloh's school being out on vacation, time seemed to go by incredibly slowly. Each day I would find myself not wanting to just remain in slumber, letting the warmth of my bed envelop my heart. I took off the shawl, returning it to its place, and went to my family quarters, a soldier spent from defeat of another failed mission. I was beginning to believe that I would be a terrible warrior if I were always unsuccessful in every task.

On my bed was a package, the one Madja had in her hand when she left the study to allow Master Tali and me to speak in private. The feeling of maturity hadn't set in yet, but the late gifts that arrived over the past few days brought smiles to my face, if even for a few moments. The package was in the shape of a large book. Its casing was hard and leathery. I rolled my eyes at the thought of receiving another novel or journal out of the many I had already received. Keeping your thoughts by writing, an outlet used by many she-elves, was seen as something cultured to do, while I felt that I would rather do the things I was writing about. I began unwrapping it anyway, untying the leather belt and letting the flaps of the cloth fall to all sides of the package.

It wasn't at all what I expected. In fact, it was everything I could want, even if it was my only gift from my Kei. The breeches were a dark black, apparently used before judging, by the fading around the knees. The thick shirt was collarless, resembling the kind that Segun and Rayloh wore when escorting the prince to my Kei, but of the same color as the breaches. This was warrior garb, more specifically the lads' uniform used at the School of Talents. *Why would Master Tali give me this as a gift?* I unfolded the tunic, holding it to my chest. It would be a little bigger around the areas where it should be fitted, but it would do. I tucked the parcel under my cot, careful to keep it out of sight, and made my way to the main hall for midday meal, anxious now for my first training session.

I awoke early, the sun's light preceding its nearing appearance. I had to hurry. My eyes took their time adjusting to the dark room. When they finally did, I could see Madja, tucked in the corner of Mira's bed, her untied hair leaking from her crown like petals surrounding a flower's pistil. Mira was snoring, something that I had never known her to do since I never slept in our family quarters.

I grabbed an overshirt made of wool, and the training attire from under my cot and slinked out to the grooming quarters. I wiped my face and braided back my hair. I was in a rush and didn't feel the need to find a Dwala, who were all likely in the kitchen at this hour, to do it for me. I put on the breeches and the tunic, which were heavy on my body. After adjusting the clothing in the mirror, I picked up the wool overshirt. It came just short of covering the black tunic fully but it wasn't noticeable that what I wore was a warrior's training uniform, so I didn't worry.

The streets were quiet. My slippers made tiny claps as I treaded the stone slabs. Guards weren't at their usual posts. A lazy bunch they were, unless it came to evaluation. Still they had no reason to be fearful, most of them having seen nothing other than a rowdy oral disagreement in the markets or city squares during their term. They were probably slumbering at their headquarters or eating an early breakfast in their homes. Either way, being alone, walking in the dark wasn't scary because Segun and Rayloh weren't there to escort me, but because the darkness hid so much. *Like the owner of the yellow eyes.* I shivered at the thought of the beast being within the city walls, abducting whom it pleased during the dark hours. I attempted to make my steps quieter, the patting of my feet against my shoes softer, attempting to sink into the hard stones with every step.

The sun was rising, but not fast enough for my comfort. This was the in-between, when the sky was the darkest, right before the dawn. Sweat drenched my collar. A twig snapped, probably from one of the brittle saplings that had succumbed to the dryness and cold ground brought on by the fall, but my mind wouldn't allow that to be the conclusion. I froze, the sound seeming to echo through my ears and again and again in my head.

Flutters of wings cut through the air. Up above, bats returning from a hunt in the edgewoods headed to their roosts in the upper parts of our mountainous terrain, ever so often sending trills through the air. I had learned that they couldn't see well during the night and that for them to operate in their surroundings, they used the echoes from their voices to know what lay ahead. Looking at them now, their eerie shrills made me nervous.

I made it into the blue ring, my shadow growing longer as the darkness began to lighten. The last patch of black squirmed together, behind pillars and arches, and beneath great stone coverings and statues in an attempt to outrun the inevitable sun. My eyes finally came upon the school and I was soothed a little.

Being somewhere familiar helped. Homes and cottages began to stir, mothers and fathers waking to prepare for work. The smells of spiced vegetables and seasoned mushrooms slipped from cracked windows and small vents into my nose, and slowly I began to fall back to earth. The sun kissed the hills and I quickened my pace. The school was still a quarter mile off from where I stood.

Something darted to my left, next to an old cart, its movements seeming precise and otherworldly. I stared but promptly wrote it off, deeming it as probably some large stray or a lost domestic. The darkness was disappearing, and with it, it took the dangers I felt it hid. I didn't want Master Tali to regret her offer of training me by being late. My foot had but just touched the marble steps when two strong grips ensnared both sides of my overshirt. I squirmed and sucked in air to let out a screech of alarm, but the figure, with a quick, precise jab, knocked the air from my throat, causing the sensation of choking. I couldn't summon a sound. With their jabbing hand, they covered my mouth, their body wrapping around mine. My eyes shifted from left to right, searching for help, but no one emerged to save me. The figure moved their face close to my ear. They smelled of citrus fruits and honey.

"You're late."

Chapter Thirteen

The weather was cold, adding to the weight of the tin buckets I carried on each arm, full of icy water from the pond in the courtyard. Small, colorful koi and goldfish flickered about under the surface, like fireflies in the night sky. I had been instructed to move this pond to a hole across the courtyard. I dumped my two pails into the hole, each time the water seeping into the ground. What little progress I had made was unnoticeable.

"This is a waste. This isn't possible. The ground is not frozen yet and drinks as if dry. We should wait until after a storm, when the ground is full, and then try again."

Master Tali sat in the corner of the courtyard, a few yards from the pond. Her legs were crossed and her palms were pressed together, as if in prayer. Her black cloak covered her form, keeping her warm and dry, something I would have burdened all stars to have right now. She ignored my complaining, so I continued. I dipped the tin buckets into the pond, careful to wiggle the tins a little when they touched the water's surface, to scare the fish out of the buckets' suction. The cold water nipped at my knuckles, making my hands number with every trip. The bails of the buckets sliced through the dry skin of my fingers, the air chapping the places where they weighed the most. I gritted my teeth, bearing the cold. The torment went on and on. I couldn't count how many trips I made back and forth from the pond, but as far as progress, there was none. Finally, the sun crept over the courtyard's wall, warming my cheeks. I found that in the cold, my body immediately responded to the slight change in temperature. The heat warmed my face and I stood for a moment, my buckets filled with water, now causing little smears of blood to stain the tin containers.

As soon as the sun engulfed Master Tali's entire body in its rays, she unfolded herself like a flower in bloom, standing up, allowing her hood to fall to her back. She stretched her limbs, her joints cracking loudly enough that I could hear them from where I was standing. She pulled from her sleeve a small book and tossed it to me. I dropped my buckets to catch it, sloshing water in every direction, drenching my feet and calves.

"Study this. Learn the words. We'll resume tomorrow. Don't be late again."

It was still early morning by the time we finished. I was excited to be done and at the same time sorry that I had agreed to this. I couldn't rescind my acceptance now. That would be dishonorable. I dragged my body, hardly able to keep my head up as I wandered up one of the paths leading to the yellow ring. The sweat from my scalp was now nothing more than a cold layer of viscous fluid. I didn't expect our training to go as it did. This was bitter work, something that a team of servants should be assigned or even a strong band of he-elves, but I alone was left to accomplish. It was impossible.

Back at the Remni, I crept into the grooming quarters, and slipped into a changing stall to peel off my damp garments and took a soothing, hot bath. After that, I stuffed the training uniform inside a pillowcase, along with the book, and wound it tightly, ensuring that most of the air had been pushed out. I pushed the bundle into the gap between my bed and the wall. I covered a protruding end with another of my decorative pillows and pushed it out of my mind for the moment. Madja kept to her household duties, and if I kept the uniform in the family quarters, it most certainly would be discovered. but she had just changed my bed linens, so I figured that this spot would do for now.

I headed to the main hall for breakfast. The table where we sprites usually sat was nearly empty, only Mira occupying it now. She sat quietly, as usual, pouring peach syrup and prune preservatives on my favorite appetizer, foxtrit biscuits. One of the special things about the weather changing was the uncommon desserts that were brought out during the cold seasons. Special jams, sweets sauces of vanilla and strawberry, made my favorite foods even more delectable. Mira seemed to be in her own world most of the time. I wondered if she too missed Rayloh and Segun. Did she miss their harmless teasing, the pointless bickering, or even the imaginative discussions of what we wanted to be when we grew up? I would never know by looking at her. There was no telling if her thoughts included the lads, the adults, or even me. Lord Fueto, Rayloh's father, bellowed, nearly toppling out of his chair with laughter, snipping me away from my thoughts.

"There she is!" he boomed at me, waving his hand, beckoning me over to his table. "Here!" He shoved a chalice of red spice wine into my grip, wrapping his arm around my shoulder. Even sitting down, he was just short of my height standing up. His biceps bulged around my neck, his pulsating veins matching my own body's rhythm. "You're a mistress now. No longer a sprite . . . but not a lady either. Nope, you've got a ways to go," he said dramatically, nodding his head at Madja. The table chuckled and giggled; even I cracked a smile at his banter. "You'll make a fine wife. Well, if I were still courting, there'd be no question." He winked at me jokingly and I blushed. "Well, go ahead then."

The table looked back at me and I to them. What were they waiting for? He tapped the foot of the chalice with his index finger. I immediately understood. I put the brim to my lips, taking a small sip. It tasted bitter, the spice causing my face to redden. I scrunched my nose and mouth together and the table laughed, apparently amused by my reaction to my first drink—well, my first to everyone's knowledge. It felt warm inside so I decided to give a go again, while in their company. As I pressed the brim to my lips again, one of the other adults sitting to the right of Lord Fueto pushed the glass slightly, forcing me to take in a huge gulp. I almost spit the whole lot of it onto Lord Fueto, but with great regret I forced it down. My head became a little light and my blood seemed to grow hot. The adults laughed again and I curtseyed, felling a little silly but enjoying the moment, taking it as my initiation into elfhood.

"Told you, Alyawan," Lord Fueto said to Madja. I looked at her, her expression motherly. Then she smiled at me. I wonder if Madja suspected that he had given me spirits to the lads and me before this and decided to test this theory. When she looked at me and smiled, I figured it wasn't about that, but Madja's motherly instincts have proven to be more than capable of seeking out truth in most instances.

"Won't you join us this morning?" one of them asked. I looked at their pleased expressions, their eyes anxiously waiting my response. It would be nice to be thought of differently, to leave the sprite's table and join the high-ranking elves that assembled at the fancier, more elegant table. I looked behind me at Mira, who by now had looked up from her plate and was listening in on all the excitement. She seemed to be anticipating my answer. I turned back to Lord Fueto.

"I feel honored by your respectful extension but I believe I'll have my breakfast with my sister. With Segun and Rayloh gone, she's all I have left." The adults returned to their side conversations, not really caring either way, a few expressing warm sentiments at my answer, but out of the corner of my eye, I could see Madja's eyes sinking in, making space for the wide smile on her face. I took a seat right across from her.

"You know I would have been perfectly fine sitting alone?" She tilted her head back, trying to seem mature and tall all at once.

"Yes, but I wouldn't have anyone to throw honey grapes at if I left."

She giggled and I knew she appreciated my gesture. I realized I had carried the chalice with me from the adults' table, a swallow of wine sitting at the bottom of the glass. I looked over my shoulder to see if anyone had noticed. The adults had returned to their banter, and again I returned to being Lord Meoltan and Lady Alyawan's daughter, seen but not noticed. I brought the glass under the table and nudged Mira's knee with the tip of my slipper. She looked up, puzzled.

"Your turn." I pointed twice with my finger and brought just the brim up past the level of the table so she could see what I was alluding to. Quite truthfully, I thought she would deny it, she being the golden sprite of our family, but she took it and didn't smell it or sip it for taste but in two gulps emptied the glass of its contents and returned the chalice to me under the table. If this was her attempt at showing me her adventurous side, she had gotten my attention.

I grabbed five biscuits from the platter. Even Rayloh couldn't eat that many, but I was starving after training. I filled each of the biscuits with goat cheese and honey grape preserves and began scarfing them down. By the time the last bite of the fifth one entered my mouth, I was full, feeling as if my stomach were going to tear from my body, sending my organs spilling in every direction, dashed with torn bread and honey grape chunks. After eating, Mira and I talked about everything, from the upcoming unveiling to the success of my Kei. I told her that I had been working with Master Tali without divulging any important details, showing her where the buckets' bails had cut into my skin. I thought about showing her the bow—maybe having someone to shoot with would be fun—but I figured she wouldn't be interested. I didn't want to run the risk of her telling Madja and her taking those away from me, too, just like the sparring set. More importantly, I wanted to ask her about the day I found her in her bed, when she lashed out at me. I wanted to know if she remembered who had been in the room. If it had been Lord Calo, but I couldn't bring myself to ask. If she didn't know, what then? I recalled how she lashed out at me when I tried to touch her and how she was dazed and confused. I would need to find out on my own. I would need to make sure it never happened again. The next opportunity I got, I was going to be sure to make an effort to find out these truths.

After sitting for a while I thought I would get the book Master Tali gave to me and begin my studying. I climbed onto my bed, pulling a portion of the pillow casing's mouth out into the open. I reached in, feeling around for the book. I pulled it out, examining its weathered and vintage leather hide. I hadn't spent long periods of time in the study alone since the lads left, feeling that too many things in there would remind me of all our wonderful adventures, but I was attempting to turn over a new leaf. Reading the book Master Tali gave me in the study would be a good first step.

I opened the door, the scents of Rayloh and Segun still lingering. I sat on the love seat, kicking my feet up on one of the decorative pillows and knocking the rest onto the floor. I cracked the book open, heavy and worn pages making the spine creak, like a cat stretching its back after a long nap. *Cernidonu* was written on its first page, in archaic handwriting thick in ink stain. Beneath it, in the modern language of the Keldrock elves, was *A Guide to Sifting*, its handwriting different from and more recent than the pages it held.

This book wasn't what I expected. I flipped through the pages, seeing elaborate headings signaling a change of subject and beneath them their translation, it seemed, done in the second writing that had been the same on the cover. Under these words were two lists; running on the left was the weird language, and on the other, the common tongue. I assumed that words on each line were related, translating one another.

Cernidonu must mean "sifting," I concluded. But what is "sifting"? I passed one section that I found interesting. After *Bosqudeli* it said "Wood." I peered over the list of words, some I didn't have the faintest idea how to pronounce.

- *Cortezyil* . . . Bark
- *Hojyill* . . . Leaf
- *Ramyil* . . . Limb

- *Arbomai* . . . Tree
- *Viendeli* . . . Vine

The pages contained other headings. Some pertained to fire, the skies, people, animals, earth, actions, dreams, the body, and so much more. The categories were endless. In the course of our vacation from school, Master Tali wanted me to learn another language on top of the labor I was to perform. I sat back, frustrated. *You can do this!*

I picked up the book and began again, pushing the task's length out of my thoughts. The heading read:

Lumai . . . Light

I read for about three hours before stopping. All the words seemed to flutter in my head like butterflies in a garden, as I had memorized some and forgotten others. Afterward, I took the book back to the family quarters, returning it to the pillow casing. On my way I passed Lord Calo, who didn't even glance my way. It was always like that, him speaking when he wanted to, being extremely kind but at other times, ignoring me completely. His behavior made me a little on edge, but I found comfort that he didn't know I knew.

Somehow the glass doors leading to the balcony had been propped open. I slammed them tight, ensuring that the latch was returned to its proper place. A scratch on the bedpost caught me off guard, making me whip around in a flurry of astonishment and high nerves. When I turned I saw a red bird, much like the one I'd seen in Kala's home a few days prior, resting on Madja's bedpost. I stood quietly, watching it hop from the bedpost, to the bed, to the headboard, eventually making its way to the dresser.

What does it want? I stared at it questioningly, careful not to take my eyes off of it. This creature wasn't as predictable and simpleminded as most birds were thought to be. It skipped over the clumped strands of Mira and Madja's hair in their respective hair runners and brushes; the strands would be great when it came to building nests. It landed atop my jewelry box. With its beak, it pushed the top handle of the case forward, opening the drawer that kept my necklaces. Its head dove into the wide compartment, pushing things about. When it emerged, it had in its grasp the snake necklace from my Kei. I laughed. It must have confused the silver serpent in the drawer for a meal. It pulled it out, and began fluttering its wings, flapping loudly, trying its hardest to ascend with the heavy load.

It headed toward me in wobbly flight and I stepped back, unsure of what to do. The bird delivered the necklace to me, and I looked down at it, confused. What could this bird want me to do with this accessory other than wear it? It perched itself gently in the groove of my shoulder, its head twitching as it peered into my eyes and back at the necklace I held in my hand.

I looked down, studying the engraved scrapes zigzagging intricately, imitating the scaly skin of a snake. Its gem eyes seemed to glow on their own, the light of the room just accenting their beauty. A twinkle of silver at the snout of the serpent broke my trance. I turned back to the bird, wondering what it could possibly mean to prove by bringing me the necklace. A hiss shot through to my ears, seeming to come from all directions, bouncing off the walls. I spun about, seeing what could have made the sound. A firm and unbendable grip tightened around my wrist, hooking like a lock on a chain. I brought my wrist to my front to see a silver head, a tongue flicking, eyes fixed deeply on mine. Its mouth slowly opened, sprouting silver fangs, tongue pulsating beneath them like a cave's creek under stalactites. The snake reared its head back and lunged.

Chapter Fourteen

The forest was quiet and still. The sounds of strings and flutes played in the distance. The trees seemed to sway in time with the beautiful sounds. In front of me, about a quarter mile from where I stood, I saw a massive tree, much different from the others, like a queen ant among her drones. I approached it, the sounds of the flutes and the strumming of the strings growing louder as I drew closer. Even at a distance I could still see the tree's detailing due to its gigantic size. It was covered with red bark. It sat atop a hill in a clearing, the trees at the hill's edge bowing with the music at this miraculous marvel.

A figure with hair as black as night stood, staring at the tree. His dress was of nobility, his robe white. I approached cautiously along the figure's left side, his hair blowing ever so lightly in the cool breeze, covering his face. He turned his head to me sharply. His eyes were diseased, the whites and color of his eyes consumed by black.

"Prince Alag. Your highness."

He didn't utter a word. He simply smiled and turned back to the tree. Leaves fell, fluttering about like tiny boats coasting uncontrollably down a waterfall, as the strings and flutes continued to play. I was startled when the bass of drums interrupted the peace, shifting the sweet melodies to dissonant

*sounds of sadness and suffering. Screams filled the air, and I
watched the tree become engulfed in flames.*

*I turned to the prince, hoping he would have some
explanation of this catastrophe, but he stood still, the glow of the
flames flickering in his black eyes. Leaves that once glided down
gracefully were now plummeting torches from the heavens. The
bark was burnt black, with a twist of red, resembling fresh blood
splattered on an already rotting corpse. Screams came from every
direction. Frantically I looked around, finding nothing. The
drums, the strumming, and the whistle of the flute warped into one
voice of desperation.*

"Alya!"

I awoke to find Kala standing over me. Her ebony skin
glistened with sweat and her fiery red hair drooped over her face. I
sat up, my head throbbing.

"What happened?" I rested my forehead in my palm,
trying to gather my thoughts.

"I came in not too long ago. You were on the floor . . .
screaming. I was cleaning the vent in the hall and just happened to
be near enough to hear. Thankfully." She placed a warm, damp
towel on the nape of my neck to help ease the tension locked in
my body.

"I remember . . . not." Everything was distorted. The tree,
the flames, the flutes, drums, and strings were all one and . . . the
snake. I shot up like a swallow to the sky, startling Kala so much
that she flung the towel in the air and yelped. I opened my jewelry

box and spotted the silver head with beautiful green emerald cut eyes. It hadn't been disturbed.

Kala stared at me. "Are you all right, Mistress Alya?"

"Yes . . . I believe so." I grinned as if nothing were the matter, but inside I was worried. This nightmare was familiar and distant at the same time. Considering the imagery of Prince Alag and the screaming, I had more than enough reason to keep the vision, along with the animation of the silver necklace, which I still wasn't sure about, to myself.

"Well, then." She approached me warily. "Midday meal has been prepared. You are hungry, aren't you?" I nodded.

Kala helped me down the hall, even though, as far as physical strength went, I was more than capable, but a struggle with her would just make her even more inclined to mention this incident to someone of authority, and I wouldn't want to bring any more unnecessary attention to myself than I already had.

The smells of the midday meal reached me as I came down the corridor to the main hall. Another special thing that the cold weather allowed was the consistent preparation of hot meals, which were uncommon during the hotter months. The familiar scent of gourds and squash marinated in aged vegetable broth made my heart jump for joy. The hall was already filled with the other residents. Mira was sitting with a sprite from one of the other estates at the opposite end of the table where we normally sat. Kala pulled out my chair, supporting my arm as I sat down. She offered to fix my plate and I sat back, giving in to whatever would

205

calm her inclinations about what had happened upstairs. She came back with two bowls, one with squash and the other with rice, a small plate of thumb cherries, a tiny saucer of honey placed next to a line of crackers, and a large cup of hot chocolate. It all looked quite delicious, but after all that had happened, my tongue rejected even the thought. Kala stood waiting at my side.

"Honestly, I'm quite all right. It was just a horrid dream. Nothing more." She didn't move. She was waiting for me to eat something. She seemed invested, as if my health were personally important to her.

I reached for my butter knife. Of all the heavy foods on my plate, I would have the most fruitful effort if I attempted the crackers and honey spread. My mouth was dry, causing the crackers to stick to the roof of my mouth. After swallowing, I turned to Kala, smiling and shrugging, seeming as nonchalant as I could bear.

"See?" I struggled to swallow the remaining cracker, trying not to cough or show any signs of distress. "I'm fine." Kala smiled, bowing her head slightly and cheerfully striding out of the main hall.

I heaved a little, trying to clear my throat of the salted cracker bits. A water flagon had yet to be brought to the table, so I picked up my mug of hot chocolate and had a sip. It steamed my mouth, causing the moisture to return, like a hot water basin sent to extinguish the ice and snow that builds on windows and door stoops during the midwinter season. I ate two or three thumb

206

cherries and forced down another cracker, but that was all I could do at the moment. I left the rest of my meal at the table and didn't bother to go to the other end of the table and introduce myself to Mira's playmate. It looked like I would be spending my time alone more than ever now that Mira was making friends her own age.

When I arrived back at the family quarters, I noticed my father's robe hanging at its post. He wasn't in the main hall so he was most likely locked in his private chambers, hard at work. All these strange occurrences and all the information that kept me looking for answers. *Was this dream the universe telling me to back off?* I thought the nightmares that plagued me following the edgewoods incident had ended, but they came back, and this time without the monster at all, just the prince. *Would the prince know about the mongrowl?* It was such a simple thought and a likely place to start, since things at my Kei had gone so well.

Like a scene in a play, Madja walked in, carrying some supplies, I spotting rolls of yarn and a few patches, and assumed it was one of her new hobbies. She dropped them off, smiling at me kindly as she noticed I was there.

"Madja." I put on my best beckoning voice. She came over, expressing concern. I had never talked to Madja about love interests, and to be honest, I had never quite had one that was even remotely realistic. The very idea of marriage was off-putting, but I couldn't help but want companionship to some degree. Just not in the way it was outlined in my life. Still, this was irrelevant to getting an audience with Prince Alag, so this would have to be a first for Madja and me.

"Do you think I could speak to the prince?" I asked. "I haven't seen him since the Kei." Madja smiled, placing her palms dramatically against her chest. I wanted to laugh but I held my composure.

"If only, my sweet angel. That's not quite how things work." I didn't understand. "For one, the unveiling is approaching, and news from the blue ring has taught that the prince and his company have been all but dedicated to the Guerr barracks. Even still, outside of that, in a formal sense, his majesty doesn't accept audiences for the sake of having them. The only reason he came to your Kei is because your father saw an opportunity and took it. You see, the prince is to be married, and if you're lucky, you'll be selected."

Her face searched mine and before I could ask what she was looking for, I noticed that my face was tense, my brows stern, and my lips tightened. I was that disgusted by these words that I'd broken character. Madja only took my reaction as strong disappointment at the news.

"I'm sorry, Alya, but I'm glad to see that you are . . . interested in the prince." She smiled, and leaving her basket, left me to myself, likely giddy inside. I sank on the bed, another round of defeat taking more and more of my days and closing the door more and more to my youth. All of the reasoning I sought, the questions I had, didn't matter because I had no power. As mighty as I felt, I had nothing that could make a difference. I felt like I was living. I wanted to feel like I had a life. Had I ever. Would I ever. I wondered how long my father had waited to pawn me out to the highest bidder and what he had done to ensure that I would be considered an option. My stomach lurched. I sank deeper into the bed, tears silently trickling from my eyes. I stared at the ceiling until my mind went blank.

Chapter Fifteen

The skin on my hands was torn apart by the end of the next morning's training session, and my lips were starting to chap. I had awoken extremely early to ensure that I wasn't late, in aid to the fact that I couldn't sleep while being plagued with the woes of elfhood. Master Tali arrived to me stretching by the pond. She immediately set down the buckets she carried and took her seat in the corner once again, eyes closed, legs crossed. She quizzed me on a few words just to see that I was studying the book she gave me, and I was proud to say that I didn't get any wrong. I was one of her best pupils, and even though I was alone in this experience, I would still be the best I could be.

Each day after, I considered quitting, but I had to believe there was some reason behind this madness. The hole would not hold the water, but still I heaved these pails of water from the pond. The next day was the same, and so were the next days, and the days after that as well. By now, large blisters formed around my feet and ankles that Kala had to nurse with vinegar twice a day. A week passed by, then two, then three, and still there was no progress in moving the pond. I was beginning to lose patience.

One day I awoke to the sound of leaves rattling against the balcony door. It was pitch black outside. It would be a while before the sun would be up, but I had a lot on my mind. I grabbed my housecoat and eased to my feet, my soles hard, having acclimated to their new regime. Kala had been so helpful. She surprised me with her vast knowledge on treatments of wounds and mending broken skin. She took plants from the garden—passionflower had proven to be the most efficient—and showed me how to make a supplement from it. She also used herbs and spices to treat the cuts and breaks and help shield sickness from my nose and throat while being out in the cold. I soaked my hands in warm salt water, soothing the healing skin.

Fall decorations had warped my home into a pumpkin patch. Horns of squash sprinkled with autumn leaves, and sweet vials of pumpkin spice were littered about the house. The ladies, even some of the younger elves of the Remni, made custard cakes and pies, something I had always enjoyed doing with Madja and Mira, oddly enough. Instead of enjoying my vacation, I was laboring like a slave with Master Tali. I couldn't bear it anymore. Today I planned on confronting her. I thought of all the possible questions she would ask. Why had I accepted her offer if I wasn't ready for the task? Why had I wasted her time for so long? I didn't want to disappoint her, but lugging pails of water wasn't what I had in mind for training.

In the halls, the little incense vents along the halls now fumed with burning logs, heating the entire Remni. I put on my warrior's training uniform and headed for Shiloh. The streets were wet from a cold downpour earlier that week. The sun hadn't come out long enough to dry them up, so the water just held for days. Not that any progress was being made on emptying the pond, but the rain wouldn't help.

 I arrived as the sky began to lighten. I began toting water immediately upon my arrival, still thinking about quitting and how I would go about it. Master Tali arrived as usual, bidding me a good morning and sat down without needing to tell me what to do. I had done four trips before she had arrived and it was ten before I was fed up. The water was down my boots, making annoying, sloshing sounds like rags being repeatedly dunked into cleaning pots. My hands were tired of the abuse. I was pushing myself beyond anything I had ever known, and the worst part was that it was all in vain. Just as I was about to reach the hole to deliver my two buckets of water, my hands let go. My whole body gave in, releasing the dams. One full bucket fell directly on my foot while the other fell alongside my leg, the rim of the bucket scraping at my breeches, cutting the skin within them. I cried out, not so much from the pain but out of anger and frustration.

 Master Tali didn't flinch. She continued to sit, legs crossed in the shadows of the wall. Rage grew inside me and my foot kicked, sending one of the buckets sailing through the air, directly at Master Tali. Her arm, like a frog's tongue, snapped to the air, catching the bucket at its rim, right in front of her face. She threw it to the side with such force that it crumpled into the ground, her strength uplifting the grass and the soft layer of dirt. I had never seen such force that I started trembling, but I was still enraged, so there was no backing down now. She stood, pushing her hood back like she would normally do after we concluded our lessons. I stared, still angry. My tongue couldn't hold itself any longer. I had reached my breaking point.

"I'm done with this . . . this waste." I hurled. Master Tali unbuttoned her cloak, gathering it into one hand and tossing it over the crumpled bucket, all the while never taking her eyes off of me. Her expression was blank, unmoving. I couldn't tell if she was upset, amused, or just as fed up with these lessons as I was.

She crossed her arms and requested of me, "The word for water?" Her voice still sounded like beautiful crickets and the wings of butterflies. It angered me even more.

"What?" I shouted, surprising myself with how much anger was in my voice.

She sighed, bringing two fingers to the bridge of her nose, massaging it, as if annoyed with my question. "Incorrect! The word for drain?"

"Are you mad? Your mind is clearly clouded. I'm done. You've wasted my time for the last day. You're deranged." I reached and pulled from my side the leather-encased manual. "I don't care about this meaningless old book." I tossed it at her, and it landed just at her feet, where the grass was still wet with the dew of the morning and the leftover rain. The sun had just begun to peek over the courtyard wall, the brightest of the beams shining into the pool, where the fish swam through the rays, their scales twinkling shades of orange, white, and red, and every so often a shimmer of pink.

Master Tali shot forward, pausing for a second at the edge

of the pond, her hair flying around her shoulders. I braced myself.
I was extremely fatigued from heaving the buckets, and adding to
the problem was my now injured foot and scraped leg—not to say
that if Master Tali wanted to deal me a swift hand that I, in my
best health, would never stand a chance. She seemed weightless in
the air, landing in the center of the pond. The water appeared to
run from her, her feet landing on solid ground. I stood in awe at
this spectacle. Not even the elves with water talents could
manipulate it in this fashion. How could she?

"*Ui Aguayil drenu.*" She turned around and leaped from
the pond, opening up the earth in the uncovered ground, coming to
rest just opposite from where I stood. The water, the fish, even the
lily pads warped around the depression she left. Within seconds it
was emptied; even the very soil that once held the pond was dry.

Master Tali turned, slowly walking to her right. I just
stared at her, unsure of what she was about to do. I tried to move
away, but my knees were locked. I thought to pick a bucket and
try to use it as a defense but my body wouldn't respond, not that
the bucket would be a formidable weapon anyhow. I replayed the
words I had shouted at my teacher in my head. I was insulting and
unnaturally disrespectful, especially to one of her caliber.

Her steps remained in a rhythm as she walked around the
pond's edge, but instead of coming toward where I stood, she
made a hard right. She walked along the small patch of grass
between us and stopped just short of the empty hole, where mud
and water clumped together in brown puddles from my weeks of

effort. She stood at the edge, her feet looking like cliffs at the edge of a grassy pit. She turned her face toward me, smiling in a way that unsettled me. She stood there, still looking at me and I looking at her, unsure of what I should do. Without fully coming to a decision, my feet took action, and before I knew it, I was standing right next to her. Like corkscrews, we shifted, peering into the hole. The hole that sucked down every haul of water I brought to it.

"The word for fill?"

I thought for a moment, remembering the words in my head and gathering together its pronunciation. *"Llenu?"* I responded questioningly. She nodded excitedly, the warmth returning to her eyes. I felt the same pride that I felt every day during lessons in the front row of Master Tali's hut.

She closed her eyes and her voice came out like sweet honey over warm milk. *"Ui Aguayil llenu."*

The ground trembled slightly. I started to back away from the hole, but Master Tali grabbed my hand, preventing my escape. Somehow I felt safe even though her actions, to me, lacked sensibility. The ground shook more aggressively and I could feel the unknown force coming. From the center of the hole, where the larger puddle had gathered, bubbles began to surface, popping and inflating in a constant dance, like hot water boiling over a fire.

A single spring of clear water shot into the air. It went as high as twenty feet, almost reaching the break of the courtyard's walls before crashing back down, filling the crater. The shimmering of colored scales came as well, the fish like crystals in the water, shining in the sun that now graced the entire courtyard just as the pool came to rest. The pond had been moved. Master Tali sank to the ground, returning to rest, her legs crossed. Her breathing was faster than normal, as if exerted from a long walk.

"Are you all right, Master?" I sat on my knees next to her, peering into her eyes.

"Despite my old age, it had been a while since I've sifted at that capacity."

"Sifted?" I remembered the title of the book she had given me. I waited patiently for an explanation. Due to her slight exhaustion it took her a few moments to gather her thoughts.

"Sifting is manipulating the energies of your surroundings. These words that you learned are sacred in meaning and on the tongue. They transcend all."

"But you're a beast talent. How can you manipulate the earth and water?"

She rotated her neck, making large popping sounds from the areas where stress had gathered. "Sifting"—at a high capacity, anyway—requires a number of requirements to be achieved in alignment with the action you are trying to perform. The languages of these words go beyond time, life form, and understanding. The water has its own energy, and in understanding that energy, the water will accept your command and do as you have wished it to do. When I asked you to move the pond—"

"You could move the pond and day after day you still had

216

me carry those buckets? Blasted beldame!" I didn't mean for the words to slip out, but it was too late.

My chest seared in pain, from the impact of Master Tali's hand. Her strike was as powerful as I had seen just moments before, when she sent the bucket sinking into the ground. I lay in the grass, still wet but drying in the sun. I had spoken out of turn one too many times for her liking. After catching my breath, I sat up and apologized, and she continued.

"The first part is the mind. To truly understand the power of sifting, your mind must be unhinged. Since every being, every thing has energy, then there is life and understanding even when there's no equality of will. You must understand that, for you to sift the energies that aren't within you. You must release any doubts or limits about yourself, your beliefs, and your own energy."

I nodded in understanding, intent on making up for my lack of respect. It didn't take much artificial effort because I was deeply intrigued.

"The second is your own body. Sifting takes a lot of your own strength, and having the stamina is just as important as, if not more important than maintaining an unrestricted mind. For example, it would take exceedingly more energy and expend a larger portion of your physical health to move the water into the air and then to the hole than letting it take one of its own normal courses of action. An important element of sifting is working along with the natural course of things in an unnatural sense." To me that didn't make sense, but she hadn't paused for questioning, so I held my inquiries.

"The third is, of course, the words themselves. These words were formed by the first of our being. Taught to our ancestors by the nymphs of Olörun. These beautiful beings are similar to us in many ways, but are bound by no limits, physical or mental. Some of them still exist today, sometimes in the forms of mountains and streams, but most have faded into the heavens, leaving this world behind. Their words are the quintessence of all language and should be treated as such because once entangled in your mind's visions and your own strength, cannot be taken back. They must carry out their purpose, so it's important that you construct these phrases so as not to suffocate and eradicate yourself from existence."

Uncertainty and fear surged through me, and Master Tali, seeing my distraught expression, responded caringly.

"I assure you that if the proper precautions are taken and great dedication is applied to your training, that you will excel in ways beyond your wildest dreams, with no harm coming to you. Sifting is one of the most beautiful things in this world, and few are blessed with such capabilities."

So I was a prodigy? How did Master Tali think I could do this? I looked down at the ground, away from her cheery face. I had so many questions of my own. She was teaching me to sift, something that I had never heard of until now, and probably for good reason, considering the awful things that could happen to me if I didn't exercise it with great caution. There were books, teachings, scrolls, even expressions of art that had long been outlawed, since my people decided to hide behind the walls of our city when it was first veiled. Master Tali could be teaching me something that could put my family and myself in danger. Still, this sifting intrigued me, and it was something that was part of me as much as it was part of my ancestors. Still, one question burned my insides.

"Why me?" I looked up into her deep, reddish-brown eyes that in the sun showcased their iridescence.

"Pardon?"

"Why me? Why have you chosen me to teach sifting to? I'm sure there are other, more qualified students who are farther along in the mastering of their talents than I. So again I ask, why me?" Master Tali hesitated before answering, rubbing the bridge of her nose as she had before while she gathered her thoughts.

"I chose you because you differ from the others. You have a mind of your own guiding your beliefs, an asset unique to those who can easily develop this ability. I can feel your spirit shifting, questioning all you've known to be true your entire life. You're not like the other insolent sprites whose beliefs and worries only go so far as what they will wear to the next gala. No; you, my dear, are special." She sighed and simultaneously stood and took me by the hand, facing the pond. "All will be revealed in due time, but for the moment don't burden your mind with such trifling thoughts. Now I must go. Your lessons are concluded for the day.

219

I will see you bright and early tomorrow morning."

I nodded, even though I was still unsure about my decision to continue training with her, even after all I had seen. In fact, these new factors are what pushed me closer to that line. She holstered her cloak, letting the hood remain at her back. "You've had the book for some time now. It's important that that be the focus of your time when you are home. Our preliminaries are over, Mistress Alya. The real work begins now." As she left, she turned abruptly to add a last remark. "Now that you have been cultured, more so than the other sprites at Shiloh, I think it best that we keep our training sessions secret. We wouldn't want them or the Courts burying their noses into the curriculum that I have set outside of the normal rotation. That could prove rather . . . *devastating for the both of us.*"

If her warning had been any more evident, it would have taken the form of a knife and dug itself within my conscious. No one could know about what went on during my training sessions. Was this book outlawed, as well as this skill? I imagined the pages I had yet to embark upon. I would go about memorizing all of them, attempting to become better versed in this powerful language. I had to keep the book secret. I had to keep it safe. A lot depended on it not being discovered. A lot depended on my decision to continue or to quit.

Chapter Sixteen

When I arrived home, the sun was full and bright, making its ascent into the sky. The Remni was beginning to stir with rising residents. I was filled with new ambitions—and new worries, but mostly new ambitions. Master Tali selected me to be taught a craft that was nearly nonexistent now. She trusted me to keep her secrets, now *our* secrets, and given our relationship that had been built over this past year, I had no problem trusting her as well. This has to be enough reason to continue these lessons. I was going to need more time to convince myself. My body was sore as usual but I believe it could sense my relief that it wouldn't be lugging bails of water aimlessly anymore. Still, it wouldn't calm itself completely. Tomorrow would be when *the real work begins.*

When I arrived at the family quarters, Mira was already up, and to my surprise, she had done something drastic: her long, beautiful hair had been cut short. The longest strands fell at the front, framing her face, and became shorter along the back, just above her collarbones. It made her look years older. Her beauty, already at the young age of nine, was already incomparable to many of the older adolescent misses that I saw arrogantly prancing about Keldrock. She was a sight to see, but in me it stirred something more. My shadow was gone and she was coming into her own. Mira would soon no longer be Alya's younger sister.

"Good morn, Mira," I said cheerfully. Normally a start of

conversation initiated by me would spark a light within her, like an invitation that she had long been awaiting, but she just turned and nodded.

"Good morn, sister," she replied flatly. She had no reason to be mad at me, but I reacted more gingerly in my words so as not to push her away.

"Are you headed out to the garden?"

"Yes. Madja isn't feeling well this morning, so I'm going to set up the display for our table." I looked at our mother's sleeping form in her bed. I didn't even bother looking at her cot when I came in because it was her natural course of action to have been up before I returned home.

"Why don't I come with you? I'm sure you could use some company."

Mira smiled, picking up a small pouch and heading for the door. "Of course, Alya." She leaned in. "It's not a trip to the edgewoods, but if you want to come, I'd be delighted." I giggled, remembering that tragic night out—the humorous parts, at least—that happened long enough in the past that it seemed like a distant memory. Mira didn't know everything that happened, so I made sure not to seem so tense.

It had been a while since I'd been to the yellow gardens. Since the intense cold had begun to creep within our city, a glass dome had been erected for about a week now, mainly to keep the vegetation safe from the harsh winds and unforgiving storms that were to come. It was interesting to see Mira grow from a youth to an adolescent sprite in one short season. I realized that I should savor the moments I would have with her before they were all gone and I became the bothersome older sister, just as Mira was my bothersome younger one.

The glass dome was grand in every way. Of course the yellow ring had to be extravagant in all its designs and used the finest of materials in construction. From a distance, as we walked, I could see inside it through the shiny, clear panes of glass. All the brightly colored flowers were still full in their beauty, new saplings shooting through the soil preparing to form buds and blossom alongside squash, tomatoes, and other fall treats that tasted delicious in warm stews. The orchards to the rear were full of fruit as well, due to the dome, even though they were out of season. The only time I even cared to look at the garden these days was to see if Madja and Mira were there. It had grown vast since my absence.

I noticed great beams of oakwood extending above in spaced rows inside the dome, supporting the grand structure internally along with poles, rounded and slightly hollowed, making it easier for them to enter the ground and hold. *These would be great targets for practicing my shot*, I thought. I hadn't been shooting a lot. Between the effects the weight training had on my body, the early mornings, and the stress of memorizing another language, I was just too exhausted to practice.

Mira went straight for the flower plot. While she made her decision on which blooms to use for the table setting, I explored the garden, beginning in the orchards. There stood trees of oranges, apples, and pears broad and healthy, their fruits plentiful. *Their branches would be a great place to hoist a target as well.* The garden, being a place too open for shooting before, now with the enclosure, would be the perfect facility to spend some free time shooting and developing my own talent, and if learned properly, to practice sifting. I took this realization as a gift for coming to the garden with my sister. I eventually made it back to Mira, who had just finished plucking a bunch of tulips and red hydrangeas.

"I like your hair," I complimented. She paused for a moment, staring away from me, before ruffling through her pockets and turning to me.

"Here." She handed me a small pouch. It was frilly, made from a lace cloth, probably one of Madja 's old handkerchiefs.

"Such a beautiful gift," I said as convincingly as I could, careful to show appreciation at my sister's kind gesture.

"The real gift is inside," she said, giggling.

I peered inside to find seeds. They were an interesting type I had never seen before, smooth ovals of icy sapphire blue.

"Thank you," I said. "But I wouldn't say gardening is my kind of outlet, Mira."

"I know, but maybe we can do it together. It'll be *our* little venture." I smiled, she returning it with a slight giddy chuckle. "You're an earth talent. Maybe these will come of use to you in time." I nodded, tucking the pouch into my pocket, in the back of my mind knowing that I resented gardening because it was one of the occupations the she-elves with earth talents were pushed to partake in. I made it a point to everyone that that wasn't the path I would choose. Mira and I made our way back up to the estate, her basket full of flowers.

A difference had arisen in me thanks to Master Tali's assurance, and now I looked forward to studying instead of dreading it. I was going to continue with these lessons, regardless of my fears. I needed this chance. I needed this opportunity to define a new path, and if sifting would do that for me, then I would embrace it. I reached in the corner pocket of my bed and pulled out the sifting book. After memorizing a section, I was irritated, my eyes watering from staring at the old handwriting and weathered pages. I closed my eyes. In the silence all I could hear were my thoughts and the cool winds whistling outside.

You have to open your mind to the possibilities. I repeated Master Tali's wise words in my head. The last I had left off was in the *Aquyil* section. I learned words for waves, sea, river, lake, tide, and many others that weren't even remotely applicable to the climate we lived in. I hadn't seen an ocean or gotten to experience the tide or even heard the whispers of the sea. The closest I got were through the books I'd read, or the accounts I'd heard passed down from ancient elves. Even the artwork that glistened on stone walls or on fine parchment told stories that I hadn't come to know. Still, I was quizzed on these words each and every day after lessons. A waste of time, maybe, but I didn't want to cause any ill will that may put a dent in my progress with Master Tali. I would like to see the ocean stretching as far as the eye could see, or maybe meet the merfolk, who were said to be so beautiful that no one could resist their charms. I wondered if they were real or just myths to spark the imaginations of young sprites.

By dinnertime I had finished the *Aquyil* section. I put on breeches and a sweater, with my leather boots. I was to go out tonight, but I didn't want to make it obvious by changing late in the night when my family was around. I pulled off my housecoat, taking out the pouch of seeds Mira gave me and tossing them into my satchel. I unbuttoned my nightgown, letting it fall to the floor. I walked around naked, loving the feeling. I had discovered this freedom the night of my Kei. My body was changing, and it made me all the more excited to flaunt it, even if it was just for myself. I walked across the room toward my chest. I caught a glimpse in the mirror and stopped.

My shoulders had gained a slight build and my biceps were almost as rounded as Rayloh's. My calves and thighs were sculpted like thin hourglasses, and my hips were chiseled, leading up into the sketched abs of my stomach. My body had become fine-tuned. The work I had been doing with Master Tali wasn't entirely in vain. In fact, I think in some twisted fashion, it was entirely good. She taught me a lesson: that in everything, there is worth. There is an answer. *You have to open your mind to the possibilities*, I said to myself.

When I arrived in the main hall, Mira wasn't there and I had suspected that she was with her newly made acquaintance. She had been spending a lot of time at the Menstrom, an estate much like ours but smaller. Her acquaintance, whose name I came to know was Miliki, lived there, and after a few supervised visits, Madja permitted Mira go to the Menstrom on her own. Mira, who used to long to be at my side, was now finding her own way, and for a brief moment I missed her slightly annoying presence. She was distancing herself. I remembered when I used to follow behind Madja, hardly ever out of her sight, then wanting to grow up, seeing the lads and wanting to join them. I used to scowl when I saw them, labeling them nuisances and hooligans until I woke up one day and realized that I wanted to be older and so began acting as so, leaving Mira as my replacement for Madja. Now Mira was finding her own as well.

Although they had been spending a lot of time together, I thought it was too early to start referring to Miliki as Mira's friend. That was something my father always said: *"A friend is a stately term and should only be used when most certain the individual has gained your trust and that can only be achieved through time. Much time."* He taught me a lot of lessons when I was younger, some of which I still held. Others I learned from my own experiences. *"Sometimes the friends you make can earn your trust, and sometimes the family you have can lose it."* I realized that when my father grew cold and our talks began to become passing nods.

After dinner, I went into the family quarters, retrieved my bow, arrows, and the sifting book, placing it in my satchel. I grabbed a small container of red paint, and a brush as well. It was the perfect time because most residents were still in the main hall, including my parents. I slipped into the study. It was empty. I thought to put the bow and arrows in the chest, but remembering Madja's discovery of my sparring equipment, I felt that it would be better to just slide them under the love seat. I began another section in the sifting book and ate corn leaves until I was nearly certain that everyone had retired for the night.

I peeked outside the door of the study. The corridor was dark. I looked out one of the skylights. The moon was high in the sky, resembling a half-filled saucer sitting in the heavens. The night wasn't as cold. The wind that blew was warm. The weather never ceased to surprise me. My sweater actually made me feel hot, but I wasn't going to go back into the Remni just to change shirts. I would just have to ignore these small aggravations.

I scanned around for guards. I didn't want anyone to know I was shooting arrows in the community garden, lest word gets back to Madja and she confiscate my bow and arrows set. But the dome made me feel all the more secure. The hardest part would be getting there without the guards seeing me. I'd assumed someone had complained about their absence at posts or the slackers had been discovered and reprimanded because there were a few patrolling the path in front of the garden. One even stood a few feet from the dome's door. I ducked, crawled, and scaled the small trees and bushes along the path until I was right across from the door. All I could do was wait. It would be easy to shake a vine or a tree, but they would suspect foul play, and if they didn't, the very least they would do is investigate the surrounding area, a hindrance as well. It had to have been nearly an hour before they started moving down the hill toward the blue ring.

As soon as I couldn't see their heads over the crest of the hill, I shot from the shadows to enter the dome. Water kissed the petals and leaves of the flowers and trees inside. I pulled the red paint and paintbrush from my satchel. The wooden poles would do nicely. They were rounded and larger than the thin trees that dotted the terrace of the Remni, and they were also hollow. The arrow would be able to pierce these much easier than the slender tree trunks. I dipped the brush and painted medium-size circles of red on the beams, something that would be deemed harmless, at the most odd but ignorable, if noticed by a servant or one of the housewives. After doing three others the same way, I pulled an arrow from my quiver and drew it in the bow. I decided to start back about ten feet. I released the arrow, it easily piercing the wet red target. I was proud, especially after my first attempts at the end of the summer. Not only did I hit the pole but also I hit the red mark. I retrieved my arrow and added five more feet in distance. I missed the pole altogether on the first shot, but the second shot hit its target. I gave it a dozen more attempts before deciding to distance myself even more. At twenty feet, it got more challenging. I would aim at the target, the tip of the sharp arrow

229

pointed straight at the red sphere, but each time it would descend into the ground, or into one of the nearby vegetable patches.

An hour passed by and then another, and then another. I had to have shot more than one hundred times and had hit the pole only a quarter of the times when I decided to call it a night. I still had training and should get in a few hours of rest. I slept in the study. It was where I felt most comfortable, and it didn't take me to such a sorrowful place anymore. I laid on the love seat. There was no reason to sleep on the floor anymore, now that the lads were gone. We used to all sleep, clustered together, because we didn't think it fair that one of us sleep on the love seat and didn't have the patience to plan a time to take turns. It made us closer, us sacrificing the more comfortable option for the sake of each other's company.

Once my muscles had relaxed, it felt as if bricks were attached to my arms. I was sore around my shoulders and my upper triceps and the muscles around my neck, but no matter how still I laid, I still managed to remain tense. I slept on my back. I didn't feel like using the energy or going through the pain of turning over onto my stomach. I drifted off with nothing but the warmth of the lantern and the wall of books to keep me company, plus hopeful visions of whishing arrows hitting bright red spots.

Chapter Seventeen

Master Tali tossed me a thick branch that had been stripped of twigs and nubs and sanded smooth. It almost went over my head, but I caught the end of it before it was out of reach.

"I assume you've had some experience with the sword since you're becoming acclimated to the bow and arrow." My eyes widened. *How did she even know that I had the archery set?* "Bring that to your next session. Now ready your sword."

She launched at me, her hair flying, catching the air, lifting from the sheer force of her speed. She came down on top of my head and with my right hand I caught the stick before it collided with the top of my brow. She turned around, digging her elbow into my side, knocking the wind out of me, causing me to release her stick and drop mine in the process. Having gained her ground, she took this opportunity to stab the point of the stick into my lower spine. I fell to the ground with one loud yelp. She laughed as the thud of the stick hit my back.

"Again!" she ordered. I got up, stick in hand. I was angry. Master Tali lunged and our sticks collided. I whirled around in an attempt to take a shot at her from behind, but she quickly turned, simultaneously meeting my strike with a block. Her foot met my chest, sending me tumbling to the ground. Pebbles nudged my back, scraping the points of my elbows. I gritted my teeth. She was good. That was an understatement. She was an expert. But how? "Who would think an old elf could take on one so spirited?"

Her remark resonated within me, boiling like water in a covered pot. I was a formidable opponent when dueling with the lads, and I would like to think that I was well acclimated to the sport, but right now I was flung about like a toy. Surprisingly, the words sprouted from my lips, blossoming into a confident imperative.

"*Guijanu a wa cabeyil.*" A pebble lifted, striking her square in the forehead. She stumbled a little, dizzy from the blow.

"You're learning. In a duel, you must fight with all you can. Anything can be a weapon, but for the sake of your training, let's keep to the sticks and away from sifting. You might overextend yourself past your strengths and abilities." I smiled and nodded, proud that I had received praise. She reached down and pulled me up and we were at it again.

We sparred for another two hours before ending the session. I could feel my body beginning to welt from the bruises. Master Tali seemed fine. I had only managed to strike her one or two times with too little force to be deemed commendable. She picked up her cloak from the ground and pulled out a water skin. After taking a few sips of water she tossed it to me. I caught it and gulped down the water eagerly, ignoring the surprised stare from Master Tali. I wiped the residue from my lips and tossed the skin back to her. She laughed, tucking the skin back into the pocket of her cloak.

"Come! Follow me. I have something to show you."

She took me to the back of the school, where we stopped at a thick wooden door. As she moved, I caught the scent of mint and sweet greens emanating from her body. Even after an exhaustive sparring session in the middle of the fall, she still smelled of a bright summer's day. She reached in a pocket within her cloak, returning with some sort of key. The door opened to a stairwell.

Closing the door behind us, we climbed a spiral staircase. It was dark, the light fading as we continued to ascend. Finally, we reached a small ladder that led to a wooden hatch. Master Tali pushed it up, letting in the bright rays of the sun. I blinked my eyes in discomfort.

"I apologize; I should have cautioned you to close your eyes."

Still squinting from the light, I said, "Yes, I believe I've not gone blind, thankfully." She let out a small chuckle while I grunted.

We climbed out through the hatch, Master Tali going first, and then assisting me up. Finally my pupils dilated, adjusting to the bright sky.

I could see everything: the edgewoods, the black ring, and even Kala's home by the mines. I could see the elves and the Dwala marching about, attending to their daily tasks, like ants in an anthill. I inhaled, taking in the fresh air. It seemed like we were almost among the clouds, just out of reach of the glorious sun.

"The school houses one of two watchtowers. This used to

be the last means of protection should danger arise. You see, the city once extended past these walls into miles and miles of woods, fields, even the sea. We shared it with other creatures, each having their own lands allotted for the sake of peace and fairness. This fortitude served as a keep in times of war and peril should the woods ever become unsafe and our people had to retreat. This keep also was the basis of the alliance between us and the humans."

"The Dwala used to be our allies," I recited.

"Correct. They were, before the end of the world. Well, I should describe the event as the end of *our* world rather, and the beginning of a new."

"What do you mean by that?" We peered around, now facing the purple ring. I stuck my head through one of the parapets that provided space enough for archers to shoot and watchers to peer from all sides. The school seemed but a little box below. It made me nervous being up so high, but I gathered myself, sinking to the floor, as Master Tali continued her history lesson.

"Until that point, we believed the world would end tragically, possibly in flames, or some terrible flood. Maybe the tides of the sea to the east would swallow up the forest and wash away all life, but that was not to be. We were unaware that there were other worlds, other life that coexisted within our domain. There were even more men and elves." She still stared off into the distance toward the purple ring, the tower's reflection in her pupils.

"When those worlds split, and the forces that kept them separate collapsed, our world collided simultaneously with others', dispelling all time, disrupting the flow of energy, and the physical world as we knew it changed forever as well. Lands, claimed once by elves, were scarred by fire in other worlds, and the same came to pass in ours. People in other worlds were at war among each other, and the same came to pass for those of this world. Protector Shiloh grew tired and angry with those who sought to conquer lands for their own, slaughtering in the process. Specifically a human lot, from the land of Meric, were greedy in their pursuit of power. Shiloh, in an attempt to stop their bloody conquest, requested an audience with their leader, sending to speak on both of our behalves a Dwala, who sat on the treaties council between the elves of Keldrock and the humans of Dwaland. Her name was Manu. She was headstrong but often made her point, summoning the best response from those she was attempting to convince."

Master Tali seemed unnerved from the telling of the story and sat down across from me. "The day before Manu departed, they had a feast in her honor, wishing her good tidings as she made her journey. The next day she headed for the open plains, which the Merics had claimed as their domain. Along with her came two he-elves, who served as escorts and defense should she need defending. A week had gone by and they had yet to return, and concern arose among us. We feared that we had been naïve in our thoughts of peace and sacrificed innocent parties, but on the next sun, word arrived. One of the escorts returned, battered and scarred. He told us that Manu had betrayed the elves to keep the Dwala safe and that the Meric army would descend upon the woods by the next sun.

Word traveled quickly, spreading like fire among the bramble. The Dwala left in the night, breaking our treaty. They had chosen to align themselves with the Merics. As the battered escort had reported, the issue of battle was raised and our people stood off at the border of the woods in defense. She-elves and sprites were sent to the keep, which we now call our fair city. Even from the long journey, they could still hear the fighting, the cries of agony, the cries of death, but we pressed on toward the keep, Shiloh and the treaty council leading the way. Once they were all gathered within the gates, Shiloh went to the first watchtower, this one being the second, which we now call the chamber of light. My mother remembered seeing him, brave and noble, forced to lead the future of his people instead of fighting alongside his brothers. After days upon days of fighting, a flame so great rose to the sky, its billow of smoke making the very day turn to night. Shiloh knew the inevitable had occurred, that our home had been destroyed, and with great sorrow he did what he had to do to keep his people safe. A surge of energy, a power unlike anyone has ever seen, shot to the sky and spread in all directions, pouring over and eventually into the woods surrounding the mountain where our keep sits. That was the day the veil was lowered, the top of the tower was named the chamber of light, and no one dared enter for fear the veil would fall, Shiloh be destroyed, and the end of our people be undeniable."

"So if the Dwala left to join the other humans of Meric, why do we have them in our city today?"

Master Tali sighed. "Some Dwala retreated with the she-elves and sprites, honoring our treaty and the peace we had forged over the centuries. Some even fought alongside our brothers. Still, the matter of betrayal lay within their kind, and the Courts, which were in charge until Shiloh's line bore an heir, were willing to let them live alongside us—but as lesser beings, not as allies. Then life began anew. Few still live who remember the details of that day. We had our troubles while living behind these walls—illness and plague. The woods as our home and everything we needed to live and multiply were not resources any longer. We lived behind the veil, forbidden of even the edgewoods. The new school, this second watchtower, was renamed in honor of Shiloh, and the Courts have ruled ever since."

"So in all this time, an heir hasn't come after Shiloh, other than Prince Alag?"

"*They* would have us believe it were so. Soon after the veil, the rings of separation were created to keep order among the people. Anyone who stepped out of line, specifically the Dwala, was severely punished. Shiloh's wife and daughter were kept within the purple ring. It has been nearly eighty years since the veil has been raised. Perhaps it is destiny that Prince Alag is the only heir to be born of Shiloh, and in that, the Courts had their way in his raising, warping his mind to be similar to theirs; or perhaps not. Perhaps another will come. Now that is a little extreme—far-fetched, even—but one has to consider all possibilities, Alya. Power is desired by more than just the pitiful and downtrodden. I would like to, however, caution you to not be so hasty in your judgment of character. Once that hand is dealt, it cannot be undone."

"By what do you mean, Master?"

"I mean there may come a time when you will have to decide what side you're aligned with. Life isn't fair for all, and after hearing this bit of your history, as well as mine, all is not what it seems. The rules we limit ourselves with most times are the most ridiculously imagined things in this world."

I didn't quite understand what she was going on about. Since I had been training with her, I'd noticed that she would speak in roundabout ways. It was something that annoyed me about her.

Chapter Eighteen

The weeks that followed were challenging but in a wonderful way. We sparred almost every day, and eventually I bested Master Tali. We began incorporating sifting elements into our battles. It was harder fighting while sifting. The exertion from waving around a sword and using up potential energy would drain me during battle, so it was only to be used in the most simplistic of ways and only if there was little to no chance of your opponent stopping the attack. We also practiced sifting things around the courtyard. I brought my bow and arrows and Master Tali showed me techniques to better manage my shot. I would still slip out at night and go to the yellow gardens and practice, and I could now, in the dark and at a great distance, hit a red circle the size of a doorknob.

I didn't quite spend my days alone anymore. Kala would keep me company. She slowly became a good friend of mine, and surprisingly my father didn't have anything to say concerning it and so Madja didn't object, either. Mira helped me to start my own plot in the garden. I didn't use the pouch of flower seeds that she gave me—I wanted my garden to consist of only fruits and vegetables. It gave me such a marvelous feeling to plant something and be able to watch it grow into something I could actually use, even though I would never openly say it. Kala kindly took on the task of teaching me how to cook some of my favorite dishes. Some were fairly simple, easy enough that I could make them on my own. I was happy I had found an interest in the work she-elves did and that Madja was delighted as well. But it was more to me than that. The more I learned from Master Tali, the more I felt like the warrior I dreamed of. The more I felt like a warrior, the less scary the edgewoods seemed, and by the same token, I wanted to learn survival skills. I wanted to learn how to grow and cook my own food, and find out what things were safe in the wild and how to tell if they were poisonous and other things I figured I'd need to know if I were to actually leave Keldrock. On any front, Madja, Mira, and Kala didn't need to know that those sparked my interest.

The Remni was starting to stir with life again. It was bustling with smiles and laughs, something I would see only when an event was approaching and people had a reason to dress up, drink, and mingle with each other. The unveiling was days away, and there was to be a celebration for the Guerr. I was extremely excited because Rayloh and Segun would be allowed to return to the Remni before setting out into the edgewoods for this special mission. I wondered if they had changed as I had.

The day finally came and I was beyond elated. I awoke early, naturally, since I had been training with Master Tali. Today, however, training had been canceled for the Guerr celebration. It was hosted in the blue ring's square. The warriors would walk out formally from their barracks and be welcomed with high praise, the waving of flags, and random shouts of blessings.

I decided to go out to the garden and select some flowers

240

for our table. I wanted everything to be perfect. I put my housecoat over my nightgown and made my way outside. The sky was still dark but it was lighter over the eastern hills, where the sun was slowly rising. The mornowl chimed its call and I smiled as the song that normally irritated me now filled me with joy for the lads' homecoming.

I picked a basket off of the wall of the garden dome and waded carefully through the flower plot to a group of lilies. They looked like fire sitting atop a grass torch, the blends of orange and yellow imitating the flapping of a flame. I thought to make the lads a pumpkin medley from my garden to show them what I had picked up while they were gone, especially since nothing pleased them more than food.

I moved on to my garden plot, crouching among the gourds and carrot sprouts. I examined the fruits and vegetables, checking them for bruising and signs of decay as I always did, deciding, as Mira and Kala had shown me time and time again, which were ready to be picked. I heard rustling behind me. I turned around, still crouching. A feeling of uncertainty came over me. I tried hard to rebel but my imagination took hold. I couldn't help but assume the worst. I dared not move. I began trying to convince myself that nothing was there, that my mind had conjured the sound itself—until the branch of a nearby apple tree shook. The purpose of the dome was to keep things such as pests, vermin, and the elements out, but it also kept things in. It was keeping me in.

I looked at the shaking branch and squinted my eyes, trying to make out any figure that might be near. If the sun had been up, its light would have been an aid and I would not be so uncertain. Finally I formed a possible silhouette in the darkness. It was confirmed when the branch shook again and a shadow tumbled out of the tree. The thud seemed to resonate in me, shaking the ground. The figure stood. I didn't move a muscle. The figure didn't move either, its silhouette fuzzy to me, mixing with the surrounding shadows. I flipped through the pages of my memory, trying to recall some animal I had read about or seen during my missions in the edgewood that could stand upright and climb trees. Only one came to mind, and it was something I had pushed out of mind for so long.

With a quick jolt of my neck, I looked at the dome's door. The beast had come for me. I couldn't escape the thought anymore. For a few seconds I looked at the door, contemplating my means of escape, before turning back to the anonymous visitor. In those few moments, it had begun advancing in my direction, covering half the ground that was between us. I felt vulnerable, scared, forgetting all I had learned during this vacation. Other memories forced those lessons away. The yellow eyes, the scraping of the base's trunk, and the cry of the monster filled my head and made me panic. I stumbled clumsily toward the dome door. Air escaped my lungs faster than normal. Just as I reached the latch, I felt arms around me. I screamed. Only a small, high-pitched shriek escaped my lips before my mouth was covered. My eyes felt as if they were going to ooze out of my head. The hand tasted of sweat and soil. I closed my eyes, not accepting my fate, but hoping that I would somehow be saved. Then I realized that the figure and I were lying calmly on the ground. It was holding me, and I was breathing heavily.

"It's me."

I instantly began to relax as the hand moved away from my lips. The hand was strong, I realized, but soft. I looked up.

"Nazda?"

Chapter Nineteen

A guard burst through the garden's dome doors. It was the same guard who rudely nudged me to the sprites' section at the lads' Guerr ceremony not too long ago. I aligned shovels and picks in the corner, attempting to pass innocently as if nothing had happened, a quick reaction to an already suspicious situation. A Dwala girl and an elf miss, alone in the yellow gardens, before the sun.

"I heard a scream. Is everything all right, miss?" He glared at Nazda, who was sitting eating an apple, cutting chucks of it with her ivory knife with the beautiful maiden handle.

"I am quite fine, my good sir. A pick fell out of place and nearly speared my foot is all. To my embarrassment, it was quite a dramatic reaction but I assure you that we are fine." Nazda peered up from her apple, smirking sardonically.

"What a fine dagger. I wouldn't think a . . . ." The guard lingered for a moment, staring down Nazda until she looked away. I could tell he felt something was wrong or in the very least felt challenged by this resilient girl. He examined the dome, ensuring that everything was in order, before leaving us to our own company, but staring down Nazda one last time.

"What are you doing here?" I screeched in a quiet exclamation. "Are you trying to be killed?" Nazda stood up, dusting off her worn breeches that stopped just short of her calves.

This wasn't the ideal weather for her to wear something that barely went past her knees, but I didn't want to bring up the fact, considering she likely didn't have many other options. She picked up her sackful of apples, which was made from an old shirt with tied sleeves, before answering my inquiries.

"Actually, although terribly ironic, I should ask you what you are doing here. The garden is normally empty around this hour." I didn't laugh like she anticipated so after a moment, she continued. "The beginnings of the cold season have been somewhat harsh, and all the more causing a shift in the already unpleasant character of Mr. Harmon. He has cut our rations and payment in half. It was already a struggle before, so I'm doing what I have to do."

"How long have you been stealing from here?"

Her face scrunched, as if she were infuriated by the very alluding to the act as stealing. "It's been about a month since I've been *using* the yellow gardens. I take what I need for the orphans and myself to survive another day. Not that you would know anything about surviving, princess!" I looked away, giving thought to the situation. I wasn't there to argue and I considered Nazda somewhat of a friend, even though her comments at this moment stacked against my beliefs.

"Tonight is the celebration honoring the Guerr. The whole city will be in attendance, and well, I'm sure no one will be tending the garden—or guarding it, for that matter—during that time. An empty potato sack might serve you a lot better than that

245

shirt anyhow," I said, nodding at a pile of empty potato sacks in the corner, atop a wooden pallet. "For your safety, this has to be the last time, so take your fill and this stays our little secret." Her arms gripped my body, lifting me into the air. For a moment I thought that she had grown enraged and had decided to display her anger by wrestling me to the ground until I looked down and saw her eyes beaming with joy. What was a small gesture by my token was meaningful to her. Apparently she had surprised herself with her reaction, because she immediately returned to her reserved state.

"I meant to say . . . thank you," she said, looking away. "You know, I never apologized for hitting you. I was too hasty in my judgment."

"As was I. I would say that in more than one way, I deserved it." I smiled at her and she at me. Perhaps the same harsh judgments held by elves about Dwala were held in the inverse as well.

"Yeah, you did deserve it." She picked up her shirtful of apples and headed for the door, peeking out first to ensure the guard wasn't around. "Thanks, Alya. For caring, that is. My friend."

With that she was gone, nothing left of her but her smudged footprints in the soil and the wonderful feeling she had given me. I picked my flowers off of the ground, along with the fruits and vegetables I had selected, and headed for the estate.

It was still quiet inside. Light from the start of the day

hadn't filled the halls yet. I went immediately to the main hall, creaking the old decorative doors open. The enormous, empty room was cooler than the rest of the Remni. I sat my possessions on the sprite's table, and picking up one of the vases, began arranging the flowers I selected. Mira had taught me how to choose the larger ones to go in the middle and how to break the stems of the others to situate them better around those. She took it so seriously and now that I had learned the craft, it was hard not to want my floral arrangements to look perfect. It was less of a domestic duty and more a gift. Something beautiful that no matter what issues circulated within closed quarters that the one space we all shared would always be filled with beautiful flowers. A tradition I had seen performed as long as I could remember. In a world where she-elves weren't given many options, it only made sense that what was permitted was done stunningly.

I requested Kala to meet me here early. I wanted to bathe before everyone else and get a head start on this pumpkin medley dish. While I was confident enough that I had mastered the recipe, I would feel better having a second pair of expert eyes and hands present. Kala was waiting in the kitchen. I took the liberty of washing the fruits and vegetables. She took over then, removing potatoes from the cupboard and starting the tedious process of delicately peeling them. I made my way to the grooming quarters, taking off my house robe. Kala had prepared my bath the way I liked it, so I took no time to dive right into the warm water. Something that was more a chore in the warmer weather was a special treat in the winter. Still, today I didn't have time to sit and soak up the steam, as usual. I had way too many tasks I wanted to get accomplished. I washed my hair, adding fresh oils and lotions for smell and texture. Sometime during my bath, the halls had filled with residents. I assumed they had plans for this grand day as well. I finished rinsing the soap off of my body, dried off, and put on a housedress.

The main hall had filled with servants and hired help. Kitchen staff, housekeepers, and friendly elf kin had all come; even the coordinator for my Kei was in attendance. I was hesitant about speaking to him, since our last meeting brought more stress than he probably had anticipated, but when he spotted me shooting toward the kitchen, he called my name and I had no choice but to stop.

"Mistress Alya. How good it is to see you again."

"Good to see you again as well, Sir . . ." To be honest, I hadn't ever gotten his name.

"It's Nicon. Sir Nicon. I'm sure you're delighted your friends will be coming back this day. Thanks to the success of your Kei, the residents have decided to hire me yet again." He winked at me. His face was smooth, wrinkle-free, and he smelled of peppermint with a subtle hint of lavender. He was dressed for the day's events in a turquoise kurta with remarkable detailing. His hair was braided into one single rope, which lined his entire spine. I hadn't noticed before, since his hair covered all of his ears but the tips, but he had three piercings in each of the lobes of his ears. He seemed to me in this moment to be kindly enough, and had we not met under such stressful circumstances, and had he lived in the Remni, he would have intrigued me as one of the adults I would have liked to get to know.

"Well, Sir Nicon, congratulations on the assignment. I know it will turn out great. I very much enjoyed my Kei. It was nothing less than what I dreamed of. Even better." He smiled and bowed gracefully. Then he spun around, clapping his hands, assigning tasks to his personal team.

I laughed at how Sir Nicon poured out his entire creative genius into his work. It was admirable while all the same overly dramatic. The kitchen was bustling as usual around this time. Breakfast was being made. The servants were cubing fruit and mushrooms while others sliced bread and butter. As of late, we had been having hot breakfasts on the cold days, but it was a simple breakfast today so the staff could put more energy into preparing food for the feast. The food had to be prepared earlier than the celebration, which began a little after the normal time for midday meal. The days were growing shorter and it grew darker much sooner, so it was important to have the celebration during the light of day. Kala had been moved to a corner of the kitchen, now that the staff needed the majority of it to move about. She had already started emptying the contents of a pumpkin.

"I apologize, Alya. I've peeled half of the potatoes before they urged me aside but I put all of the ingredients you will need inside of the gourd. We can go to the servants' kitchen. While it's not as nice as this one, it'll serve its purpose." I nodded and she opened a hatch in the floor, one that reminded me of the hatch that led onto the top of the watchtower at Shiloh's school. "I should go first." She picked up the pumpkin and a few kitchen supplies and stepped through the opening. I followed, closing it behind me. We were on a platform, connecting the kitchen and the wall to a set of stairs leading downward.

"Careful. They are worn," she said, nodding toward the stairs.

The planks of wood under my feet seemed to sway as if alive, creating the feeling that they would collapse under me at any time. I realized too late that one was cracked when the plank broke under my planted foot, plummeting to the empty space beneath. I instinctively grabbed for the railing but there wasn't one. I felt myself losing control, sinking. I almost let out a scream when I felt Kala's grip on my hand pulling me up, lifting me back to reality. I used my leg that hadn't fallen through the stairs to heave myself up. I heard the plank crash into the stone floor, sending dust and debris into the air.

"Many pardons. I thought you saw me pass the step. It's common knowledge to us servants to skip it. I should have said something."

"It's fine." There was frustration in my voice and I didn't want Kala to think it was directed at her, so I added for confirmation, "I'm quite fine. Thanks. No worries." I gingerly tapped the hand she used to catch me and we continued down the stairs after I took a moment to catch my breath. It was really my fault for not following her movements as she had instructed. It seemed to always be like that. Someone was always saving me, someone catching me unprepared or off guard. Even after all the training with Master Tali, all of it seemed to not make any difference. I always wanted more than this life, but maybe it wasn't to be because it wasn't meant to be.

The staircase ended and we turned a corner to find a small room where a single lantern hung over a rickety table. There weren't any ovens or vast pots and shelving, only a table, some wobbly chairs, a fireplace, and a few tattered pans and dishes. Kala increased the heat of the lantern, brightening the flame. She cleared off a portion of the table and sat the items she grabbed from the main hall's kitchen onto it. Surprisingly, she had managed to carry a cutting board and a pot, along with the pumpkin filled with vegetables and seasoning. Her work had made her stronger than most, the same result that came about my training. Kala was truly remarkable.

Being in this limited kitchen would add more time if I were to have everything prepared for the lads. I began chopping the fruits and vegetables. After a short focused time, the two of us had everything chopped, peeled, seeded, and mixed in the pumpkin gourd. It was almost filled to the brim but when the water was boiled and added to the concoction; it would make everything congeal, lowering the contents away from the brim. Now we would have the task of seasoning. Time had elapsed faster than I expected, and soon the horns would blare, signaling the city to assemble in the blue ring. We mixed in black pepper, lemon juice, parsley leaves, oil, salt, and a handful of corn kernels for sweetness. As I added each ingredient, Kala stirred, so that the ingredients would fall evenly among the fruits and vegetables.

"You know I can't express my appreciation for the effort you've been putting in. I know without additional pay, it must be a burden to always have to spend any spare time with me. I must say that I do quite enjoy it."

She smiled. "Mistress, it is I who should thank you. The groundskeeper has seen your favor and has insisted on keeping me. I consider our time together most fruitful and I desire nothing more than to serve your house."

"Please. 'Mistress' seems too formal for two friends." I gripped her hand and she gripped mine back. "I have something for you." I reached into my pocket, pulling out the gold necklace given to me by Rayloh's father, the sun charm twirling slowly at the end of the gold chain. "It was given to me by Lord Fueto. I figured you would enjoy it just as much as I have, especially since you favor him as much as I do." We giggled and for once it felt natural, like the bonds I had with the lads. "It isn't this easy making friends with the drones in my rotation at the School of Talents. I often feel that I am surrendering parts of myself when even interacting with those snarky sprites, but with you I found a comrade in the most unlikely of places. I hope this shows my gratitude." I handed her the charm necklace, coiling it in her hand.

"I don't think—"

"Mira has a crescent moon and says that she is wearing it to the celebration. She hopes you'll wear yours in unison with her, but if you don't want to, it would mean no harm. She sometimes imitates or matches me and it can get quite annoying but it comes from a place of flattery."

"I don't think I can accept this."

"What do you mean? I'm giving it to you."

"I don't believe I've been as forthcoming about myself as I should have been."

I recoiled, unsure of how to take this news. "Whatever do you mean?"

Kala settled down into one of the chairs, pulling it from under the table. I followed suit. She kept her head down. I was good at looking in the eyes of anyone and seeing their intentions, a taste of their thoughts, but Kala never gave me that luxury.

"You know, if something is wrong you can tell me."

"*I'm* the something wrong, Alya. I'm not who you think I am."

"What are you talk—"

I heard the slam of the hatch door open, it interrupting our conversation. I turned around in my chair facing the stairwell, expecting a slew of servants to rush in like a stampede, but instead I saw Madja.

"There you are. I have been looking all over for you." She stepped into the room, letting the lantern light cast shadows on her face, making her appear angrier than she actually was. "If Sir Nicon hadn't told me he'd seen you with a servant girl in the kitchen, I wouldn't have even checked down here. It's time for you to get ready. The horns will sound at any moment and you have yet to get dressed."

"Kala and I were just preparing my gift for the lads."

Madja didn't seem to be extraordinarily pleased, let alone like she really cared. "Well, if you haven't completed your little meal by now, it will have to wait until after the celebration or the servant will have to complete it for you. Where has she gone off? I hope she didn't leave you down here alone." I turned around in my chair.

"She's . . ." I couldn't believe my eyes. Kala wasn't there. There was just an empty chair. I looked around the room. There was no hidden door. No secret hatch. She had gone. The only opening was a hole in the window, barely wide enough for a small bird to pass through.

"Well, you must get ready," Madja said. "I won't have my little elf appearing unkempt in public. The House of Meoltan will not be shamed while I am its keeper." She hurried back up the stairs. I looked at the hole in the window.

"Impossible."

I turned down the lantern and headed for the main floor.

Chapter Twenty

The square was filled with the sound of beautiful flutes and harps playing for the Jalla dancers' winter performance. The ice talents had trickled icicles from the edges of buildings, and wrapped laces of snowflakes around poles and columns for this wonderful occasion. The Jalla dancers skated in the center of the sunken platform that had been transformed into an ice rink. People lined the sides while sprites stacked on each of the four staircases, dangling their feet as they watched the beautiful performance. The Jalla dancers wore white leotards and silver tutus, their movements imitating snowflakes like a rain dance of sorts, summoning the snow that was to come. Each stroke of the harp and each blow of the flute mesmerized the audience, sending visions of winter bliss in the forms of snow angels, prancing white stallions, and winter lights that lit up the sky. The music talents' gifts were one of the ones I enjoyed the most. The fact that their music could create such imagery was something I always envied as well as desired. As soon as the performance concluded, applause rang through the entire market. Elves of all trades came out donning their best for this reunion of the entire city. The Dwala walked about as well, many not straying too far from the blue ring's path. They didn't get close enough to watch the ice-skating or listen to the harpists and the flutist. Most came wearing anything from housedresses to smiths' garb. I spotted Master Tali talking to a few of the misses in my rotation from a distance. She wore a purple dress that fully extended to her ankles and began just short of the upper portion of her chest and neck, where spirals of patterned ribbons took its place. I maneuvered toward her anxiously. After all the training sessions, I had grown even fonder of her as more than just a mentor but a friend as well.

"Master Tali!" I curtseyed, bowing my head to her. She responded in the same manner as was customary.

"Well, aren't you as dazzling as the northernmost star, my dear. Are you enjoying this event? I figured it would serve as quite a splendid recess." She alluded.

Out of the corner of my eye, I saw Nazda slipping through the crowd. I wouldn't have known it was she if I hadn't remembered the torn breeches I had seen her wearing in the yellow gardens. She was just about to start up one of the paths leading to the yellow ring. She must have taken my offer. *I should make sure everything works out*, I thought. I excused myself politely from Master Tali and began crossing back around the sunken platform when the trumpets sounded.

"Introducing Olörun's chosen sons, the heart and the strength of this great nation. The shell that guards Shiloh's pearl." I stopped my pursuit as the crowd, even the air, grew still. Guards split the path so the procession could begin.

"I present to you, your nation's legacy, Prince Alag."

Roars of cheering came from all sides. Prince Alag stepped forward, leading the congregation in our nation's pledge.

He then gave a speech seeking to instill hope upon the ears the words fell upon, and from the reactions of those around me, it seemed they were quite effective. The sprites, including my comrades, as well as the he-elves who had taken the oath of the Guerr previously, were introduced by rank and afterward were released to join their families in the crowd. Alag began with the commanding officers. They seemed lifeless, like some inanimate objects that had been reconditioned to only do one thing, like a once wild animal being now confined to a cage and taught to do tricks. Even when joined with their families, their smiles and displays of joy seemed forced and unnatural, some sort of mirage for what they really and truly felt.

I didn't care to stay around and watch the list of names with attached biographies. I hadn't finished the pumpkin medley, and since Rayloh and Segun would be announced almost last, assumedly since they were the last to join the Guerr, I thought it best to head to the Remni and finish cooking, not to mention that I wanted to be close to the yellow gardens to ensure Nazda's safety. I ducked down, strategically maneuvering through the crowd, trying not to be seen by the guards. They too were hypnotized by the ceremony, so it was much easier than I had anticipated. Halfway through my trek, I became a little bolder, moving a little faster. Some of the older citizens snuffed as I passed them, deeming my behavior rude or disrespectful. They, being aged, were judgmental when it came to matters of the state and displays of allegiance and respect.

I slipped down a set of stairs that descended onto the sunken platform. Most of the sprites had cleared the steps and were padding around on the ice. As long as they were quiet, the Guards of Candor let them be. I took off my slippers. I couldn't pad the ice. I was in a dress—one, that if torn, would send Madja into an uproar. The only option was baring my feet. The cold picked at my toes as I took my first steps, seeping into my blood like the stinger of a mosquito. I could feel my pulse in the ice. The thumping seemed to echo louder and louder as my feet grew numb. By the time I had journeyed a little more than halfway my body felt unsupported, my knees trembling, putting up their greatest fight to keep from buckling and sending me crashing to the ground. I used my left hand to prop myself against the wall, scaling it and using it for support. The stairs soon were upon me and I collapsed on the first one. Without attempting to continue climbing, I turned over on the steps, letting my body rest. I put on my slippers again, waiting for the feeling to return to every toe before beginning my ascent. Those who watched me as I made my way across turned their attention back to Prince Alag or the crawling sprites they were chaperoning.

I cut down a side street, looking over my shoulder as I put more and more distance between the crowd and myself. I turned one more corner and I was out of sight. I paused, taking in the glory of my feat, relishing the rush of excitement.

"Do you need accompanying, Mistress?"

I turned to see Kala in a ghastly red dress. It was a little outdated for my taste. The closest garment I had ever seen that could match this was on the rare occasion when the older elves of our city would tell stories of their Keis to young sprites and attempt to demonstrate by stuffing themselves back into their gowns, which they held on to as prized processions, right under their betrothal garments.

"I was just heading back to the Remni to finish the pumpkin medley. I know it only needs boiling since it's been seasoned and prepared, so there's no—"

"Well then! You'll want me to accompany you." I hadn't uttered another word before her arm was tucked under mine and we were on our way.

I had hoped Nazda was already in and out of the garden dome by the time I made it to the Remni. I walked a little slower, stalling to give her a little more time to finish collecting her goods. For the exception of Nazda, I would have wanted nothing more than Kala to accompany me back to the Remni, especially after our awkward interaction in the servants' kitchen. I thought it better not to bring it up now, unsure if she had heard what Madja said, especially since we would be putting the finishing touches on my dish together. I sensed she would rather not either, so I abided.

The estate was quiet when we arrived. Everyone was gone, but it was weird not hearing any sounds of life. It was as if I had entered an abandoned home, haunted by the spirits of its deceased owners. This was the only home I had ever known, but in this instance I felt insecure and frightened, so in a twist, I was

thankful Kala was with me. We went down to the servants'
quarters and brought the stuffed pumpkin upstairs into the
Remni's kitchen. We sat the pumpkin on a metal pedestal above
the furnace so the mixture within it could boil. It took careful
maneuvering not to burn us or drop our prize among the dancing
embers. We did it with success. I exhaled deeply, not realizing that
I had held my breath in my concentration. With that done, all we
had to do was wait.

"I think I should return to Mira. I was with her before I
found you and it would be only right that I seek her and
accompany her home. They should be nearing the lads' listings.
I'm quite sure that the pumpkin medley will be fine and should be
fully cooked by the time when or soon after everyone returns to
the estate. Would you like to come back as well?" I thought about
it for a moment. The large, empty estate was haunting in some
aspects but the kitchen felt normal, if not more inviting, due to the
array of foods laid out and the pleasant smells of different dishes
mixing together. It was warm and soothing, tingling my skin like a
hot summer's day, when the sun heats every part of your body. I
also wanted to check the yellow gardens to assure that Nazda was
either wrapping up or had already left, and I couldn't do that with
Kala around.

"I think I'll stay here but go ahead. I'll be fine."

The Remni was so quiet that I heard the front doors close
after Kala left. I sat at the cooking table, listening to the bubbles
from the pumpkin medley slowly begin to form and pop.

I waited a few moments before deciding that surely Kala had made her way far enough from the Remni for me to check the yellow gardens, so I stirred the pumpkin medley for a few minutes and then exited the kitchen. I noticed the main hall was filled with light as I passed through the kitchen's threshold. I marveled at all the decorations that I hadn't bothered to notice before.

"Beautiful, isn't it?"

I turned from the elaborately creative walls toward the main hall's entrance. Standing there, in his red tunic, was Rayloh. I nearly shrieked with joy but kept my composure as best I could, which wasn't saying much. It had been so long since I had seen him. His hair was in its tight little curls, like I remembered. The ends of his red hair, almost yellow, appeared to surround his head with an angelic halo. He looked so stately. His eyes were different, too. They were softer and affectionate.

"Yes it is, my lord, or should I address you by some other name?" He smiled, sending chills down my spine. The way he looked at me now was somehow different than before. His gaze lingered slightly, locking my eyes, and I didn't want to look away, but I did. It wasn't in my nature to be nervous, and yet here I was. "Where is Segun, friend?"

"He is out in the front of the estate, watching the sun set."

"Well then, we should join him," I said. I started for the main hall's doors when Rayloh caught me in his grasp.

"I have something for you." From his pocket he pulled out a chain necklace with a large red link in the middle. It was rustic and seemed worn, as if owned by a couple of others before it stumbled into his possession. "I know it may not be much, but it's important that you wear this. It's my promise to you, my dear Alya. After the unveiling tomorrow, I am to set out for the edgewoods, and I don't want to leave without letting you know how I feel. May I?" He held up the necklace, an end in each hand. I turned around, putting my back to him. I felt his hands going up my back, the touch of his fingers feeling like dewdrops through the dress. I felt his hand touch the snake necklace I was wearing, picking its latch. He snatched his hand away with a hiss of agitation. I looked over my shoulder.

"Is something the matter?" He looked defeated and vengeful all in the same expression.

"I have underestimated the durability of the latch. You're more familiar. Perhaps you can remove it?" I had never known Rayloh to ask for any form of help, even if the solution would come easier that way. I peered down at the necklace, seeing the last of glowing eyes fading out.

That's odd, I thought.

"Of course." As I picked at my necklace's latch, I noticed through the skylight that the sun had set. Stars were twinkling. The tint of dark purple went perfectly with the settled black in the sky. That's when I realized something was awry. It was just pure day. And Segun wouldn't wait outside, especially not to watch the sun set. The snake necklace slipped into my hands and I watched as Rayloh closed in behind me, bringing the new necklace over my head and in front of my face.

"Wait." I nudged the necklace slightly, but Rayloh wouldn't abandon his goal. He continued bringing the ends around my neck. I slipped underneath the barrier of links.

"We should go and meet Segun." I smiled at him, but his face remained stern. The emotion I had seen before, of defeat and resentment, returned. He moved in closer. I stood still, unsure of what to do. He brought his hand to my face, pulled me in, and kissed me. It wasn't like to Rayloh to be aggressive in such a way. Such behavior was unattractive and I would never expect it of him. I attempted to pull away but he held me, his strength like that of a grown he-elf. Finally he released me, smiling into my face. His eyes were large and crazed and his face was blushed. His smile wasn't his own, but appeared lustful and perverted. I wanted so badly to run away but I couldn't.

In one fell swoop his grip was unhinged and his eyes filled with water. I couldn't tell what was the matter. His expression reeked of pain, and with it came a mixture of grunts and small gasps that escaped his throat. I examined him, unsure of where this display stemmed from. It was as if he were being tormented by some demon. I moved away and looked past him toward the door. There, Nazda stood with a torch in her hand, rage engulfing her body. Her eyebrows were furrowed and her lips quivered in anger. I turned back to Rayloh and saw, sticking out of his back, just behind his shoulder, her dagger. The ivory handle's engraved woman was splattered with blood.

"What have you done?" I stood shaking, unsure of what to make of the situation. Nazda had stabbed my best friend. The same friend who introduced me to her. Tears trickled down my cheeks. "Rayloh!" I screamed.

"He is no friend! That is he!" Her teeth gritted, just as Rayloh fell to the floor.

The room filled with the light of day. I was slowly floating back to reality while at the same time challenging everything I had witnessed, deeming it a lie. A cloaked figure lay in front of me, now appearing much larger than Rayloh, his breath harsh but stable. A wrinkled hand clutched the pierced shoulder. The injury wasn't serious but assumedly painful nonetheless. I didn't know if I should console, attack, or retreat, but all I could do was stand there and wait. One thing for sure was this wasn't Rayloh.

I looked up from the injured frame to see Nazda slowly approaching. Her steps were wary and quiet. She came up behind him, aiming to retrieve the dagger, which was still fused to his back. She was scared, but I didn't know why, and in my confusion, as much as I wanted to demand an explanation, I observed, hoping that this was just a horrible mistake. Nazda had but touched the tip of the ivory handle when the figure's hand shot from the wound, grabbing her by the wrist. The snap of his grip caught her off guard as well as myself. He lifted her into the air, prying the torch from her hand, and coursed her through the air. Her foot hit my face, spiraling me toward the youth table. After using her to pummel me, he cast her back toward the main hall's entrance.

My face throbbed from the blow. My vision was blurry, objects on the table running together in blended images, but I made out a flicker of light attached to a cold, dark silhouette. It was a torch he had retrieved from the wall. I made out the vase and the toppled flowers that I had placed just this morning. I lifted my head toward the figure. He was fully standing now, the light of the moon reflecting on his bald head. He turned toward me. My realization was a whisper of an unsuspecting fear—the obvious trapped within the unobvious. The other mirages I'd had before, the night in the backyard of the Remni and waking up in front of his quarters' door.

"Lord Calo?" My sight was still blurry but it was he.

He turned toward me, leaving Nazda on the ground, tormented. He was intruding her mind as he had done to me, but judging by her distress, our visions were nowhere near similar. The dagger was now in his hand. His blood still stained the ivory blade and handle. An unsettling grin emerged on his face—the same look I'd seen on what I thought was Rayloh's. It was just as perverted. Just as wrong. Nazda began to wail, screaming.

"An interesting characteristic about visions." His voice was harsh and cold. The kind but somewhat indecent old elf I had come to know was not what he seemed. He was a puppeteer, using his talent as an advantage over his victims, like young sprites that hadn't experienced the world enough to know the lies from the truths. "Some can be just as bad as some are good. Some can invade the very soul."

I couldn't bear the tormented sounds of her screams, but in his eyes I saw his mind. He was losing control of this situation. The residents would soon be returning. He held his gaze on Nazda and began to slowly approach her, the knife in his hand ready to inflict the revenge he sought for his own wounds. I looked at the toppled vase and back to Lord Calo. A plan came to mind. I had never seen this side of him, and to proceed without caution was a mistake I had made too often and couldn't afford to make now.

"So you can create visions? That's your talent?" My voice was high-pitched due to my nerves, but I still managed to sound intrigued. Nazda's wailing ceased, and all I heard from her was heavy breathing, her body stilled under the torchlight. Lord Calo had stopped, for the moment. I prepared for him to turn to me, closing my eyes and gritting my teeth, unsure how to deflect his attacks. Nazda knew this he-elf and his danger and even she wasn't prepared, but I was an elf with talents of my own.

"That's my talent. Yes." Nothing happened, so I allowed myself to relax. He was looking at me, his eyes returning to the normal gray pupils I had seen every day in the Remni from the strange old elf.

"It's quite a talent, Lord Calo. I'm sure you can conjure some very beautiful visions." A smile pursed his lips, and his face turned red. It was as if he were two different people. Within him a demon and cherub in constant battle for control of his consciousness. Right now the cherub was winning. He continued,

"I can help you experience your most vivid dreams. It's the perfect blend of reality and imagination. Still, there's one thing not even my visions could fulfill." I felt his expression change, even though he had hung his head when saying this. The demon had regained its upper hand. So I cautioned myself as I inquired, allowing a brief pause before I continued.

"What is it? This thing?" He looked up, anger returning to his gray eyes, clenching his fists.

"It is she and she is you. You ruined this. You ruined us." I had no clue of what he spoke of but I didn't want to anger him.

"I apologize for my treachery, but I assure you I never meant to betray you, my lord." His face eased and he smiled. He swept toward me, almost leaping as if to strike. I recoiled, but he only gently stroked my cheek.

"It truly wasn't your fault. If I had only been observant and you had been in your quarters that day. The day I prepared your gift."

"What gift? I'm sure it would have been something to behold." He ran the tips of his fingers through my hair, all the way down to the curled ends of my locks.

"A hair runner. I came in while you were asleep, but it was not you in the bed, but your younger self. Your sister." I recalled the missing hair runner being replaced by an intricate new one. Just as the thought crossed my mind, he pulled it from his cloak, stroking its teeth. It sounded like a distressed instrument, strummed with its strings too tight. "I heard someone outside of

267

your quarters that day. Your sister did as well, for she was
disturbed in her sleep. So I had to do it. I had to make her forget."
I thought of how Mira reacted when I came in and saw her on the
bed. I grew sickened and vengeful but I had to be wise, so I
calmed myself and continued. I had an objective and I couldn't let
this sudden rush of emotion get the better of me.

"Such a pity I didn't get it. I'm sure there is something
else you could bless me with, my lord." His eyes gleamed. I had
understood what he wanted all along. All he wanted was me, and
if he thought he had a chance to have me, he would do anything.

"I do." Lord Calo turned around, heading for the main
hall's doors.

He passed by Nazda, who was sitting up now, having
witnessed our entire conversation. She wasn't pleased with the
back-and-forth but I hoped that she would remain still and
unnoticed. He had but crossed the threshold when Nazda sputtered
the thing he hated most. Words that he had heard before but
thought he'd outrun.

"You are a sick creature. Preying on the youth. Pathetic."
He froze in his steps and I immediately regretted her words. But
she didn't, because she continued, "You'll never escape this."
Lord Calo twitched, the knife now pointed at Nazda, the demon
fully in control.

"I can escape it!" His voice was raised. "You scum. You
Dwala scum."

He pulled her up by her hair, her body sinking, weak from

her tormentor. "I took what was owed to me and you didn't hold your tongue then and you didn't hold it now." He brought the blade to her neck. I cringed. I looked around, unsure of what to do. *Why did she speak?* I thought. *Why did I come back to the Remni? Why is this happening?* I thought of my time with Master Tali, and all I had learned and might not ever come to learn. How soon would he turn after killing her and killing me? My mind panicked, rushing to find a solution. I bumped the vase, causing it to rock a little before coming to a stop. "I tried fixing you before. It looks like you're broken for good." He drew back the blade, burying the ivory lady in his sweaty palm.

"Guijanu a wa cabeyil!"

The vase lifted and whirled in the air, hitting him between the eyes just as the pebble had done to Master Tali during my first sparring lesson, except harder. A lot harder. Lord Calo stumbled back, the knife falling to the ground as he landed in a terrible display. His body was sprawled and his head's contact with the marble floor echoed throughout the hall as the vase smashed in shattered pieces around him. I stared in horror. I had always imagined myself as a warrior, able to defy all odds and slay one thousand beasts with a single shot, but I somehow had never included death in the equation. Watching the life in someone's eyes leave their body. Maybe in another circumstance it would be easier, because I felt he deserved death, but this wasn't premeditated or calculated. I had just used something that I had been taught by Master Tali not as a last resort, but by impulse. I

269

could have screamed, or rushed him, or possibly sifted in another way, but instead I killed him. He was dead. I killed him. We sat in the quiet for some time; both of us staring at his still form sprawled on the main hall's floor.

The sound of consuming flames interrupted our observation. They had reached the ceiling, none of us having noticed the fire growing and climbing in the chaos, from the toppled torch. The flames had caught a long tapestry, encouraging the flames' consumption. Glass from the skylight shattered and tumbled to the floor, tickling our heads. Nazda somehow had gotten to me in the madness. She was pulling me, seemingly unfazed by what had just happened. She almost appeared relieved. And why would she be? I was the one who had just murdered an elf. His face seemed distorted and pleasured all in the same glance. I stopped. Staring into his eyes, those now lifeless gray eyes. His wrinkled cheeks and crow's-feet under his eyelids made him appear meek, unable to inflict harm. I finally came to when Nazda tugged at my arm again, nearly causing me to topple forward.

There, in the main hall's archway, Lord Calo's sister stood staring at us in her housecoat. She began to laugh. Her chuckle, mixed with the crackles of the burning wood and tapestries, was a soft breeze to my ears. Until this point, I believed her to be mute. Why else wouldn't she speak? As she looked upon her dead brother, tears ran down her cheeks, but an unhinging laughter still filled the air and a smile still wrenched her face. She waded past us, kneeling by his head. I could see her tears pecking his skin, like a leaked ceiling on a tabletop.

"We have to get out of here, Alya," Nazda urged.

We passed through the archway. I didn't want to leave the poor she-elf, but what more could I do? I could see the despair that I, her brother's murderer, had caused. Her flood of emotions, the dead body, the now darkened gray eyes were all my doing. And even still, there was something else there that I feared to even assume. Nazda grabbed the sack of fruit that she had gotten from the yellow garden, tossing it over her shoulder. Then we were off, a murderer and a trespasser, sprinting down the Remni's path.

Chapter Twenty-One

I didn't have to do anything but run, but even that seemed like an impossible task. Just placing my feet one after the other. All I wanted was to lie down and fade into nothing. In that moment, my already stressful world became engulfed in flame and was burning down before my eyes, quite literally as well.

She didn't let me go. Nazda moved for both of us. She navigated the streets. She told me when to be quiet and continued pulling me. I never heard her. There were no words in me that could summon the emotion I felt. I wanted to scream, just to be sure that I was awake. I wanted this to be some terrible dream. I couldn't have killed someone. I couldn't have allowed the Remni, my home, to burn.

I don't know how long it took us to get to the black ring or how many streets we crossed and how many people we dodged that I may or may not have known. I sat in the barn's loft now, the children sitting across from me, staring, much in the same fashion as we had when we first met. Their eyes were concerned, especially Rose's and Meca's. Cadon only looked at me disapprovingly. Feeling eventually returned to my body, and I realized I was extremely cold. I had almost forgotten about the lovely dress I wore. It was torn and stained, and I had lost the shawl mother had given me to wear with it. Muck from the streets clung to the intricate threads. Much like the life I had known, everything I had changed. I was a pure, clean sheet, soiled and stained.

I had done the unthinkable. I couldn't hold anything back now. The swells of indescribable emotions had gathered together and were now plummeting toward me all at once. I began wailing. From the deepest dungeon of my soul I wept. Tears swelled in my eyes, blurring the sight of the children. They didn't move. I'm sure it was awkward for them, unsure of how to handle this odd she-elf in their loft. Nazda nearly knocked me over as she rushed to cover my mouth, but I couldn't stop. I couldn't reseal the doors of hurt and regret, so I continued wailing. If this hadn't been such a horrible situation, I would have found my behavior quite comical and her reaction even more hilarious.

"Quiet! If Mr. Harmon hears you, we'll be out on the street. Especially if word spreads about what we've done."

I was surprised that Nazda took some of the responsibility when the entire crime was mine, but maybe she blamed herself. Maybe she pitied the effect this situation had on me. Maybe she's been in similar situations. I wasn't sure, but the least I could do was stop wailing. I quieted, and in my silence I felt silly. I pulled the towel from my mouth and lay down on the cold bean sack. I drifted and soon I was gone, warped by despair into a deep slumber.

Chapter Twenty-Two

I awoke during the morning time. I don't know how many days had passed. If I had to guess, it would have been a little less than a week, maybe five days. I hadn't eaten anything this entire time. I had just awoken and then slept and then cried and then slept again. I had lost my feeling of hunger. Over the course of these few days, the only times I awoke were by Nazda's doing. She made me drink water, for that she wouldn't yield, but she allowed me to refuse the food. They didn't have much to go around, so I'm sure she was somewhat grateful, even though she would never admit it. She changed my clothes, discarding the dress, and put me in some rugged breeches, worn boots, and a large overshirt that was two sizes too big. I patted my neck for the necklace. It was still there, unmoved.

I sat up this morning, having soaked up all the pain and sorrow of the past few days. I looked up at the barn's loft window and saw that the sun was high in the sky. The loft was empty now. Nazda and the children were working for Mr. Harmon, earning their keep. I didn't want to go outside. I didn't want to see, rising from the yellow ring, residual smoke, though I realized that was highly unlikely at this point. I was calm but not cured, and anything could send me back into a state of panic. Still, I could use the fresh air and decided an appropriate compromise would be to stay within the black ring. The day was cold and bright. I went to the side of the barn, between it and the house, and took a seat on one of the old crates. Wandering chickens and scurrying rats kept me company as I stared off into the sky.

A horrible pang came from the door of the house. I heard voices and then I heard my name. I thought I had dreamed it at first. Then again, why wouldn't my family be frantically searching for me? It would only make sense.

"Alya Lightstar. Have you seen her?" I could hear the urgency in his voice and I could picture him holding up one of my family's painted portraits, or some sort of sketch that had been created from it. I held my breath and stood up. I wasn't sure what was to come of the situation but I couldn't hide forever. To be honest, I missed them more than anything. These past few days had been hard enough, and for the first time I wanted to be a sprite again. O to be an immature elf-miss wreaking havoc and it being pardoned easily with a ruffling of the hair and a pinch of the cheek. I inhaled and began creeping along the side of the house. "She's wanted in association with the murder of a high official."

I paused in my tracks. This wasn't a missing search call but a bounty hunt. I was wanted. I could picture the sprites in my rotation turning up their noses, laughing at my misfortune. I could picture Master Tali shaking her head in disappointment. I could picture my father, even my sister and Madja, torn by anger at me. I waited to hear what was said.

"I haven't seen no elf 'round these parts." This answer came from Mr. Harmon.

"Well, she was last seen with a girl. A guard, who reported to the scene, saw the murder weapon, and recognized it as a Dwala girl's he ran into a time before. He remembers the elf miss being with her. It was a knife of ivory, carved on it, a woman."

There was silence before an answer came. "This Dwala girl I'm not sure of, but an elf in the black ring I'm certain is hearty news, especially now that she is an associate to a crime. I will keep an eye—no, two eyes—out for these two and if anything is discovered, I will report directly to you." I was grateful to Mr. Harmon. He had seen an elf miss in the black ring before, and he knew I had come looking for Nazda, a Dwala girl, but he didn't say anything. Likely for his own sake, as it was safer to disassociate.

I slipped back into the barn and hoped that Nazda would show up soon. My wish came true but it was not due to my wanting. She came in rushed and panicked. In her hand was a notice with my name and face on it. In bold were DWALA and MURDERER; I was described as a simple witness, little more than a hostage. My stomach began to burn and I vomited on the bean sack. I couldn't believe it. I had put Nazda and myself in danger. I was the one who had killed Lord Calo, not Nazda, but I was considered the associate. My life, thanks to my father's place in the Courts, would be spared, while Nazda would be severely punished for a crime she didn't commit. I don't know if her intent in stabbing Lord Calo was to murder him, but whether or not it was, she was innocent. She had done everything she could to save me, and she was the one who clearly needed saving. I couldn't sit in self-pity while she went down in destruction. I owed her that much. I gathered myself, putting on a face of confidence and control, as she had done for me. After a moment, I spoke.

"We'll need to leave." She looked at me. The children emerged from the hatch and stopped in their tracks. Nazda was crying, tears streaming down her cheeks and along the sides of her soot-covered nose. They must have been cleaning chimneys today because the children looked identical.

She smiled. It was one of those smiles that were a way to comfort those around you rather than yourself. "Where will we go?" she asked as she wiped the tears from her face. I mulled over the idea before responding.

"We'll go to the edgewoods."

Chapter Twenty-Three

Nazda prepared Cadon, briefing him on all that he would need to know to care for Rose and Meca. It wasn't as dramatic as I would have guessed. It was as if emotion—sadness, that is—wasn't tolerated, or perhaps they were reasonable enough to know that this was her only option. There weren't any tears, even from Rose. Rose wasn't old enough to know the extent of danger we were in but she understood that Nazda was leaving for a long time, possibly forever. Still, they only hugged. With the cover of darkness we fled. We didn't have far to go to get to the outer wall and we were thankful for that. On almost every post hung wanted posters. The award for our capture was sizable; not that much would be needed to convince a citizen to turn us in. Probably the next morning, once Mr. Harmon caught wind that there was money to be had for our whereabouts.

We made it to the tunnel undetected. I went through first. Murky water had settled in the hole, claiming my boots, sloshing about, making my feet damp. Nazda was right behind me. We looked around at the end of the tunnel, taking in our surroundings. The woods didn't seem to recognize us. Mist settled around it, sealing it from view. We moved slowly, careful to not alert the guards on their post nearby. Small drops pounded the tops of our heads. It was going to rain tonight—yet another adversary. We made it to the bridge and got across with ease, and eventually the wood's edge came into view. The woods weren't filled with sounds of life, as it normally was. The winter had sent most of the animals either into hibernation or into caves and burrows for shelter from the cold. The ground was hard, and the air was harsh. We came upon the hollowed-out potbellied tree, the base, but it was too obvious a place to seek refuge, not to mention we weren't the only ones who knew of its whereabouts anymore since the masked warriors discovered us.

We kept moving, unsure of where to go. I thought a cave would be perfect, a place where we could build a fire and be concealed from view. The rain had picked up and was falling on us in heavy sheets, soaking our clothes and making our already freezing forms colder. I regretted not taking shelter at the base and at least waiting until the rain passed before continuing, but I couldn't focus on that now. We walked northwest for a few miles before discovering a small mouth in a hill. The hill was covered with dead grasses and mud. It looked artificial, as if it were made by some beast, but we had no choice. I was tired and wet and I could tell that the same was true for Nazda. We climbed in. The air inside was humid from the rain, not to mention it would be impossible to find dry kindling during this storm. I looked around the cave but found only two or three twigs and an aged, dead branch. So we settled down. I sat against the smooth wall of the cave, with Nazda next to me, her head leaning on my shoulder.

I watched the outside. The cold air and the sheets of rain that fell sounded like a never-ending flow of rice into a bowl. I couldn't see past it, but I could somehow feel the city. There were so many things that I wished I had done. I wished I had a chance to see the entire city again, from the school's watchtower to the shops in the blue ring. I wished I had the chance to tell my family I loved them. I wished I had seen Kala and the lads before I left. The patter of the rain continued as I finally drifted off into sleep.

I rubbed my eyes, trying to end the blurriness. My back was aching. The sun had yet to rise high enough in the sky to dispel the darkness completely. I could imagine that around this time I would be headed off to training with Master Tali. I looked out into the rain. The pattering of drops on top of the hill echoed inside the cave. It was comforting, and our clothes had semidried, and it seemed that everything would be fine even though it wouldn't. I stared out into the rain to see eyes coming in my direction, floating like little star beetles. Yellow eyes. I rubbed my eyes again, hoping that it was just my paranoia conjuring them.

"Nazda, wake up."

She leaned up, squinting. She looked tired, as if she finally had just drifted off to sleep after all this time. She peered out of the cave and saw them, too. I could tell by her reaction. It was those eyes—the ones that for a long time I thought I had escaped. They were growing closer, the mist concealing the beast's body.

I immediately reacted. My training had quickened my reflexes and doused my fear in some aspects. My mind and my will to live had become my most valuable assets. They were all I had now. I grabbed the branch that I had thought to use for kindling and called to Nazda.

"On your feet." The eyes were almost to us, by my estimates, a few yards. We had to move.

I stepped out into the rain, holding Nazda's arm. I wished I had my bow and arrows. I wished they weren't still tucked under my bed—well now, most likely charred in the heap of destruction that used to be the Remni. There was no time for regret. I scanned the area quickly but knew I couldn't make it to any of the nearby trees. *The hill*, I thought. I circled around to climb up the side, thankful the rain was shielding us. I helped Nazda first, allowing her to get up halfway before making my ascent. The stick was our only protection and the hill our vantage point. It was a slippery slope but we made it to the top just in time.

I braced myself, predicting that the monster, which I had come to know to be called the mongrowl, would leap in all its might from the front of the cave, and I, in all my strength, would bring the branch crashing down upon it. If our demise was to come this day, I wasn't going to go down without a fight. I had run too many times. I had felt sorry for myself for far too long. The mongrowl wouldn't pity me. It would only see me as prey and it as predator. I stood in the center of the hill, unmoving, every part of my body tensing in anticipation. Nothing came. Minutes passed, and still nothing. Not a howl or the sound of claws scratching at the sides of the hill. I had seen it. Nazda had seen it, too. When my nerves had eased somewhat, I decided to go down to the ground. I could hear my surroundings better that way.

It wasn't difficult to get down. I simply slid. I heard slush behind me and saw that Nazda was now alert and just as ready as I was. She held in her hand a rock from the many that sat atop the hill. She wasn't giving up, either. We crept along the side of the hill and looked off into the distance. Nothing. No eyes. There was only the smell of wet animal. The mongrowl had definitely been through here. I peered into the cave and froze. The mongrowl was in there! It was wrestling with something much smaller than it. Nazda knelt, so she could see in as well. It was a child. I stared at its face. Then I realized who it was, and so did Nazda.

"Niegi!" she screeched.

Nazda rushed forward, but the beast was now made aware of her presence and assumed her to be a threat. She stopped in her tracks as the monster lunged at her, toppling her to the ground. She screamed, her shrill voice echoing throughout the cave and the edgewoods. The creature was very doglike in appearance and catlike in structure. Its fur was black and glossy, its tail short and stubby. It had hands that could grip along with its feet, not paws, like elves and humans, but its snout was almost like that of a bear. It seemed a lot different than I had imagined, not nearly as hideous and evil as I had anticipated, if at all.

"It's all right. He won't hurt you," Niegi called from the back of the cave.

Its ears twitched and it began licking Nazda excessively. Nazda, in her confusion, wanted nothing more than for the

282

creature to stop, to retreat to Niegi, but it held her down and continued licking her face. I entered the cave, relaxed by this display of affection until its eyes looked upon me. They still had their yellow gloss; the narrow slits of black of its pupils, catlike, cut into my soul. Its wet hair arched on its back. It snapped its teeth, wrinkling its snout, and started walking toward me. It stood on its hind legs, baring its chest. I was terrified. I knelt to show my surrender, to demonstrate that I came in peace, but it didn't stop. I wanted to scream. He was inches from my face when Niegi appeared, a stick in hand.

"Here. Go get it, Komai." The mongrowl snapped to attention, its anger turning to bliss, at the thought of the prize Niegi held in his hands. Its eyes didn't even remotely consider returning to me. Niegi sent the stick flying into the woods, and with it, the mongrowl. He helped me up, brushing me off. I took a few moments to collect myself before addressing Nazda's lost friend.

"We thought you were dead. The monster lifted you into the air. I saw it. I saw it fling you." I stared at him in disbelief.

"That's how they protect their young, I would guess. They toss them to their kin in an effort to keep them out of harm's way."

"So it thought you were one of its own."

"No. Komai knows I am human. He's actually relatively young. Probably around our age by their standards." He paused, looking back to the outside of the cave, checking on the mongrowl. It was busy grinding its teeth on the stick without a

283

care in the world, so Niegi continued. "His mother was the one you saw. She was protecting me, I believe . . . from you."

"Protecting you from me? Why would she think that I would hurt you?"

The mongrowl returned, gripping the stick within its paws as it made its way into the cave. It tossed it to the side and sat behind Niegi, digging its large snout under Niegi's arm, beckoning for a scratch or a treat. Niegi scratched his chin before answering my inquiry.

"The Guerr has been hunting these creatures, for what reason, I do not know. You and Segun were with me, and I assume, in her obligation to her young, she took pity on me. She recognized that you two were elves, and to her, that spelled danger."

"That must have been why she came to the base. She wanted to drive you and the other elflings out," Nazda interjected.

"What reason would the Guerr have to hunt these animals? My people attempt to live in peace with all creatures. All of our clothes are spun from silk, or shaved from the wool of our sheep. If any hide were used in anything we have, the animal would have had to pass from this world naturally. Even our talents serve the world we live in and were gifted to us by Olörun to do so. Why these animals?"

"The ladies of the wood have told me that it's been many years that they have hunted the mongrowls. The Guerr have hunted them almost to extinction. Even the ladies don't know the reason. If I had to guess, it would be for their teeth. Maybe they use them for target practice. I've lived behind Keldrock's walls just as long as you have and I know very little about the goings on within the soldier barracks. They have even silenced Komai's mother." I could hear the anger in his voice at my reticence to believe him but he had to understand that this was a lot to absorb.

"I'm sorry for its mother, but the Guerr are our protectors. They are yours as well as mine. They protect us from the dangers behind the veil."

"How do we even know that what lies beyond the veil is dangerous?" Neigi threw his arms in the air in a crazed motion, grunting. "For all we know, there could be peace on the other side of the veil. It's been years since the alignment of the worlds, when the bridges intersected and there was a new beginning. Who's to say that things haven't changed? The veil is open for just a few moments. That's not long enough to witness what's on the other side, if there is anything on the other side."

"You knew this entire time? You knew that Niegi was taken and believed him dead?" Nazda's words stilled the cave, even the beast, who had taken to rolling on its back on the ground, now sat still, resting on its belly. "Were you ever going to tell me?"

I couldn't help but turn away. I couldn't look at the hurt in her eyes. "I wanted to tell you. I wanted to tell you so many times, but I saw the pain it would bring, so I—"

"So you lied?"

I paused, unsure of what response I could give. I surrendered.

"Yes."

I expected something dramatic and emotional to happen after that. Some form of aggression. I almost wanted it. I wanted her to hit me, shove me, and curse me. I wanted her to show me that I was wrong and that she expected more from our friendship, but she just turned and sat in a pocket of the cave, retreating within herself. This experience had been a lot for her as well, and trust was something she couldn't afford to lose in this moment. I could see that and I felt horrible for it. I continued talking with Niegi.

"Who are these *ladies* you speak of?"

"Even I'm not sure of that. I haven't spoken to them much. I met them after I had been separated from you. The mongrowls seemed to trust them enough, but after they explained the state of the creatures and what Keldrock had done with them they offered to escort me back to the city." He turned, scratching behind the ear of the beast. "But I refused. Komai needed me here."

"I want to meet them. These are very serious accusations and they seem to know more than you on this matter."

Niegi's eyebrows furrowed, he offended.

"Very well. We'll set out under the cover of darkness, after Komai has fallen asleep. It's too dangerous for him to travel with us and it's only a few hours' journey. If he wakes up and we're gone, he won't leave the cave until we return."

"Very well. Under the cover of darkness," I agreed.

Chapter Twenty-Four

After two hours of traveling, I realized I was weaker than I thought. I was hungry, near starving. Niegi assured us that we would eat once we arrived at our destination. I was thankful the rain had stopped, but it had been days since I'd eaten, and now that my appetite had returned, food was all I could think about. Nazda hadn't spoken to me since we left the cave in the hill. I thought it best to give her some time and room to forgive me. After all, she was someone I cherished, and if I were to make up for my transgressions, I was going to give her time to heal.

"Can we stop for a moment, Niegi? Just to catch our breaths."

"Come on, Alya. We've stopped plenty. You'll never be a warrior with that attitude, or have you discarded that dream so easily?" One thing I had forgotten about Niegi was his snarky remarks, and now that we had reunited with him, I'm sure he would never let me forget this little trait about him again.

"I'm more than capable at keeping up," I huffed at him.

I pushed on without remorse for my body. I couldn't satisfy the beliefs Niegi had about me. That I was some spoiled, rich elf who would never have a sense of the world and forever lived among the clouds. If I had but the time to describe to him the chain of events that had happened until this point, he'd bite his tongue. Still, this was no time to compare wits, and my current state of affairs was nothing to brag about. I noticed a difference in the sky. It felt as if the atmosphere were heavy but lifting. As told by the heavens, tomorrow would be the day of the unveiling, something that had somehow slipped my thoughts. The moon was full, and with that, was ready to eclipse the sun, come the morrow and cause the veil to fall. I hadn't quite calculated the days until this point, but now I was certain, and beyond petrified. Maybe seeking refuge with the ladies of the woods, who might know about the masked warriors as well, would be a better option than a lowly cave with no defenses.

We traveled for a little more than an hour more before coming upon a cluster of trees. They grew together strong, their branches interweaving into one single canopy that sheltered the grassy space below.

"We're here," Niegi announced, like a proud tour guide.

As we walked into the grassy meadow surrounded by the grove, I looked around, expecting to see some race that coexisted with the mongrowls and had entered our world when the worlds collided and were perhaps the kin of the masked warriors we had encountered in the woods many nights ago. But all I saw was grass.

"There's nothing here. Are you sure you aren't lost?" I asked sarcastically.

"No. We are here." Niegi pointed up.

I looked up to see that in the lower branches were zip lines and rope bridges that connected tree to tree. Platforms of wooden planks and sheets had been built in the branches as well. It was a beautiful network of architecture. I was dumbfounded until a sharp prod to my back drew me back to a familiar state of fear.

"State your business, elf." I didn't dare move, and although many words wanted to escape my lips, I thought it better to say nothing. I eyed Niegi in the dark.

"I would love to see you spear the little princess, but she is a friend." He laughed while I grimaced as the sharp pain subsided.

"My apologies." I turned to see the masked warriors. I had guessed their affiliation correctly. Their voices were harsh like before, altered by the hollows of their masks. "Welcome to our camp! We will take you to our leader. I'm sure she'll be both surprised and pleased by your arrival." The warrior tucked his knife back into his sheath. "Stand down." I turned to see that we were surrounded. I hadn't sensed any of them or heard their movements, and for that I was impressed. They were well trained.

They led us to a tree. At the base, they tapped several times, the sound echoing against the other trees in the grove. Dim lights soon emerged in the treetops and new life seemed to be born within their lower branches. Apparently they saw our approach before we were even remotely upon them. From the platform, a wealth of ropes fell down, coiling at the base of the tree.

"Grab a rope. Tug twice when you're ready to ascend."

I braced myself, for heights were a fear that I had yet to overcome, but would have to eventually. I let out a breath, and before I knew it, only the warrior whom I assumed to be the leader of the troupe by their assertion, and myself were still on the ground. I looked up to the branches to see that Nazda and Niegi were already climbing onto one of the platforms.

"When you're ready." I closed my eyes and tugged twice. I was whisked into the air with great ease, a rush of cool wind chilling my face. Once among the branches, two warriors helped me onto the platform.

We crossed a series of rope bridges, heading into a large hut that sat in a cluster of branches in the middle of a round of trees. It seemed to be the mother of all the smaller huts that ran along the circumference of the grassy meadow in the canopy. Inside was a woman, fierce in appearance. Her hair was black, dreaded down her back. She was a beautiful masterpiece, her maple skin warmed to perfection. Her body was sculpted and rippling with muscle. Her shirt was torn in places, revealing the sides of her abs beneath her weathered breastplate. She approached us with a gentle smile that reminded me of Madja.

"Greetings, youth of Keldrock. Welcome to Wood Haven, the home of the ladies of the woods. My name is Amazja. I am the head of this community. Whom do I have the pleasure of greeting?" We bowed our heads in respect. She seemed friendly enough.

"I am Niegi, of the Dwala clan."

"I am elf mistress Alya Lightstar, from the House of Meoltan, and this is Nazda, of the Dwala clan." I wished I had been quicker to stop my tongue. Nazda bulged her eyes at me. I

291

didn't mean to speak for her, but I had been making such horrible
headway in seeking her forgiveness that I thought this gesture
would ease some tension. My impulse was mistaken, and I
immediately regretted it.

"Well, make yourselves at home. My daughter Yann will
escort you to a hut for the night. I'm sure you're hungry and in
need of rest. We would give you the option of returning you to the
city normally, but since the day of unveiling is upon us, we think it
best we remain in seclusion." She turned to the head of the
warriors. "Have the cooks prepare a meal for our young guests and
ensure that something that has not felt pain is served to the sprite."

The head warrior removed his masked helmet, revealing
long black voluminous curls attempting to be tamed by a red
ribbon. The other warriors followed suit, and I couldn't believe my
eyes.

"You all are—"

"Yes. We are all women. Once Keldrock citizens, but
exiled to the edgewoods by your kin," shot one of the warriors,
who had a piercing driven through her septum. I paused for a
moment, unsure of what to say or how to respond. Such a raw
comment would be hard to nurture. Then it hit me—the most
obvious answer of all. They were banished, just like the woman in
the story whom the Courts sent to the edgewoods in response to
the Dwala protest. It was interesting to see that the banished sisters
Master Tali told me about were still among us, not burned in the
edgewoods long ago. Staying here would have been their best

option, considering that the Courts wished them dead, but their colony exceeded anything I could have fathomed. This was a whole new way of living.

"You had to know I had no choice in that matter. It was an error in judgment of my people. You have to know that," I said softly and as kindly as I could. Their faces remained unchanged, and for a moment I feared for my safety.

"Of course she does." Amazja shot the head of the warriors a look, warning her to calm her nerves. "She meant no offense and we do not hold you accountable, young sprite. You are beyond welcome in our confine, and we will hold you in the same high regard as our own. A friend to these children couldn't mean harm to any one of our people." She turned to the warrior's leader, with the dark voluminous curls attempting to be tamed by a red ribbon. "Yann, you may be on your way. Ensure that our guests are taken care of. You are their host."

We went over a rope bridge and rode a zip line that was quite enjoyable now that my body had become semiaccustomed to the heights of the trees. The hut was small but better than the cave or even the rickety barn where Nazda and the other children lived. In the center, from the zenith of the hut's shrubbery ceiling, hung a small lantern. We gathered around it, sitting in a circle, as we waited for the food to arrive. Yann returned shortly after alerting the cooks of our needs and I thought it the perfect opportunity to get some answers not only about the ladies of the woods' long survival in the edgewoods but their theory concerning the mongrowls as well. Yann was young, possibly a few years older than Kala, but would hopefully know some of the answers I sought. She removed her breastplate, setting it next to her helmet. I soon began.

"I can't believe women built all this. It's quite breathtaking."

She smiled, bending one of her legs upright and placing her elbow on her knee in a bragging gesture. "Yes, it is, isn't it? And to think we built it all from fallen wood. It took many attempts, from what I'm told, but by the grace of the earth, we have survived." Small wooden bowls of cold berries, skewered rodents, and nuts were set before us along with a skin of water to share. "Sorry it's not what you are accustomed to, Alya Lightstar, but since our banishment, we have had to make certain sacrifices." I nodded and thought to quickly change the subject, trying to avoid the tension that my very existence in their camp caused.

"And those magic ropes are—"

"They are not enchanted. There are no such things that exist among the Dwala. The ropes are harnessed by pulleys," she said abruptly, answering as if my guess was moronic, which caused an awkward silence to ensue. I decided not to inquire any further into pulleys, having rather felt offended at her mild bite at me.

"You seem very young, Yann. It must be a great honor to hold such a high rank among the warriors of your order."

"You should train with her. She can probably teach you all

that you would need to become a warrior." It was actually a
suggestion, though I couldn't tell if Niegi was being snarky
or sincere.

"That will have to wait," Yann said. "While I would
enjoy spending more time getting acquainted with you all, I
retire for the night. We must rise early to prepare for the da
unveiling in case our borders need defending. Good night."
seemed that she wasn't keen on the idea by her reaction bu
more concerned that my questions would have to go yet ag
unanswered.

After eating, we each grabbed one of the thin, mu
pallets that had been brought to us and prepared to rest. N
wasn't speaking to me, and I felt before bed was the best
hash out any negative feelings we had toward one anothe
was standing outside the hut on the platform, while Niegi
already fallen asleep, so I decided to join her.

"I never expected this. It's quite a marvel!"

"You know he deserved it. The old elf deserved
than anything."

I nodded, content in the fact that she was now s
me. "I try not to issue such judgments, especially for on
as myself."

"You don't understand. It had to happen or he
have stopped! He didn't stop!" I couldn't see Nazda's
could hear her sobbing. I moved closer, patting her sho
kindly. "If it weren't for him, this would never have h

Her hand moved toward her chest. I remembered the first night we met, her being so open and revealing her scars to me. Now it had come full circle. She didn't go any further as to the specifics of exactly what happened to her and I didn't need her to. I pulled her in, letting her head fall on my shoulder. She let go, releasing her guard, and for the first time I saw the girl that she was, like the many I'd seen working in the Remni. Just like Kala or even sprites like me. I began to cry, too. We just held each other, not wanting to let go. After a few moments we came to calm, crashing back down to reality, where we had to maintain our emotions just to function. "I'm sorry you had to kill him. I really am," she whispered low enough so that Niegi couldn't hear if he was eavesdropping and not really sleeping.

"I'm sorry too but I'm more sorry that you were hurt. I'm sorry for lying. For not telling you about Niegi. I'm sorry about—

"It's all right, Alya. You're my friend. We're in this together and we're going to get through this." She laughed a little and nudged me in my shoulder. "You're forgiven this time."

Chapter Twenty-Five

The tunes of strings, drums, and music filled the air, awaking me from my slumber. I walked out onto the wooden platform to see the grassy meadow in the center of the grove burning. Not a single blade of grass remained unscathed. I zip lined down to the ground like it was instinct, forgetting my fear of heights. The ground was black, small sifts of smoke rising and disappearing in the air. It was like a huge scar in the center of the grove, like war and pain warped all into one.

Then, in the center of the meadow, I saw movement. The drums grew harder, matching the beat of my racing heart as I approached. In the center of the burned grass grew a sapling. Breaking through the decay of its fallen cousins it grew, somehow finding life amid this destruction. Its beauty was so breathtaking that I didn't see what curled beneath it, coming. If I hadn't looked twice, I would have thought it simply to be a root shifting and maneuvering with this springing piece of life. Its silver scales wrapped around the green trunk of the sapling, and before I could move it snapped its head, showing its fangs.

I awoke in a sweat. I grabbed my neck to feel the warm metal against my skin. I ran my fingers over the slender, pointed head and touched the gemmed eyes. Somehow, over these past few days, it had become part of me. I thought to take it off right then, to toss it away into the night in the hope that these nightmares would end, but it wasn't the necklace's doing. That would be a stretch even if I thought it to be true, which I didn't. It was just a continuum in my dreams; the celebrity appearance. I had a lot on my mind, and the changes over the past few days were likely the causes of my tormented slumber. I decided a little fresh air would soothe my angst.

The edgewoods were lighter, the night fading into softer colors. I could see the thin purple hue in the sky and knew morning was coming soon. I had slept most of the night—for that I was thankful— but could use a little more rest, considering the day I had before. I walked onto the platform and peered down at the meadow in the center of the grove. The grass was shifting ever so lightly in the wind. Some looked dead from the hints of cold winter winds that stole away fall, but none was burned, like in my dream. I stretched my arms and lower back as I sat on the platform, my feet dangling from the sturdy wooden planks.

Alya?

It was almost inaudible, and sounded like a question; a confirmation of whether another had heard right. I looked to my left, along the assemblage of huts, platforms, and rope bridges that looped through the trees and saw one with a light flickering.

Something to drink would probably ease this tension? I convinced myself.

I cautiously crossed the rope bridge, careful not to shake too much. I didn't want to wake anyone but mostly I didn't want to fall to my death by moving too swiftly. Soon I was on the platform of the little hut, about to cross its threshold into the lantern light when a hushed exclamation stopped my tracks.

"I told you to be quiet. Do you want to wake up the whole camp? Are they ready to leave? The unveiling is upon us and Guerr are days away."

"Yes, they've departed, and by this time should be waiting at the cusp of the edgewoods, waiting for the horn to sound. We must make sure the veil has fallen before we attack."

"Perfect. They have no idea, correct? What has Niegi told you of the sprite Alya?" There was my name again.

"He says she's of a high rank. Her father works in the purple ring, under the Courts."

"She might prove her worth after all. Go and bind her. I don't want any complications. In a few hours, we will ensure the veil never rises again." I gasped loudly, not catching myself in time before I heard the sound of feet scurrying out onto the platform.

The splintered wood cut into the insides of my fingers, making it hard for me to hold on as I dangled over the edge. The feet paused right above my fingers and I just knew I had been discovered. I waited for the figure to either look over and identify me as the eavesdropper or to crush my knuckles under the might of their foot and send me tumbling to my death. I closed my eyes as I awaited their decision, which seemed like hours. Then I heard the creak of the planks as they moved away, retreating into the hut.

The darkness had been my ally.

I couldn't hang on much longer but I couldn't climb back up. If I were discovered, I would surely be eliminated. These warriors were going to invade the city. They said they were going to make sure the veil never rose again. As the only elf in their camp, I most likely was to be their insurance should complications arise in their plan. I was no more than a casualty to them. I had to escape. I had to warn Keldrock. I had to get out of there.

I looked for a nearby branch. It was still dark outside, so it was hard to see most things if they weren't right in front of me, but in the hushed shadows I made out a branch, and hanging from it, by the grace of Olörun, a rope. I bent my elbows slightly, pulsing the muscles in my arm. I only had one shot to swing and get it. If I wasted too much time gaining momentum, I could alert the figures in the hut and meet my demise. I swung back and the planks cried. I lunged forward with all my might, reaching for the branch. I missed.

I began swiping at the air, trying to find reason as I fell to the ground. I swung my arms widely and slapped the rope. I had missed the branch but had made it within the reach of the rope. I clasped it, burning my hands as I slid down. I cringed from the pain, gritting my teeth to keep from screaming. I felt warm drips on my hand and knew I was bleeding as my feet safely touched the ground. Ripped skin was a small price to pay for my life. I darted into the edgewoods just as I heard the rush of zip lines. I ran without looking back. My strength had returned with rest and

food, and I could only hope that they couldn't keep up. They wer remarkable, I must say, but I was still an elf—a trained elf who had spent many a night trolling the edgewoods. I darted through the woods like a doe, the wolves too few in number and unprepared for my catlike reflexes. I ran as fast as I could. For two hours I continued to run, unable to stop, disturbing sleeping reptilians from their sleep and uplifting the last of the roosting birds from their nests.

Finally, exhausted, I stopped to catch my breath, unsure of where I was. The sun hadn't peeked through the trees yet. It was quiet, with only the chirp of crickets and the ever so often flicker of fireflies. I let out a deep breath and turned to navigate toward the city when an arrow whizzed through the air, just missing my head, the sheer force uplifting my hair from their roots. I moved again, darting faster than before. *How are they keeping up with me?* I thought.

I ran without direction, shooting through the woods onl in an attempt to keep my life. I heard the drawing of another arı on its bowstring and dodged to the left, hoping that my pursuer shot to my right. This was it. This was how I was going to die— like an animal. The once proud doe that dodged between the stumbling wolves was now stumbling, the wolves' tactics overpowering her grace and speed. I thought to surrender, to out for mercy, but that wouldn't still their hands. I pressed on wildly as twigs broke off from nearby branches, cutting my f could hear myself sobbing, panting, and screaming uncontro

the face of death almost upon me. It was a game of shadow man, like the lads and I would play, except this wasn't a game. My pursuers were shiftier than shadows, almost spirits if it weren't for their arrows trying to find their mark. I shot through a small thicket of bushes and I saw it. The cave.

I looked around as I ran, hearing a dense movement of a being among the treetops. I looked up and saw the yellow eyes peering down, watching the warriors hunt me like pawns on a chessboard. The eyes began to fall. They looked like shooting stars plummeting to the earth, burning brighter as they gained momentum. I knelt, balling up, and it shot over me, capturing in its grasp one of my hunters and sending her flying through the woods, colliding with a large tree. She looked like a rag being tossed, her body meshing into the wet soil beneath it. The creature roared, shaking the woods with the might of its voice. I heard branches snap and leaves rustle as the other hunter retreated, making her way back to the pack. I had just barely made out her identity, as a glimmer caught in the little light of the morning sun, her pierced septum. The fallen warrior quickly followed suit, making her way with her injuries as fast as her legs could carry her. The woods soon were quiet again.

Then the yellow eyes were focused on me. They were open and full, sucking my soul into their magical orbs of gold. *You have to be open. Let them see you. Let them know you.* This is what Master Tali would tell me if she were here. I dropped to the ground, letting my breath escape to the open air. I took a deep

breath, which I prayed wouldn't be my last. I opened my eyes. I stared into its eyes, its mighty face, with its wrinkled nose and sharp snarl. I didn't blink but let it feel my thoughts and my intentions. I didn't want to die. I didn't mean it any harm. But even more, I needed help. I needed to save my people, my city. I didn't close my eyes. I would accept whatever came my way but I would show it my full self. It sniffed around my hair and my neck and ended at my torso. It circled around, still watching me, its teeth bared. It made its way full circle, meeting my eyes yet again. Komai the mongrowl had decided.

Chapter Twenty-Six

We tore for the city. Branches to the mongrowl were like petals in the wind, ripping from their stems. The sun was peeking over the horizon just as the moon was about to pass its form. They would meet in a heavenly kiss and the unveiling would begin. A horn blared, shaking the trees and the ground, and even the young mongrowl knew that we had to move faster now. That the horn meant we were running out of time.

Almost an hour into our sprint, we passed my abandoned base and soon we were upon the path that was etched out by the lads and myself from our adventures in these woods. As we approached the ends of the trees I could hear the growing sound of battle cries. I heard the clash of weapons and the wisps of arrows. We flew over the stone bridge to the city gate that lay in ruin, reduced to twisted metal and splintered wood. The mongrowl lunged forward through the streets, I directing it by tugging on the long hairs of its back, which didn't seem at all necessary. It was as if it knew my thoughts, as if my memories were its.

The streets of the black ring were empty; not a single hinge or post was disturbed. It had been passed over. Soon we were upon the gate of the blue ring, and that's when I saw that a great harm had occurred.

It was a terrible sight. The Guards of Candor were unprepared for this surprise attack. The Guerr, who had been trained for tasks such as these, were far away from the city, a few days' journey, and the city defenses weren't a match for these skilled warriors. Bodies of guards and he-elves that tried to defend were littered like timber on the streets of the blue ring, along with fallen warriors of Wood Haven. Blood stained the stone slab roads. I could hear sobs coming from inside houses, while some were engulfed in flames, their wood cracking as dark smoke rose to the tinted sky. We raced on, through the gore and destruction, a few of the guards and other he-elves still attempting to defend their homes and their loved ones. I had to find my family. I had to make sure they were safe.

We sprinted up the path to the yellow ring, the same path that I had walked so many times with the lads, Madja, Mira, and Kala. We were soon upon the tired heap of burned wood, fallen stone, and crumbled columns that used to be the Remni. I could almost see the many rooms and chambers. I could picture the walkway and the flowers that lined the outside of the estate. I looked high above the ground, at my family's chamber, with its beautiful balcony, the autumn leaves drifting from its detailed stone etched railing. Everything was gone.

Just as I had deemed all lost, I saw a glimmer in the rising sun. I had thought nothing could have survived this fire. None of Madja's jewels, or the necklaces that Lord Fueto had given us could have resisted the flames or surfaced through the heavy heaps of stone and marble. I slid off the back of the mongrowl. I didn't realize how unnerved and overwhelmed I had become until I came back down to earth, both literally and figuratively. Until my feet touched the ground, maybe I thought this nightmare would end and I would wake up in a happy world, undisturbed by trouble and war. But this was a reality. My home was gone and my city would soon follow suit, but something had survived.

Something glimmered in the heaps of rubble. I climbed over stone slabs as fast as I could, realizing, in the damages, the shiny ends of something that I thought I had lost for sure. I rushed over splintered wood, and my scorched oak chest that once encased my clothes, until I reached my bow in all its glory and all its might. The bow was unharmed, it protruding from the heap of burned memories like a rose in a field of thorns. I pulled it out, lifting settled dust and ashes into the air. Hanging at the end of the bow was my quiver of arrows and a small pouch. I pulled at it, releasing it from my bow's snag, and opened it. In it were the seeds that Mira had gifted me. One solitary tear rolled down my cheek as I tucked the seeds that I never got to plant with my sister into my pocket. It wasn't much, but it had survived along with the bow. These prized memories had survived out of hundreds that were lost.

I pushed aside a piece of my cot and what looked like burned sheets to see if anything else remained. I recognized the leather that bound my sifting book. Lost. I saw singed papers and blackened volumes from my father's chambers. Lost. I even saw Lord Calo's hair runner, broken and shattered. Destroyed for good. I heard an explosion up the path and saw the silhouettes of bodies running from the yellow gardens toward the purple ring. *The Wood Haven warriors.*

I settled back atop the mongrowl and charged up the path behind the fleeing figures. No more was I going to run and not fight. All my life I wanted to be a warrior, but in all truth I was the farthest thing from it. I made a great deal of mistakes, some that could never be fixed, but I couldn't sit back idly as my city was engulfed in ruin. I drew an arrow and placed it on the bowstring. I had witnessed death, been its forced hand, but now I was its willing ally. It was time for me to stand up for those who couldn't stand up for themselves. I pulled back and let the shaft sail through the air. It pierced the warrior in the back, sending her rolling forward. The other turned in a web of fury, drawing two elven swords I assumed she had confiscated during her murder spree in the blue ring. She leaped into the air, aiming for my chest, but the mongrowl, leaning back on its hind legs, swiped her in the air, pummeling her to the ground in a broken heap. We continued up the path, passing the warrior I shot with my arrow. She was still breathing. As I looked at her, I pitied her, my thirst for death now questioned. She looked regretful, and if it was only for show, it had done its duty in making me feel all the worse for wanting to kill her. She would live.

We reached the purple ring's gates that housed the great tower from where the veil emanated. Darkness slowly began to envelop, shading the city and all the destruction around me. It was happening. I looked to the skies. The moon was aligning with the

sun. The tinted sky was no more and the unveiling commenced.
The sky lost its purple hue and darkness fell like a shower of rain
upon our world. We raced to the tower and began our ascent up
the side of the zenith of our great city, to the chamber of light. I
had to protect the source that produced the veil. If anything, that
would make things right. *Only a quarter hour*, I thought. A second
horn blared, echoing closer than before. It had to have been blown
from within the purple ring. We climbed faster, the beast hoisting
me, using the stone ledges and crevices of the large tower as
points of leverage.

The top of the tower was a beautiful spectacle. Glass
panels enclosed this lantern room, and held in its creases was
welded gold. An iron spiraled rod that was patterned for
decoration stuck from the top of the encasement like a lightning
rod. The mongrowl crashed through one of the glass panels,
sending shattered pieces to the floor. The room was empty.
Nothing. No crystal orb or gem lay in this chamber like in the
legends I had heard, producing a veil that protected us from the
outside world.

"You shouldn't have come here, young one." A voice
sounded from the shadows. I drew an arrow, placing its nock
slowly in the string, as if my pursuer couldn't see me taking arms.
"Do not be afraid, sprite. You have nothing to fear by my hand. I
am here to protect. And you're not here for the light. That would
be most terrible."

"Who are you? Come from the shadows and reveal

yourself."

A figure emerged from one of the arches that supported the glass encasement. Once he got close enough, I didn't see him as much of a threat. He was an older elf, with hair of gray. He seemed withered and worn.

"I went by many names once, some of which have been lost in the dispels of time. One, however, seems to transcend the passing of seasons."

I raised the arrow, preparing it for a shot should the truth not be produced. "I have no time for trifles. If you are some mercenary hired by those wenches of Wood Haven, I can guarantee you won't live to receive your payment. Speak your name, traitor."

A searing pain shot through my hands, a feeling of fire and ice all poured into one. My grip fell short of its hold on the bow and arrow, which landed on the ground just in front of the mysterious being. Once released, the searing pain stopped. He bent down picking up my bow, running his hands over the metal that tipped the lower limbs all the way down to the arch.

"This was claimed once, but not by you. From where did you get this?"

"From an ally." I felt helpless to answer his inquiries.

From the center of the room, a banging of the hatch ensued and I moved back, centering myself in front of the young mongrowl. An eruption of wood and smoke exploded into the chamber, shattering the remainder of the glass encasement. Shards of glass fell, stabbing at my body as they tumbled to the ground, shimmering like crystal hailstones. Blood trickled from the various cuts but I felt no great pain. I waited for the smoke to clear, in hopes that what lay on the other side of the hatch was a friend and not a foe. It was the latter.

A group of the Wood Haven warriors emerged from the torn hatch, five in total. The old elf tossed me my bow and I strung another arrow.

"How will you defend yourself, mercenary?" I couldn't believe what I saw next. Out of the air he produced two swords.

"You needn't worry, miss. I've witnessed many years of battle. You just keep up." Soon the air was filled with the clash of swords and the wisp of arrows. The mongrowl helped dwindle their numbers as more sprouted from the hatch, sending them with mighty force out of the chamber's open arches where glass had once been. A group of guards, alerted of the attack on the tower, assisted in our defense. Soon it seemed the odds were even. An arrow snipped my shoulder and in return I sent an arrow through its shooter's leg. I hadn't fully come to grips with my thoughts on killing someone.

It looked as though we would live to see another day, and that the city would survive. I had spoken too soon. A roar echoed through the floor, stopping the fighting for a moment. It was as if time had stilled. From the mongrowl's back, a spear stuck, like a solitary flag on a mountain. It turned to me for help, but I could provide it none. Those same yellow eyes that I once feared were so open now. I understood its pain and its misery and I wanted nothing more than to reverse time and prevent all of this madness from ever ensuing. After a few staggering steps, it collapsed, slipping from the tower, and I watched in agony as it fell from the chamber of light to the ground below. I turned to see its killer removing her mask and helmet. It was the girl with the red ribbon—our hostess, Yann. She turned to me, an evil smile on her face, as if she were proud to have done the deed.

I bit into my lip, trying to regain control. I reached over my shoulder into my quiver to find it empty. I peered at an arrow on the floor, which the old elf had seared from my hand. I turned back to Yann. She pulled from one of her dead warriors' grip a sword and slowly began walking toward me, still smiling as if she enjoyed this game and drew it out by leisurely striding. The old elf had been captured and was being held at spearpoint by two of the last of the invading party, while the rescuing party of my kin lay slain on the marble floor, alongside the sisters of Wood Haven.

"Why are you doing this? Can't you see you're only causing more hurt? More destruction?" I hoped reason would speak to Yann.

"We're not here to cause any more pain, elf. That's what you and your people do. That's not what we want. We want one thing and that is to eliminate the source of the veil."

"Well, it's not here. I've looked. The chamber is empty."

"Oh, but it isn't. You see the source of the veil is in this room." She turned to the old elf. "Is that not so, Protector?"

I stared in awe. This couldn't be. Shiloh hadn't been seen for years. Many presumed him dead.

"I am he. The virtue. The light." Even her troupe of warriors wasn't expecting this confirmation. Yann approached him, gleefully. She had won and she wanted to revel in her triumph.

"Tell me, O virtue. Tell me of the light." Her tone reeked of sarcasm and disrespect. "Where is the source of the veil? The moon is shifting and the clouds are lighting. Your answer should be swift. Where is this great source?"

"One should not ask questions when the answer has already been presented. I have nothing to fear." All the air escaped the room, as I was sure I would witness his demise.

Instead, the oddest thing occurred. Yann laughed, turning away from the elf, looking madly at me. She began to laugh hysterically, reaching up to remove the ribbon and letting her curls tumble around her face, making her appearance seem crazed and insane. She stared at me, gripping the sword in her hand. I closed my eyes, ready to let this be the end.

"Aaaargh." I squinted, letting the bits of light that began to escape the moon rush into my eyes. Yann held the sword in Shiloh's side, and I heard the last of his breath escape his body. I rushed at him.

He fell to the ground as arrows shot from the shattered glass encasements. Reinforcements had come. They lay siege to the remaining warriors of Wood Haven. I didn't hear the calls of

312

battle. I didn't hear the clash of swords. I just saw death in the form of the many fallen faces of my city and now Shiloh. I lifted the old elf's head off of the ground, cradling him in my arms. Tears streamed down my face and I began to weep uncontrollably. I could feel my voice crying out in pain but I couldn't hear it. Nothing was real anymore.

Suddenly the sun escaped the grip of the moon and the light conquered the darkness, sending it back to the night. A blinding light stilled everything. I couldn't see the fighting or death. I could only see white.

"The light has chosen you." A figure began to form in the cloudy thick ivory mist. It had to be a vision. "You have been chosen as my heir."

"You are mistaken. I belong to the House of Meoltan. I—"

"I am very well aware of to whose house you belong. This heir I speak of is not chosen by blood, but of spirit. You sought the light but to protect it. Not to claim it and for that it is yours to keep."

It was all so overwhelming. "I do not want it."

"And for that reason you must take it. By now you should have understood that I was the veil's source because I held the light. Now you must carry it for the protection of our people. For the protection of the world."

"So I must wait atop this tower and hold the veil." I shuddered, confused still by this sight.

He laughed, which I found to be an odd thing to do in this

313

instance. "No, that is not your purpose, and if I had the option I never would have allowed it, but now dawns a new age. You must lead on as the new Protector, and that decision is yours to make when the day comes."

"But what of Prince Alag? He is your blood, the next in line."

"My dear Alya. There is no line. I have been blessed enough that the line of our people's Protectors have been pure of heart and of my bloodline, but the course of my kin has changed. I have no more control over this selection than you do, and so it must be so." He smiled, his gray hair curling by his cheeks. "That bow belonged to me once, and so did the quiver. Do it justice, Alya, today savior of Keldrock. Now queen of the elves."

"But I . . . " With that he was gone, dissipating into the air.

I awoke in a sweat, gasping, beads trickling down my neck and along my forehead. I lay in a dark room, on top of a luscious bed. The coverings were of the finest linen.

"It was but a dream," a voice called out.

I looked to the corner of the room whence the voice came, to see two he-elves sitting atop stools in fine robes. Prince Alag sat on one, a crown atop his brow. He eyes refused to meet mine. Still he smiled from his seat. His years of royal treatment had taught him many things, and the principal forelesson was how to remain unnerved. The other seat was filled by the voice of my addresser. He stood with a black robe, gold buttons trailing down the center.

On his head were rose thorns and blackberries. My father stood, his face stern, chiseled and unmoved. I hadn't noticed at first but Prince Alag donned similar garb, black enveloping his body like a dark angel. Blackberries were pinned to his collar, and I knew that a burial ceremony was the reason behind this dress. I thought of the black dresses in Mistress Vesti's keep probably now owned by those that survived the siege, if her shop remained intact.

"The death count was far greater than any we've seen," the prince uttered. "And my grandfather . . ." He paused.

"I do apologize, my prince. I know—" I held my head in respect.

"Left something that apparently you took as your own." My words froze as his interruption cut into my conscience. How had he known?

"I assure you, my liege, that I have done no such thing."

"And I have assured him as well, daughter," my father chimed in. Both of our eyes widened in surprise. He felt just as awkward about coming to my defense as I did accepting it.

"I will have my leave. Upon the return of your health, we will consult with the Courts concerning this issue. Until then, rest. My home is yours to partake." With that, the prince left.

The room was far more beautiful than anything I had ever seen. The ceiling was painted with angels, fairies, fauns, and centaurs, creatures that I had only read about in legends and folklore. A big window let in the beautiful sun that soared now in a sea of light blue. I caught my reflection in the window and knew immediately why the prince had known what I had, for the most part, believed I'd imagined. From my temple to my back, my locks of black hair had turned an almost white, silver color, much like the strands that graced the mighty crown of Shiloh that I had deemed to be an elderly gray. I didn't recognize myself.

My world didn't even seem the same anymore. I wondered about the state of the city, more specifically my friends who had traveled into the edgewoods or Kala and her caretaker on the outskirts of the black ring. We had won the day, but more warriors of Wood Haven still lurked in the woods, and the Guerr couldn't have made their return already. What if the Guerr had been eliminated and the remaining warriors were just waiting in the shadows of the leafy canopy, to attack our city again? I dropped my head into the palm of my hand, letting my elbows sink into the quilt that covered my legs.

"Beautiful, isn't it?" My father stared out of the window, his head tilted toward the sky. "Once you're well, I'll bring Segun and Rayloh by to see you. Your mother and sister will probably stop by soon after the burials. It's a wonder how—"

"I think I'd like to be left alone." He stared into my eyes and I stared back, daring him to make any rebuttal, denying my request. He yielded and bowed his head as he made his way to the door. He cracked it and stood for a moment.

"I *am* proud of you, Alya."

I clenched my teeth, holding my breath, in the hopes that he would leave me be before a rush of insults breached my lips and cascaded in a fury of slander and disrespect. I heard the door close, and with a deep sigh I let out the breath I had been holding. I sat for a moment, letting the sun warm my face. The first day of winter had begun, and my first unveiling had been my final unveiling all in the same. I wanted to cry.

I heard a tap at the window and looked out to see a red bird with glistening wet feathers sitting on the outside sill. I got up, wanting to startle the little bird, not wanting to be bothered with anyone, let alone anything. Its obsession I did not know, but I wanted nothing more than to be in solace. I smacked the panel, shaking the entire frame, but it didn't flinch. Its head twitched slightly to the left. I tilted the panel and reached out, fluttering my hands, but it simply hopped farther along the sill, out of my reach. In my fury, I brushed something that sat on the outside sill. I picked up a pouch—the one Mira had given to me, not realizing I had lost it. I brought it inside and removed one of the sapphire seeds from the pouch. I rubbed the beautiful oval shell in my palm. The bird fluttered away, its wings gliding on the gentle winds.

I had fought for something, and gained more than what I had dreamed of my whole life. I had fought with more than swords and arrows and glory that my people praised, but for those I loved and cared about. I was the new Protector, the new queen, and our first ruling she-elf ever, and I would have to accept this responsibility as a burden and as fate. Perhaps if Shiloh felt I was the proper one to hold the light, then maybe like these seeds, I could help usher in the beginning of a new age in the way they ushered in new life. I settled back onto the bed, snuggling my worn body under the bedding. I placed the seed back into the pouch. In doing so, something coasted my fingers that wasn't a seed. Curiously, I reached inside and removed a small piece of parchment folded over a few times. I spread it open, revealing blotted ink, but the penmanship was exquisite enough that even in this fault it was quite beautiful. It read,

Congratulations, Protector Alya Lightstar. – **A. o. X.**

Unsure of what to make of this note or its writer, I placed the parchment back in the pouch, tucked it under my pillow, and fell asleep under the beautifully painted creatures of legend, my world having completely unraveled.

END OF BOOK ONE

About the Author

M.C. Ray is a creative who has just made his premiere to the world through the writing of *The Unveiled*, the first book of a series. He is a Georgia native, born and raised in Stockbridge, Georgia, and has always had a passion for the arts, especially the power of story telling in all its forms.

"Creating a fantasy with characters that look like me is more than just about inclusion. In reality we are present, so why not in the magical, fantastical, and the alternative."
- M.C. Ray